M000076847

COULD IT BE MAGIC?

"I never did tell you happy birthday." He leaned toward her, cupping her shoulder in the palm of his hand. "Happy birthday, Jake."

She assumed he only meant to give her your garden-variety birthday kiss—over the second it had begun. But the instant his lips touched hers, something happened. A jolt of pure pleasure rocketed through her, and a tiny moan escaped her parted lips as his tongue slipped inside to join her own. She didn't think, she just responded, arching closer to him, angling her head to give him better access to her mouth. She inhaled, breathing in the spicy aroma of his cologne, and another masculine scent that was distinctly his own.

Maybe it was the wine, or the fact that she hadn't slept much in the last couple of days, but her insides were astir with a mixture of awe and delight, and her skin felt flushed all over. Maybe she was coming down with Dani's flu.

She couldn't say who moved first. Honestly, she didn't care. Suddenly, she was in Eamon's arms, her mouth seeking his, her arms winding around his neck to hold him to her. This time, the kiss was longer, deeper, hungrier—as sizzling as the lightning that blazed outside her window.

**BOOK YOUR PLACE ON OUR WEBSITE
AND MAKE THE ARABESQUE
ROMANCE CONNECTION!**

We've created a customized website just for our very special
Arabesque readers, where you can get the inside scoop on
everything that's going on with Arabesque romance novels.

When you come online, you'll have the exciting opportunity
to:

- View covers of upcoming books

- Learn about our future publishing schedule (listed by
  publication month and author)

- Find out when your favorite authors will be visiting a
  city near you

- Search for and order backlist books

- Check out author bios and background information

- Send e-mail to your favorite authors

- Join us in weekly chats with authors, readers and other
  guests

- Get writing guidelines

- AND MUCH MORE!

Visit our website at
http://www.arabesquebooks.com

COULD IT BE MAGIC?

Deirdre Savoy

ARABESQUE

★BET
BOOKS™

BET Publications, LLC
http://www.bet.com
http://www.arabesquebooks.com

ARABESQUE BOOKS are published by

BET Publications, LLC
c/o BET BOOKS
One BET Plaza
1900 W Place NE
Washington, DC 20018-1211

Copyright © 2003 by Deirdre Savoy

All rights reserved. No part of this book may be reproduced,
stored in a retrieval system, or transmitted in any form or by
any means without the prior written consent of the Publisher.

If you purchased this book without a cover, you should be
aware that this book is stolen property. It was reported as
"unsold and destroyed" to the Publisher and neither the
Author nor the Publisher has received any payment for this
"stripped book."

All Kensington Titles, Imprints, and Distributed Lines are
available at special quantity discounts for bulk purchases for
sales promotions, premiums, fund-raising, and educational
or institutional use. Special book excerpts or customized
printings can also be created to fit specific needs. For details,
write or phone the office of the Kensington special sales
manager: Kensington Publishing Corp., 850 Third Avenue,
New York, NY 10022, attn: Special Sales Department,
Phone: 1-800-221-2647.

BET Books is a trademark of Black Entertainment Television,
Inc. ARABESQUE, the ARABESQUE logo, and the BET
BOOKS logo are trademarks and registered trademarks.

First Printing: May 2003
10 9 8 7 6 5 4 3 2 1

Printed in the United States of America

For Imam and Evelyn Simon, of the now defunct Mostly Magic in Greenwich Village, and for the good friends and good times found there.

And for the friends of my misspent youth: Joyce, Yvette, Yasamin, Raquel, Arnie, Jack, Gary, Brody, Oscar, Anthony, and others too numerous to mention. I loved those days.

ACKNOWLEDGMENTS

Thank you to all my readers, as I could not have made it this far without your support and encouragement.

Thank you to all the aspiring and published writers in ASAP and on my FictionFolks list on Yahoo. It is so wonderful to find writers supporting and uplifting one another. As they say, there is enough success out there for everyone to have a taste of it. Here's to all of us reaching the goals we set for ourselves.

Special thanks to sister-author Gwynne Forster for her unflagging friendship, good humor, and invaluable advice. I owe you, girl!

One

Jake McKenna watched anxiously as her taxi slowly made its way through the rush-hour traffic clogging Sixth Avenue. It was a sunny day, unusually warm for the beginning of June. Jake rolled down her window, but the infusion of outside air was hotter, if anything, than the air inside.

She would have to learn to budget her time better in the future. No more browsing in shop windows when she had somewhere to go. No more chatting with interesting-looking strangers who also happened to be looking for a cab. No more dallying of any kind. She gave herself the same lecture whenever she was late for an important meeting. If only she could get herself to listen.

It was nearly a quarter after nine when she stepped from the cab, almost forgetting to retrieve her all-important portfolio. She swung it at her side as she hurried toward the entrance of the building. She scanned the slip of paper she held to check what floor she was supposed to go to. Twenty-six. She found the correct elevator bank quickly. Once inside the cubicle, she surveyed her appearance in the reflection of its shiny silver walls.

Her auburn hair was tousled from her sprint from cab to building. Her blue linen dress was twisted and there was a smudge on her left cheek, she didn't know from what. She leaned the large, rectangular portfolio against the wall and made the necessary adjustments.

How to explain her lateness this time? Potential employers generally didn't accept excuses such as subway delays or getting stuck in elevators anymore. Damn! She really needed this job, too. Working freelance just wasn't cutting it anymore, not with Dani about to start a new school in September. The tuition was nearly five thousand dollars. She'd only saved half that. She'd never come up with the rest without a regular income. Maybe she'd just lie and say she thought her appointment was for nine-thirty.

The elevator doors opened. Jake picked up the portfolio and stepped out, fighting down a sudden urge to turn back. She'd never held a nine-to-five job in her life. The thought of accepting one now—if one were offered to her—was both frightening and daunting. She couldn't think about her own feelings on the matter, though. She had Dani to consider now.

The entrance to the floor was to her left. On the right-hand side of the opening archway, big chrome letters declared EBONY MAN. At least she was in the right place, though she wasn't sure what kind of place it was. Liza really hadn't told her much about the magazine or the man she was about to see. For all she knew, it was one of *those* magazines. She didn't object to nudity if it was handled tastefully, like in art class. Men's magazines were another story.

She strode up to the receptionist seated at the large black desk and smiled. "I'm Jake McKenna. I'm here to see Mr. Fitzgerald."

How calm her voice sounded, as if she really belonged in this office decorated in several shades of gray and black, with touches of purple for color. Even the receptionist didn't vary from the theme. She wore a black knit dress and her gray hair was neatly tied back with a lavender scarf.

"Mr. Fitzgerald is in the studio," the receptionist said without smiling. "You're late, you know."

Jake raised her eyebrows at the receptionist's presumptuous statement. "Am I?" She made a show of looking at her newly acquired watch. "My appointment was for nine-thirty," she said with as much conviction as she could muster. That was the best way to tell a lie—with conviction.

The receptionist gave her a cool look and said, "The studio is at the end of the hall on the left. Mr. Fitzgerald is waiting for you there."

Jake nodded her head. "Thank you." Jake headed in the direction the receptionist pointed, her bulky portfolio banging against her legs as she rounded the circular hallway. She checked her slip of paper again. Eamon Fitzgerald. The Fitzgerald was fine, but how did you pronounce that first name? She looked it up on an Internet site for what to name your baby. She forgot what the old Gaelic name supposedly meant, and worse, the site provided no clue as to how to pronounce it. She'd have to listen carefully when he introduced himself.

She stopped outside the studio, taking one last calming breath before opening the door. She could hear men laughing on the other side, probably at some disgustingly chauvinistic joke. That was the sort of thing you could expect from men who'd work at a magazine called *Ebony Man.* What was she doing here herself? If she ran now, no one but the receptionist would even know what she looked like.

Get a grip on yourself, her inner voice warned. *You're a McKenna, and before that a Troubat, and neither clan is known to be cowards.*

Obeying the command of the little voice, she straightened to her full five feet nine inches and gave a quick rap on the gray metal door before opening it. Immediately a man rushed toward her. His swarthy complexion and dark hair bespoke a Mediterranean heritage. "There you are, darling," the man said, grabbing her

arm and pulling her into the room. He wore a yellow
Hawaiian shirt, jeans, and black high-topped sneakers
with a big gold medallion on a thick chain around his
neck. "We were starting to worry about you."

He took her portfolio from her and handed it to another man, an Asian wearing a T-shirt that said I'M WITH
STUPID, with an arrow pointing poignantly downward.

"Nigel," the first man called, helping her out of her
jacket as she struggled to retain it. "Nigel," he repeated
more urgently, "come look at what we've got. Look at
those legs. We've got to get them in the picture."

Nigel appeared from amid the klieg lights surrounding the set to the left. He was tall and dark-skinned, with
a camera hanging around his neck from a large multi-
colored strap. His only greeting was a terse "H'lo."

All this happened in what seemed like a second to
Jake. She stood openmouthed, feeling vaguely as if she'd
been assailed by the three kings. But instead of giving
gifts, they were taking things away!

"I'm—" she began, trying to explain she obviously
wasn't who they thought she was.

"We're not going to bite you," the man with the medallion continued. He looked her up and down. "And, honey,
that dress has got to go."

She looked down at the offending conservatively cut
garment. *Oh, God! Oh, God! Oh, God!* The chant started
in her head. It *was* one of those magazines, and they
thought she was a model!

The man with the medallion kept on babbling about
her dress. Nigel was muttering unintelligibly, and the
third man merely shook his head. All the while, she
could feel herself being drawn farther into the room by
their hands on her arms.

"Stop it. Stop it, all of you." She stood firm, shrugging
away the hands of the three startled men. "I'm looking
for Mr. Fitzgerald. Is he here or not?"

"I'm here."

The sound of the deep baritone voice jolted her. She hadn't noticed there was a fourth man in the room remaining totally silent while all this madness went on.

She turned to him, her gaze immediately riveting on his eyes—ice blue or maybe gray—that stared back at her from a handsome, bronze face. She could almost feel his eyes travel over her as they scanned her body, one she'd always thought was too voluptuous for its own good. They settled again on her face, seeming to look more through her than at her. "Can I help you?"

"Yes," she said, trying to shake the eerie feeling he was staring right into her soul. "I'm Jake McKenna. I have a nine-thirty appointment with you."

If he was aware of her fib, his expression didn't show it—if you could describe a totally unmoving face as bearing an expression. Even when he'd spoken, she'd had the uncanny feeling that his features hadn't changed. She'd gotten his message by telepathy.

He rose from the tall stool he'd been more leaning against than sitting on, striding toward her with easy, graceful steps. The three kings, as she'd come to think of them, fell away, clearing a path for him.

"I'm sorry, Ms. McKenna," he said, extending a hand to her, which she shook. "I hope you'll forgive me, but I was expecting a man. I haven't met very many women named Jake."

"It happens all the time." But it shouldn't have this time. She distinctly heard the receptionist say, *"Ms.* McKenna is here to see you."

"And I hope my staff didn't upset you too much," he continued. "They can be a bit overzealous." He gave an almost imperceptible nod, and suddenly her belongings reappeared. He handed her her purse and jacket and held on to her portfolio.

"They've been waiting for an author we're doing an

article on who was supposed to be here at eight-thirty. Unfortunately, none of us is really sure what she looks like. It was an honest mistake."

She didn't say anything as his voice trailed off. She might have blurted out that she thought they were about to disrobe her for some pictures she was glad her mother wasn't alive to see.

He introduced her to her three assailants, Nick, Nigel, and Ng, usually called Kevin, then suggested they go somewhere to talk about the job.

He led her down the corridor, back past the receptionist's desk, to a corner office overlooking lower Manhattan. *This couldn't be his office,* she mused, looking around. Too much clutter, for one thing. Such an impeccably dressed man with neatly manicured hands would never tolerate such a mess. There were stacks of paper everywhere. The drafting table in the corner looked to be literally on its last leg, and there were boxes of all sizes stacked along one wall.

The only item in the entire office that looked like it belonged to him was a dust-covered plaque that read I'M THE MAN YOUR MOTHER ALWAYS WARNED YOU ABOUT. She had, and he probably was.

"Sit down, Ms. McKenna," he instructed, unbuttoning his suit jacket. He took it off and slung it across the brown leather chair behind the desk.

She sat, watching as he walked toward the window to close the blinds. From the rear she saw broad shoulders that tapered to lean hips and a firm derriere. When he turned around, she glimpsed a muscular chest, outlined against the thin material of his long-sleeved white shirt, and, well, the rest she would just have to speculate about. She returned her gaze to his face as he sat down.

"First thing," he said, without preamble. "I've been known to make appointments at nine and at nine-thirty, and I'm generally aware of which of the two I've said."

Jake gulped, feeling like she'd shown up at the prom without her clothes on. He'd known who she was all along. She didn't know how she knew, but she knew.

Then why had he subjected her to the antics in the studio? He could easily have put a stop to it if he'd wanted to. Was it all a joke? There wasn't the slightest trace of humor on his face. Or was it a punishment for daring to keep the great Eamon Fitzgerald waiting?

Either way, she was out of her league with this man, whose cool, steady eyes seemed to bore into her. Maybe she should thank him for his time and leave.

"Second, you come highly recommended by the agency, and you have an impressive list of clients, but you don't have any office experience."

He picked up her portfolio and unzipped it, laying it across the desk. He flipped through the laminated pages quickly, hardly enough time to appreciate her work. This was his polite way of letting her know he wasn't going to hire her.

Strangely, she felt more relieved than anything else. Graphic design was a competitive field, but she was sure she could easily get a job somewhere else. After all, this was her first interview, and she swore to herself she would be on time to all the others.

"Tell me about yourself, Ms. McKenna. Aside from your design work, you've had a number of interesting . . . jobs."

From beneath the portfolio he extracted a copy of her résumé. That was a laugh, calling it a résumé. It was more like a list of odd jobs with the emphasis on odd. In her twenty-eight years, she'd tried everything from teaching art in a private girls' school to delivering singing telegrams, with quite a few strange things in be-tween—whatever it took to keep her head above water. Whenever funds got low, she'd trot out her portfolio and knock on a few publishers' or ad agencys' doors. It was by far her most lucrative talent.

"For instance, what were you doing at this company Home Work, up until seven months ago?"

"Painting."

"Oh? Oil or watercolor?"

"Houses. My brother and I owned a small construction company. Mostly we did a lot of remodeling of co-ops and condos and the like. Once he'd finish plastering or whatever, I'd paint."

"Why are you looking for full-time work now?"

"My brother left the company unexpectedly, and I have a small child to raise."

"I see."

He didn't, but she saw no reason to explain that a car accident ended both her brother's life and the company, or that Dani was his daughter, not hers. It was none of his business, anyway.

He closed her portfolio and set it on the floor without zipping it. "I don't know how much the agency has told you about our magazine, but it's been privately run by my family since it started publication over thirty years ago. Over time, it's changed a lot, and I feel there is a need now for it to be revamped again. That's where you come in."

Me? she almost asked aloud. Did this mean he was hiring her, after only a cursory glance at her portfolio? She'd expected to have to wait at least a couple of weeks to hear anything, if ever, considering the unprofessional way she'd behaved. Liza'd told her she was the first candidate to be sent over for the job. This wasn't the way it was supposed to work.

"My uncle, who was the publisher for many years, treated the magazine as his own personal sounding board. Unfortunately, not many people share my uncle's view of what is good, or even interesting. Consequently, circulation is at its lowest point ever. Now that I've taken over, I want to see that changed."

He took a copy of the magazine from atop one of the piles on the desk and tossed it to her. "This is a prime example of what I do not want. If you look through this issue, you'll find that not only is the editorial content sloppy, the design is cluttered, and the subject matter is downright boring. I'm looking to appeal to a younger, more sophisticated audience of men and women than my uncle was, if you can describe this as being directed toward anyone at all."

Jake picked up the magazine, flipping through the pages, pretending to scan it. She felt sorry for this uncle, whoever he was. She could imagine how he'd taken over, throwing the poor old man out when he didn't prove useful enough.

"I'm looking for something fresh, incisive, nonformulaic, as far as the design is concerned. Of course, you'll be working all this out with the art director. My brother will be back in New York next Monday."

He leaned back in his chair. "I'd like you to start this Monday, so you can get acquainted with the magazine and the rest of the staff before he gets here."

"Shouldn't I meet him first?" This was all happening too fast. She wasn't sure she wanted to work at *Ebony Man* in the first place. Not if it meant working with the strange, abrupt man seated across from her. And his brother? She certainly didn't think she could stand two of them. Well, he wasn't asking her if she wanted the job, he was telling her she had it. Now, what was she going to do about it?

"He'll abide by any decision I make."

But would he like it? was a different question. The last thing she needed was to be the focal point of a feud between two brothers, both of whom would be her boss in one way or another.

She was about to refuse his offer, reminding herself that this was only her first interview. Then he told her how much he intended to pay her. It was even higher than the figure she would have asked for. She'd figured she would have to bargain down from that.

She toyed with the ring on the third finger of her left hand, her lucky ring, wondering if he was merely strange or plain ol' crazy. Nobody offered that kind of money for a designer, not in publishing, anyway.

"By the way," he added, "we have a day care facility in the building. It's only getting started so it's a little shaky, but I haven't heard any complaints so far. As long as you can drop your child off, the service is free to employees."

She had wondered what to do with Dani between the time school let out and her own workday ended at five o'clock.

Finding competent, affordable day care in New York was like finding a pearl in a plate of oysters on the half shell—damn near impossible. It did make the offer more tempting. So tempting that she knew she couldn't turn it down. She had to think of Dani, and practical things like paying the rent on time and having food on the table every night. The carefree days were over.

"Monday sounds fine," she said, forcing a smile to her lips.

She thought she saw a flicker of a smile cross his face, but it came and went so quickly she couldn't be sure. "Any questions?"

Plenty. Like how did I get myself into this mess? "Not really."

"Good," he said, rising, shaking her hand. "I'll see you on Monday. Nine o'clock this time." She moved to pick up her portfolio. "You can leave that here," he added, shrugging on his jacket. "I'll send it to your apartment by messenger, along with some other things I'd like you to look at. You will be home this afternoon."

That sounded to her more like a command than a question. "Yes."

He adjusted his collar. "I've got to run. I'm late for another meeting." The implication being that it was her fault. He walked around the desk heading for the door. He paused long enough to tell her, "Just follow the hallway. It leads straight to the elevators." Then he disappeared down the hallway himself.

"Weird, definitely weird," Jake said aloud as she put her jacket on and picked up her purse. Well, at least both her immediate problems were solved. She had a job and she had somewhere to leave Dani. And if working for the Fitzgerald brothers proved to be too much, she could always look for another job. After all, the best time to look for a job was when you had one, or so popular wisdom had it.

But what did she really know about either brother? She still didn't know how to pronounce this one's first name. Even the three kings called him Mr. Fitzgerald.

He was, however, one of the sexiest men she'd ever met. He showed absolutely no interest in her in that regard, though. She'd been sitting there the whole time with her long legs exposed by her short dress. He hadn't looked at them once.

Once outside, she decided to take a cab back home. After what she'd been through that morning, the thought of getting on a crowded, stuffy subway wasn't a pleasant one. She hurried to the curb, seeing an empty taxi headed her way. She stepped into the street, holding up her arm to catch his attention. She hadn't noticed the bicycle messenger that was headed straight for her.

"Oh, dear," she said, realizing there wasn't time to get out of the way.

Then she felt a hand on her arm and she was airborne, flying back up onto the sidewalk right into the hard wall of Eamon Fitzgerald's chest.

"Thank you," she said, looking up at him. Her hand went to her chest. "I almost ended up a pancake."

He stared down at her with the same unreadable expression and said, "Do try not to get yourself killed before Monday, Ms. McKenna." And then he was gone.

Two

The first thing Jake did when she got home was to call Liza to tell her she'd gotten the job.

"You do work fast, Jake McKenna," Liza said when she heard the news. "How did all this happen?"

Jake started with the three kings and ended with his leaving the office. The part about being late and the equally embarrassing part where he saved her from being run over were left on the cutting room floor.

"But what's *he* like?" Liza wanted to know.

"Didn't you meet him?"

"Yeah, the CEOs of companies come to see me all the time. I spoke with a British-sounding woman."

Jake laughed, twirling the phone cord around her finger. "Sounds like the receptionist."

"The receptionist?" Liza sounded offended she had to deal with such a lowly person in the company hierarchy. "You still haven't answered my question. What does he look like?"

"Like my brother, sort of." Jake replayed the similar features in her mind. A strong, straight nose, accented by high cheekbones and a square jaw. Deep-set eyes, shaded by long, sooty lashes. "His eyes are a different color, though. I'm not sure if they're light blue or gray. Either way, they're sort of spooky."

"What do you mean?"

"It isn't every day you see a dark-skinned black man

with light blue eyes. At one point, I could swear he could look right through me."

"You were probably being paranoid because you were late. What excuse did you give this time?"

"Not one that worked. How did you know I was late?"

Liza chuckled her normal throaty laugh. "Jake, I've known you since we were in kindergarten. You're always late. Now, tell me more about your new boss. What does he look like from the neck down?"

"Denzel, eat your heart out." An unconscious sigh escaped her lips.

"You're not planning on doing anything stupid, are you?"

"Who, me? Even if I were, he has absolutely no interest in me." Though she did feel a definite thrill from being brought up against him so abruptly when he'd saved her from the bicycle rider. Being startled hadn't been the only thing that had made her heart beat faster.

"And I'm not about to force myself on a man if he isn't interested." She'd learned that lesson the hard way. "Besides, he's a little too reserved for my taste." Reserved wasn't the right adjective, but she couldn't think of the one she wanted. She'd have to look in her thesaurus.

On the other hand, he might be perfect for Liza. Tall, raven-haired, willowy, and cool, Liza was the kind of woman Jake could imagine being with the mysterious Mr. Fitzgerald. Liza could be a little mysterious herself.

"What do you know about him?" Jake asked.

"Not much. Only what the receptionist let slip. He used to live in Boston until a couple of months ago. I get the feeling she's afraid of him, or maybe in awe is a better description."

That figured, Jake thought. Eamon Fitzgerald was an awesome sight. "You are coming to my birthday dinner next Saturday, aren't you?" she asked, a plan forming in her mind.

"Of course. What are you going to attempt to fix this time?"

"Steak. You can't mess up steak."

"We'll see."

They talked a few minutes more before hanging up, then Jake went about cleaning her apartment. She'd let several tasks slip in the past few weeks, and she couldn't have people over with the place in this shape.

Normally, she loved the spaciousness of her thankfully rent-stabilized apartment. But when it came to cleaning two bedrooms, two bathrooms, a large sunken living room, a kitchen, and a dining room, it was a big dusty albatross around her neck. At times like this, she yearned for a little cubicle with a bathroom down the hall. Or at least the little one-bedroom apartment she'd had when Dan was alive. Sometimes it amazed her how much her life had changed since then.

Two hours later, Jake flopped onto the sofa, satisfied and tired. If the apartment didn't sparkle, at least it had a healthy glow. Now, if she didn't let anything lapse between now and Saturday, she'd be ready.

Jake picked up the brown envelope resting on the rose-colored fabric beside her. True to his word, Eamon Fitzgerald had sent her portfolio back to her. It had arrived a few minutes before, along with an assortment of material that slid from the package when she opened it.

There were several copies of the magazine, including the issue he'd told her to look over, tentative copy for the first issue using the revised style, and a few sheets of paper held together with a paper clip. The first one, a job application, bore a little yellow Post-It note. *Please fill these out and bring them with you on Monday. E.F.* Small and neat, that couldn't be his handwriting. His handwriting would be large and bold and require a much bigger note to say the same thing.

She decided to start with the magazine first. A brief

scan of the pages gave proof to what Mr. Fitzgerald had said. Dani could have done a better job of laying out and pacing the pages. She turned back to the table of contents. She'd never heard of a single one of the articles' authors. That in itself was strange, as she read many and varied publications. Even the titles of the articles sounded dull. Reading them would try an insomniac's wherewithal.

She took the rubber band from around the bundle of loose typewritten pages. The first page bore the date of October of the same year. Jake started calculating backward. If *Ebony Man* followed the usual practice of closing an issue three months before publication date, that gave them barely a month to conceive and implement the new format.

She glanced through the pages until she came across something that interested her—the publisher's note. She tidied the ream of papers in her lap with the note on top. It dealt basically with the changes being made to the magazine, the new focus they were trying to develop, comments from readers were welcome, things in that vein. Jake wondered if it wasn't a little premature to be writing that, since some of these things hadn't been decided upon yet. Or maybe they had been in his mind. He just needed someone to carry them out.

What really surprised her was the humor and warmth evident in the writing. She wouldn't have expected that from the enigmatic man she'd talked to today. No, enigmatic wasn't the right adjective either.

She was about to look for the thesaurus when she heard the doorbell ring. She slipped all of her paraphernalia back into the envelope. Dani was home from school.

"Hi, sweetheart," Jake said, opening the door. She waved to her upstairs neighbor, who always brought Dani up from the bus along with her own children. Then she refocused her attention on Dani. "How was school today?"

Jake always asked the same question, but today she already knew the answer. One leg of Dani's jeans was frayed at the knee, both her shirt and undershirt hung below the waistline of her pants. To top it off, half her long brown hair hung out of the ponytail Jake had made for her that morning.

"Dani McKenna, you've been fighting again."

Dani marched past her sullenly, taking off her jacket and hanging it on the post of the wrought-iron railing leading down into the living room. "He started it!" Dani flopped onto the sofa and folded her arms across her chest. "He called me a bad name."

Jake sat down next to her, watching as the child turned doleful brown eyes up to her. Jake wasn't sure how serious this name-calling business was. To Dani, a bad name could range from something truly horrible to merely Danielle. As far as she was concerned, her name was Dani, and no one, not even the principle of John E. Dewey Elementary School, was permitted to call her otherwise.

"What did he say, and who's he?"

"This doofus in my class said I was an orphan and I should go to an orphan house. So I hit him." Dani's little fist flew up for emphasis.

Jake wrapped her hand around it and brought it down. "You can't go around beating people up because you don't like what they say."

"Why not?"

"Well . . ." Unable to think of a good enough reason, Jake decided to take another tack. "Anyway, Dani, you know that's not true." Sylvia the snake was still alive somewhere. She might not care what happened to her daughter, but Dani was not an orphan.

"I know, Jake."

"Besides, we're a team. McKenna and McKenna at large." She opened her arms wide in a silent *tada!*

Dani brightened a little, but Jake knew it was merely for her sake. The memory that their team had once boasted a third member was really what bothered Dani. She had been tremendously devoted to her father, and was not adjusting well to his absence. Did Dani even understand what death meant? You couldn't really expect a six-year-old psyche to comprehend so much.

Dani also didn't like being coddled. She wasn't a baby, as Dani often reminded her. "Why don't you change your clothes, and I'll tell you about my news?"

"You got the job today." Dani's eyes lit up. "I told you you would."

"Go get changed," Jake repeated, "and I'll tell you all about it."

Dani scooted off, apparently having forgotten the incident in the school yard. But Jake knew better than that. Dani was a brooder, even more so now than before. And if that doofus in her class didn't watch it, he was going to be in a lot of trouble.

Jake made Dani's favorite dinner that night, franks and beans. After she tucked the little girl into bed, she took out her papers again and started reading. By the time she'd read halfway through, she knew what he was looking for. The articles, written mostly by established and respected authors, were well researched, well written, interesting material covering a broad range of topics. Each of them had a decidedly male perspective, even the ones written by women, but without the hint of chauvinism she hated in most men's magazines.

Eamon Fitzgerald was either very ambitious or very crazy if he thought he could pull this off. There were already a zillion magazines on the stands catering to a black audience, many of them backed by big publishing conglomerates with more money and clout than she was sure he possessed. She couldn't imagine how he planned to make a dent in that market, particularly

with a magazine less sexy and more literate than most
of what was already out there.

But, her mind had already begun thinking up interesting possibilities. Coming up with a layout to match
the magazine's unorthodox approach would certainly be
a challenge. But she loved a challenge, almost as much
as she loved a mystery. Eamon Fitzgerald had furnished
her with one of each. His magazine and himself.

Jake arrived at the offices of *Ebony Man* at precisely
nine o'clock Monday morning. A different woman sat at
the reception desk, shorter, plumper, fiftyish, Jake
guessed. She offered Jake a smile that revealed a slight
gap between her two front teeth that made Jake think of
her as Esther Rolle with a page boy.

"Hi, I'm Dottie," the woman said. "You must be Jake
McKenna."

"Hi, Dottie." Jake smiled back. "Is Mr. Fitzgerald
around?"

"He said for you to wait for him here. He should be
along any minute."

Jake supposed turnabout was fair play. Resigned to the
wait, she might as well be nosy. She had a mystery to
solve.

"There was another woman sitting here last Friday."

"That must have been Mr. Fitzgerald's assistant Margot. She fills in for me sometimes when I'm out. She's a
nice girl, a little reserved. British, you know."

Jake nodded. "Has she worked for Mr. Fitzgerald long?"

"I don't know." Dottie made a face, considering it. "All
I know is that she came with him from Boston."

That wasn't any help at all. She already knew he came
from Boston. And she'd checked *Who's Who in Publishing*
and *Literary Marketplace* over the weekend. Neither one
of them had the smallest listing for an Eamon Fitzgerald.

Before she could ask another question, she heard the ping of the elevator doors about to open. She looked around to see Eamon Fitzgerald walking toward her. Liza was wrong about his eyes. She may have been paranoid before, but they still seemed to bore into her.

"Good morning, Ms. McKenna. I see you made it here in one piece. And on time at that."

"Good morning," she echoed, turning to face him fully. "I'm usually pretty good at dodging mad bicycle riders." She didn't say anything about the on-time part.

He appeared to ignore her comment, motioning for her to precede him down the hallway. "Let me show you to your office; then I'll introduce you around."

She walked alongside him down the corridor, watching the nameplates outside the office doors. They all bore only a Ms. or Mr. whoever, without even an initial to signify the person had a first name.

He stopped at the door immediately preceding the big corner one they'd been in before. He flicked on the light, illuminating a large space dominated by a large black desk, on which rested a computer with the oversize monitor common to graphic design. There was a credenza to the left, and a matching file cabinet adjacent to the desk.

When he'd said "office," she'd assumed he meant one of those little cubicles with the upholstered walls, not a real one. Nor did she expect to be introduced to two other employees who reported to her. She'd thought senior designer was one of those propped-up titles, used to make the owner feel good, but no such thing as a junior or regular designer existed.

After the art department, they went through editorial and production and soon all the names and faces and titles started to blur together. He left her at her office door, claiming to have a meeting to run off to.

Jake settled into the big gray chair behind her desk

and began to sort through the stack of material already piled on her desk. Her nameplate was on top. She looked at the *Ms. McKenna* written in sunken gray letters on a black surface and shook her head. So formal for a casual office where even the managing editor wore jeans. Maybe he was trying to change that, too.

She put it aside, planning to slide it into its slot when she went out for lunch. Next came a memo about her joining the company, the usual please help me welcome so and so to the staff. It was stamped rather than signed *Eamon Fitzgerald*. She had the feeling there were hundreds of these things printed up somewhere—only the names were changed to incriminate the guilty.

She called a meeting of her "staff" to make sure everyone had something to do for the day. She liked Leo immediately. Fresh out of school, he was eager for as much work and as much responsibility as she would give him. Sandra was different. She'd sensed the woman's hostility the moment Eamon introduced them. She wondered if that was due more to the fact that she'd expected to be promoted herself, or that Eamon's hand had rested momentarily on Jake's back at the time.

Probably some of each, Jake decided, heading off to the supply room to stock her office. Either way, she was going to watch out for her.

The rest of the morning passed quickly, as many of the staff stopped by to do just what the memo suggested. There seemed to be two camps at the magazine—Eamon Fitzgerald supporters and Eamon Fitzgerald detractors. Either he was the best thing to hit the office since the Xerox machine, or he was a hideous combination of Simon Legree, the Marquis de Sade, and Dracula rolled into one. There were no positions in between.

Jake didn't side with either of them, though the latter group was by far the larger. She really didn't know him well enough to make that kind of decision. Besides, doing so would surely alienate someone, and she already felt like a gate-crasher at somebody else's party. The staff were a tight-knit bunch, whether they agreed on the merits of the new boss or not. She would have to be the one to make friends if she stayed there.

The three kings took her to lunch that first day, to make up for Friday's "honest mistake." They were the only ones who were honestly mistaken, if they thought she bought that story. They might not have known who she was, but she was more sure now that Mr. Fitzgerald did. It didn't take a rocket scientist to figure out in which camp these three belonged.

By Wednesday, Jake knew Dani liked going to the day care center after school. The supervisor told her she'd made the mistake of introducing her to the other children as Danielle. She said Dani'd looked her in the eye, corrected her, then glanced around the room as if daring anyone to call her otherwise. There hadn't been any trouble after that.

Everything was going pretty smoothly, Jake noted, opening the paycheck waiting for her on her desk Thursday morning. It meant she could afford the steak she was serving on Saturday without eating hot dogs from the vendor on the corner for an entire week.

She was starting to feel less like the new kid on the block, having won over several of the more surly members of the staff to her position of neutrality.

The only thing that bothered her was Eamon Fitzgerald himself. She'd seen him every day that week during his "rounds" as she called them. At some point during the day, he'd descend from on high, ostensibly looking for someone specific. Yet he'd take the most circuitous route in getting there. He was spying on them and everyone knew it.

The others always seemed to sense he was coming. Like a herd of antelope when a predator comes on the scene, they would scurry out of sight, out of harm's way. He always caught her talking on the phone to Liza, or padding around barefoot in her office, or some other embarrassing situation. He'd merely continue on down the hall, looking the epitome of dignity in his immaculate dark suits—as if he hadn't seen anything at all.

The as-if-he-hadn't-seen-anything part was what annoyed her. Being honest with herself, Jake knew she was no raving beauty. She wouldn't really describe herself as pretty, either. Her huge brown eyes seemed out of place with her small nose and prominent cheekbones, her mouth a bit too wide to fit with any of her other features. She had an interesting face, as she saw it, one with endearing flaws rather than detracting ones.

Her body was another story. She'd matured early, and was quite comfortable with the womanly curves she'd cried about having to accept as a teenager. All her friends had been flat as boards, without a hip in sight. Now she liked to dress provocatively, showing off her legs in particular, her best asset. So why did Eamon Fitzgerald stubbornly refuse to look at them?

It wasn't that she wanted him to do anything about them. She was saving him for Liza. She wanted some indication that he was aware of her as a woman, not merely an employee. Why that should matter was beyond her own reasoning. She wasn't sure she liked him, what little she knew about him. And he was her boss, for goodness' sake. Plenty of women would kill to work for a man who didn't comment about their legs—or any other part of their anatomy.

Jake shrugged. Maybe he was gay. No. Something about that thought offended her. She suspected the publisher of *Ebony Man* was all man, down to the core. She would have to let Liza do the investigating. That is, if she ever got around to inviting Mr. Fitzgerald to her birthday party in the first place.

Jake took Dottie to lunch that afternoon. Not only had she been with the magazine the longest, she was the only staff member he called by first name. The mystery of Eamon Fitzgerald was no closer to being solved now than it had been the first day she started. And she should know something about him if she was going to have him in her home.

Dottie proved no help at all. She seemed interested only in talking about her new grandson, bringing out picture after picture until Jake wanted to rip out her own hair. Every time she tried to steer the conversation back to Eamon, and at least she knew how to pronounce it now, like Ay-mun, Dottie would laugh and kick in with the grandson again. Jake was beginning to wonder if Dottie was a character description rather than a nickname for Dorothy.

That evening, Jake went down to the first floor to pick up Dani, feeling defeated. No amount of probing seemed to produce any amount of information from anyone. Rather than discouraging her, the lack of information only made her more curious.

She stopped in the doorway to the nursery, taking a step back in shock. That couldn't be the awesome Eamon Fitzgerald scrunched down on one of the little school chairs. And, good Lord, he couldn't be smiling. Who was that child, not Dani, sitting so nicely on his lap? Didn't ogres eat little children for breakfast?

He was holding a dinosaur toy, making it do a funny little walk up her arm. Dani giggled, and Jake felt something go soft inside her. She couldn't remember the last time she'd heard Dani laugh.

"Hi, Dani," Jake said, unable to keep the emotion from her voice. "Hello, Mr. Fitzgerald." Jake nodded to the supervisor, who was erasing blackboards at the other end of the room.

Dani slid off his lap and ran to her. Eamon stood, and

Jake wondered how he'd ever fit his six-foot-plus frame
on that little chair. She turned her attention back to
Dani. "Are you ready to go, sweetheart?"

Dani nodded, putting on her jacket and slinging her
little knapsack over one arm. That finished, Dani took
her hand.

"Good night, Mr. Fitzgerald," Jake said, looking up at
him. "Thanks for keeping Dani company."

She realized this was an ideal opportunity to ask him
about Saturday, but somehow she couldn't. Not after
seeing Dani smiling after so many months. Both her
investigation and her matchmaking plans seemed so
frivolous.

For a moment, it seemed as if he wanted to say something, too. Perhaps an explanation of what he was doing
in the nursery in the first place.

"Good night, Ms. McKenna. Good night, Dani."

"Good night, Uncle Eamon."

Uncle Eamon? Jake looked from one to the other.
When had that happened? In the five or ten or fifteen
minutes they'd been sitting there together? Dani usually
wasn't that friendly with strangers. Sometimes she was
overtly hostile, and Jake would have to give her a stern
talking-to about the proper way to behave. This made no
sense at all. But Dani was still smiling and chatting happily as they boarded the D train headed downtown to
their Greenwich Village apartment. She was grateful at
least for that.

Friday at five o'clock, Jake mustered all her nerve and
headed up to Eamon's office. The only useful information she'd culled that week was its location, two floors
above. The only pertinent information she'd learned
was that Liza was depressed since the last guy she'd gone
out with turned out to be a total jerk. Who knew if

Eamon would turn out to be any better? But she owed it to her friend to invite him anyway.

If nothing else, he was incredibly good looking. And he had made Dani laugh, so he couldn't really be that bad. Not unless ogres were operating under a different set of ground rules these days.

Stepping off the elevator, she noticed immediately how different this floor was from the one downstairs. Not only did the color scheme differ—sober browns and beiges—but what would have been the reception desk was a large open area leading directly to ornate wooden double doors with a gold name plaque. It read EAMON J. FITZGERALD in letters so large that Stevie Wonder could have read them in the dark. So, the mighty were allowed not only two names, but three!

Eamon's secretary wasn't at her desk in the outer office. Jake contemplated sitting on the brown leather sofa by the door and waiting. That would be the polite thing to do, but she gave up that idea almost immediately. The door to the inner office, equally large and ornate, was ajar. Peering in, Jake could see there wasn't anyone inside here either.

What an opportunity! There was no better place to find out a man's secrets than his office, except his bedroom, of course. But those weren't the kind of secrets that interested Jake.

She slipped inside the big door, closing it softly behind her. A large leather sofa like the one outside sat against the wall to her left. Straight ahead was the large mahogany desk that used to be in the office downstairs. Two leather chairs faced it, with a larger chair behind it. To her right was an enormous bookcase that ran the entire length of the wall. It met another door, almost all the way to the windows.

Jake quickly dropped her purse and jacket onto one of the chairs facing the desk and kicked off her shoes

under the other. She might not have much time to look
around.

She walked back to the bookcase—actually, several
ebony wood bookcases, one after the other, encased in
glass and lit from behind. Funny, that was the only real
light in the room, aside from a small lamp on the desk.

Interesting, Jake thought, scanning the titles of the
books. All nonfiction, she noticed, apparently arranged
by subject in alphabetical order by author. Everything
from archaeology to zoology with a few interesting pit
stops in between. W.E.B. DuBois, Margaret Mead,
Descartes, Asimov, Edgar Cayce. Edgar Cayce, the mys-
tic? The last bookcase was devoted exclusively to an
extensive collection of law books.

The books a man owned were supposed to say a lot
about him, but what did this mean? That he was well
read for one thing. But why law books? That intrigued
her, not only because there were so many of them, but
because she was sure they were the technical kind de-
tailing specific trials and precedents and things like that.
What use could a publisher have for that kind of information? She tried to slide the glass open to examine one
of them, but the case was locked. All of them were.

She tried the door to the other room. That was
locked, too. She could swear she saw a light on under the
door, though she couldn't hear any noise coming from
the other side.

Feeling defeated, Jake let her breath out on a sigh.
With her luck, the man had already gone home. That's
what she got for procrastinating so long. Maybe she
should abandon the whole idea, which was half-baked at
best and just plain dumb at worst. But she knew she
wouldn't do that. Not now, when she at least had a good
pretext under which to introduce him to Liza.

She settled on writing him a note instead, asking him
to call her. Her purse yielded a small notepad but no

pen. She glanced at his immaculate desk. There wasn't even a piece of paper on it, only an empty letter tray marked IN, a phone, the lamp, and a covered candy dish.

Why was she not surprised? She slid into his chair, hoping to find a pen, write the note, and get the heck out of there. But the center drawer didn't budge; none of them did, although none but the center drawer appeared to have a lock. She'd heard of people having one locked drawer for their personal things, but all of them? And Liza called her paranoid.

Jake gritted her teeth. Could anything go her way? Obviously not. Maybe she'd seen too many Bond movies, but the idea seized her to check the underside of the desk for a spare key.

Ignoring the little voice in her head that told her she was invading his privacy, a privacy he obviously didn't want invaded, she got down on her hands and knees to look.

She was just discovering real life was different—no keys, taped or otherwise—when she felt a hand on her arm yanking her to her feet.

"What the hell are you doing, Jake?"

She felt a shiver run through her, coming face-to-face with a very angry, very controlled Eamon Fitzgerald. He hadn't even yelled at her. He'd spoken with the kind of quiet fury that often precedes a very messy murder.

"I can explain," she began, not that she had the slightest idea what that explanation was going to be. Where on earth had he come from anyway? She hadn't heard either door open, and both were closed now.

"There's no need to explain anything. You were spying on me. Or trying to."

He let go of her arm. Jake took a step back, willing the butterflies fluttering in her stomach to alight on the nearest branch. Their appearance had nothing to do whatsoever with Eamon's anger, but instead with the presence of the man himself.

He was Liza's, she reminded herself, if the other woman wanted him. Jake was sure she would. Being attracted to him herself would prove to be an unnecessary complication. She had no time for complications of any sort. Especially not with her boss when she needed this job for Dani's sake.

"I was looking for a pen. I was going to leave you a note."

"A note," he echoed. "And what were you planning to write this note on?"

She glanced back toward the chair that held her belongings. "I have paper in my purse." He gave her a look that said exactly how much he doubted that, but he did seem to relax a little. "Actually, I wanted to ask you something," she added.

"What did you want to ask me that couldn't wait until Monday?" He motioned for her to sit. She did so, walking around the big desk as gingerly as possible. Now was not the time to slip and end up on one's fanny. She immediately put on one shoe, rooting around for the other with her bare foot.

"Well, it's not that it's so important, it's that, well . . ." How did one go about asking one's boss to one's birthday party, a boss one knew precisely one week, who thought you were either a snoop or an idiot or an awful combination of the two?

"I know it's short notice, but I'm having dinner at my house tomorrow night and I wanted to know if you'd like to come. It's very casual. We're having steak."

Jake squirmed in her seat a little, feeling his measuring eyes on her. For his birthday, she was going to buy him a pair of mud-brown contacts, or maybe dark blue. Anything that wasn't so piercing.

"We?"

"Yes, it's in honor of my birthday. There should be about eight of us."

"Congratulations. How old are you going to be? Or am I not supposed to ask that?"

"Twenty-nine," she replied without hesitation. She had no hang-ups about age, but she added anyway, "Remember that number. It's the same age I'm going to be next year."

Not a smile, not a glimmer of one appeared on his face. "What should I bring?"

She assumed that meant he was coming. "Just yourself. I've got everything covered." She took out one of her business cards with her home address on it and gave it to him.

He scanned it a moment, then placed it on the desk in front of him. "I'll see you tomorrow night, then."

Jake realized this was her cue to leave, but she still hadn't found her other shoe. She could always get up and look for it instead of taking blind stabs under the chair with her toes. But there was no way to do that without getting down on her hands and knees in front of Eamon Fitzgerald. One time in one day was enough. Besides, if she could just make it downstairs she had another pair in her desk.

"Good night, then," she said, rising, trying to stand as evenly as she could. "See you tomorrow." She picked up her purse and jacket and started toward the door, stopping short when he spoke again.

"By the way, Ms. McKenna. Please show a little more . . . decorum in dressing yourself next week." She glanced back to notice that this time he did look at her legs. The hem of her red silk skirt fell barely to midthigh. "People are starting to talk."

What people? she wanted to ask. For goodness' sake, her skirts were short, but they weren't that bad. "Don't tell me you're a prude, Mr. Fitzgerald," she tossed over her shoulder as she continued on her way.

The elevator was taking forever to come, and the

whole while she could see Eamon standing at the door
to the outer office. She refused to look at him. She was
concentrating on looking as dignified as possible with
only one shoe on, and a face turning progressively red-
der under his scrutiny. She let out a relieved sigh as she
heard the ping of the elevator door opening.

"Aren't you forgetting something, Ms. McKenna?"

Automatically, she turned to face him, her eyes flying
open in surprise, seeing him dangle a little black shoe
from his fingertips. *That rat! He'd had it all along!*

She wondered what Liza would do in a situation like
this. Cool, calm Liza, who would have had the foresight
to keep both shoes on in the first place.

Drawing a blank, she walked back and snatched the
shoe out of his hand. Rather than use it as a weapon, she
quickly slipped it on and scurried back toward the closing elevator doors. She could swear she'd actually seen
him smile as she'd run up and grabbed her shoe. It was
funny, she admitted, though thoroughly embarrassing.

"What time is dinner tomorrow night?" she heard him
call as she stepped into the elevator. She poked her head
out, and this time the smile was unmistakable. "Eight
o'clock."

Then the elevator doors closed. As the car started on
its way down to the first floor, she could hear laughter,
rich masculine laughter that could only be coming from
one source.

Faith and begorra! Eamon Fitzgerald did have a sense
of humor after all.

Three

Eamon glanced out his large bedroom window just as another flash of lightning streaked across the sky. He'd counted four such flashes in the past fifteen minutes. The storm was getting worse.

This was one hell of a night for him to have to go out to the birthday party of a woman he barely knew and was sure it was in his best interest not to know. He'd hired her against his better judgment, and now he was stuck with her. In truth, he didn't know why he had. He'd only intended to screen suitable applicants, so his brother, Jim, wouldn't pick someone with purple hair or fifteen body piercings or something else equally objectionable.

Instead he ended up with someone who dressed as if she stepped off the runway at a Paris fashion show, with necklines down to there and hems up to here. He'd asked her to dress more modestly, and she'd laughed at him. He supposed he deserved that. The only person apparently disturbed by the way she dressed was him.

It drove him crazy, forcing himself to look only at her face, never letting his gaze stray over her lushly curved body. He might not be able to draw it back in time, not before she caught him. Then she would think him some sort of gawking pervert, or worse, the sort of man who expected his female employees to sleep with him in order to keep their jobs. That was definitely not the case.

For all he knew, she was married anyway. He finished

buttoning his shirt and tucked it into the waistband of
his pants. She did have a six-year-old daughter, not that
that proved much these days. Then there was the plain
gold band she wore. It could merely be for good luck.
But if so, why did she wear it on the third finger of her
left hand, the finger usually reserved for wedding bands?

Eamon sighed as he buckled his belt. No, Jake
McKenna was married, and therefore off-limits. He
couldn't imagine what sort of man would marry her,
though. Probably one with a strong constitution so he
could withstand that constant chatter of hers without losing his mind.

He'd heard her talking to some friend of hers on the
phone. The woman must either have the patience of Job
or be hard of hearing in one ear to put up with that. And
her laugh. He'd heard it echoing down the halls as effervescent and intoxicating as a glass of pink champagne.

Suddenly he felt sorry for this man Jake had married,
whoever he was. She obviously wasn't the stay-at-home
type. Her résumé showed she'd worked since she was in
high school—as a model, no less. That at least explained
the clothes. And any man, any sane man, would want to
keep a woman like that at home under lock and key—
out of trouble.

He didn't suspect she'd be unfaithful necessarily, but
without the lock and key part, the poor man was likely to
come home and find a note taped to the refrigerator
door. *Darling, the children and I have joined an expedition to
Bora Bora. Please follow as soon as you can.* There'd be a lot
of Xs and Os down at the bottom and maybe a hastily
made lip mark. But sealed with a kiss or not, she'd still
be gone. He'd have to offer his condolences to Mr.
McKenna when he met him tonight.

He slipped on his favorite pair of black loafers, pulled
on his jacket, and strode toward the kitchen. Part of him
was looking forward to an evening with the flamboyant

Jake McKenna. Part of him longed for a respite from duties and obligations and responsibilities, no matter how brief. Part of him hated the emotional desert his life had become.

Sure, he was a partner in one of the most prestigious law firms in Boston. He had a beautiful, poshly decorated home in an exclusive Boston suburb, and another out on Montauk on Long Island. He'd made more money than he ever intended to spend in one lifetime. He had things, but no people. There didn't seem to be any people in his life save for clients or business associates and the occasional date necessitated by his career.

But no family, no real friends, no one he considered to be more than a casual acquaintance. All the people in his life had simply slipped away. He hadn't seen his own brother in over a year, although that was not from lack of trying. For a while there, he'd felt himself dying inside by slow degrees.

Then Uncle Eamon had called and changed everything. Running the magazine challenged him, distracted him from the problems of his own life, though in truth he hadn't the faintest idea if what he wanted to do would work. At least he would have help soon. He'd tracked down his brother Jim the nomad in Florida of all places. When he'd heard what had happened all he'd said was, "I'm coming." After all this time, his little brother might finally be turning into a human being.

Eamon retrieved the bottle of champagne he'd bought as a present for Jake from the refrigerator. She was a distraction of a different sort. By the time this ended, he'd probably be a little nuts himself and broke besides. He had no time for musings about wild red hair that fell down her back in loose curls that smelled of violets. No time for daydreams about the way her outrageous clothes revealed all that luscious skin, the color of deep, rich honey, and probably just as smooth.

Still, as he drove from his apartment in the shadow of Lincoln Center to hers in the heart of Greenwich Village, her image superimposed itself on his consciousness. How fitting that the first woman he'd met in the past three years that reminded him he had something as mundane as a sex drive was also already spoken for. These days, if it weren't for bad luck, he'd have no luck at all.

Suddenly, he hated Mr. McKenna, whoever he was. Not only was he in a warm, dry house, he was there with Jake, possibly snuggled by the fireplace, if there was one. Or maybe enjoying a quick fling in bed before the guests arrived. Maybe he'd punch Mr. McKenna in the mouth when he saw him.

Walking the two blocks to her apartment from where he'd left his car, he hunched his shoulders and sped up his pace. He'd forgotten how treacherous parking in New York could be. And he hadn't bothered to bring an umbrella. He arrived at her apartment soaking wet and in a hell of a mood. He punched the doorbell with the side of his fist and waited. He planned to stay only until the minute dinner ended. Then if he possessed any sense at all, he'd go straight home, take a cold shower, and go to bed.

In a second, Jake was standing in front of him wearing a short blue terry cloth robe that barely reached the top of her thighs. Her lips were parted in an O of surprise.

"What are you doing here? Didn't Liza call you?" Before he could answer, she ushered him in the door. "You're soaked."

Brilliant observation. Eamon kept his caustic comment to himself, extending the bottle of champagne toward her. "This is for you."

She took the bottle from him, reached around him, and closed the door. "Thank you. But you'd better get out of those things. I think I have some clothes I can lend you." She led him down the hallway to the dining room. "Wait here," she said, already heading down another hallway. "I'll see what I can find."

Having nothing else to do, he surveyed the room. The beige color of the hallway ended abruptly at the archway to the room, replaced by a bluish gray paint. Here, a large multicolor area rug covered the parquet floors. Over that stood a black rectangular table and four chairs. An enormous china cabinet stood against one wall.

Perpendicular to that was a bookshelf built into the wall, crammed with all sorts of books and papers and magazines, apparently in no particular order. On the wall above the table hung a large painting, an abstract, rendered in shades of blue, mauve, and gray.

The living room lay to his left. He descended the three carpeted steps leading down to the large square room dominated by a large L-shaped sofa. The piano in the corner of the room caught his attention. He ran a finger over the smooth, polished wood. Though obviously old, it appeared to be in good condition. One silver-framed photograph rested atop it. In it, Jake held Dani in her arms and a man had his arms around the two of them.

The illusive Mr. McKenna, he presumed. Neither he nor Dani appeared to be home. The only lights he'd noticed were the one in the hallway, the one in the living room, and the one in the room Jake had gone into.

Another painting hung on the wall above the piano, but he knew what this one was. A nude woman sitting sideways in a rocking chair, so that all you saw were arms, back, legs, and the hint of a round derriere. There were others; in fact the living room walls were crammed with them. Portraits, landscapes, more nudes, even one that looked like Jake, some more abstracts. There was a similar element to all of them, hinting that they'd all been painted by the same artist.

He drank all this in, every detail, mentally filing it away in a folder labeled *things I know about Jake McKenna.* He went back to where she'd left him, not wanting her to find him snooping around after his reaction to her doing the same thing in his office.

It wasn't the snooping he'd minded so much, it was his own reaction to seeing her round derriere sticking up in the air at him like a taunt. For a crazy moment, he'd had the urge to show her a few things one could do in that position that were a lot more interesting than casing someone's office.

Instead, he'd hauled her up off the floor and nearly scared her half to death. If that kept up, Mr. McKenna would probably punch *him* in the mouth.

"Sorry I took so long," she said when she rejoined him in the dining room. "I couldn't find anything suitable at first. You can change in the bathroom," she said, leading him to the first door along the hallway. "I have to change, too. If you're finished first, I have a bottle of wine breathing in the kitchen. Pour us each a glass."

After that, Jake hurried along the hallway back to her room. Why on earth hadn't Liza called him? She'd given her his number along with those of the other guests to call when she found out Dani was sick. How could she entertain when Dani had a fever of 102 degrees? If it were anyone else, she would have sent them home, rain-soaked or not.

Then again, what was she complaining about? Here she had Eamon Fitzgerald alone—and on her territory. Too bad she didn't have any truth serum lying around. Maybe a couple of glasses of wine would serve the same purpose—in vino veritas and all that.

Jake threw off her robe and pulled on a pair of lacy panties. The night was cool, so she dressed in a hot-pink

Angora sweater with a deep V in both front and back over a pair of faded, skintight jeans. She brushed out her hair, arranging it in a loose ponytail high on her head. Her hair still hung past her shoulders.

After checking on Dani, who slept peacefully in her own room, she went to look for Eamon. She found him in the living room, standing at the piano, the picture of her, Dan, and Dani in one hand, a glass of wine in the other. Dan's clothes fit him almost perfectly, except for the shoulders, which were a little too snug, and the legs, which were a little too short. He still managed to look undeniably sexy.

But it was only his mind she was interested in. That sounded terribly trite, but it was true. What kind of man would go out on a night like this to the birthday party of a woman he barely knew? Any sane person would have called and canceled. What was he thinking as he stood there perfectly still, unmoving, as if it were a Gorgon he faced and it had turned him to stone?

"Dani looks like her father," he said, startling her. She hadn't realized he knew she was there.

"Yes," Jake agreed, descending the stairs to stand beside him. She noticed the second glass of wine resting on a crystal coaster atop the piano. She reached for it and sipped from it deeply.

"I think she has your eyes, though." He placed the picture on the piano.

"That's impossible," Jake said, adjusting the picture just so. "Dani looks exactly like her father."

"Where is he, Dani's father, I mean?"

"He was killed in a car accident seven months ago."

"I'm sorry."

Jake managed a tiny smile. Somehow, those universal and expected words of condolence sounded sincere coming from him. "There's no need to be."

"Has it been hard raising Dani by yourself?"

"She hasn't adjusted well to her father being gone."

"And how about you?" Eamon asked. "How have you been adjusting?"

Jake shrugged. "I'm okay, I guess." She'd given up grieving a long time ago, but the feeling of absence took a long time to go away. "I miss him, especially with Dani. He was the disciplinarian in the family. I'm lucky if I can get her to go to bed on time."

Jake managed a faint smile, realizing how intently Eamon watched her. "I'm sorry about that. I didn't mean to depress you with my family problems."

"You didn't depress me," he said softly. "Are you all right, Jake?"

"I'm fine." She took a sip from her glass. "It's been a long crazy day and Dani is sick and I thought Liza was going to call you." She'd purposely asked Liza to call everyone, knowing she'd have to talk to Eamon. It was the least she could do if she had to postpone their meeting.

"As I see it," Jake continued, "we can either stand around being maudlin, or I can fix us some dinner while your clothes dry. I vote for the latter. How about you?"

"Dinner sounds fine."

"Good. Make yourself at home. Dinner should be ready in less than an hour."

Once in the kitchen, Jake was happy to have the evening back on track. So, she'd slipped and told Eamon a few things she would rather have kept to herself. At least he was sympathetic. Some men bolted for the nearest exit the minute a woman showed the slightest sign of getting emotional. To some men, learning your middle name was a big deal.

She opened the refrigerator door, taking out all the ingredients for their meal. Once everything was cooking on its respective burner, she turned to take a peek through the kitchen door to see what Eamon was doing.

She nearly jumped, finding him standing directly in front of her.

"Can I help you with anything?"

"I may need CPR if you keep sneaking up on me like that." Jake placed a hand on her chest and let out a long breath. "If you mean with dinner, I've got everything covered: steak *au poivre, carottes a la ciboulette,* and *pommes persillade.* In other words, steak with peppercorns, carrots with chives, and potatoes with parsley and garlic."

Eamon leaned a shoulder against the refrigerator. "You have a beautiful accent. Did you study French in school?"

"*Sacre bleu!* When I was little, I wasn't allowed to speak anything but French at home. My mother thought I would lose what she considered to be my cultural identity if I didn't. My mother was born in France and lived most of her life there. She came to America right before I was born." She tore off a piece of aluminum foil and laid it on the counter. "These are authentic French recipes I'm making."

Eamon took a sip of his wine. "If anything I'd have figured you had a touch of Irish blood in your family tree."

"Why would you think that?"

"The last name McKenna, for one. The red hair. It seemed to fit."

"Appearances can be deceiving," she said with a mysterious smile. She wrapped the loaf of French bread in foil and popped it into the oven. "My uncle Jake had red hair until it turned completely white a few years ago, and believe me, Maurice Chevalier had nothing on him."

Eamon laughed softly, a pleasant sound to Jake's ears. "Isn't Jake an unusual name for a Frenchman?"

"It's Jacques, really, but being a lowly American with poor pronunciation, it always came out Jake. I was named for him."

"So Jake is short for Jacqueline."

Jake nodded. "Funny, I would have thought the same of you, given your name and the blue eyes."

"I was named for my uncle who was named for the Irish cop who delivered him on the subway when my grandmother went into premature labor. Where the eyes come from is anybody's guess. Probably the same place my family picked up the name Fitzgerald."

He shrugged. "You wouldn't believe the looks I would get from the Irish or Italian teachers at school when they would call the roll for the first time and I'd raise my hand. They were definitely not expecting me."

"I bet." And now that she'd finally gotten him talking, she hated to admit that everything was ready. She issued Eamon into the dining room and followed a few minutes later carrying two steaming plates.

"It looks delicious," Eamon said, unfolding his own napkin.

"One can only hope," she said more to herself than to him. Jake sliced into her steak and brought a small piece of meat to her mouth. Now she knew why the recipe called for *ground* peppercorns. The whole kernels crunched loudly between her teeth. Liza was right. You could mess up steak.

They ate mostly in silence, Jake breaking into occasional laughter at the rigors of eating the crunchy meal, and Eamon smiling. More of a half smile, really. And if a half smile could do such wicked things to her insides, she wondered what an ear-to-ear grin would do.

When the meal was over, Eamon rose to help Jake clear away the dishes. Retrieving the chocolate mousse cake she'd planned to serve as dessert, she suggested they open the champagne Eamon had brought her.

"Jake McKenna, I think you're trying to get me drunk."

"Don't be ridiculous." She rooted around in her miscellaneous drawer for a scissors to cut the string on the cake box. True, she had thought of trying to get him a little tipsy in the hopes of getting him to open up, but the only one who seemed to be doing any talking out of turn was her. "I only thought it would go well with the cake."

"Are you trying to take advantage of me, or are you planning to pump me for information?"

He was standing behind her and she turned to look up at him. Curse his unreadable eyes. It was impossible to tell from his expression whether he was serious or not. "I don't know what you mean."

"You spent the entire week interrogating the staff about me. Then I found you snooping in my office. Now it seems I'm the only guest at a supposed birthday party. I was wondering, what, if anything, was the point of all this."

She turned back to the task of removing the string from the cake box. "I was curious about you, that's all. No one at the magazine seems to know anything about you." Or more likely was willing to tell her. "And there was nothing in the library."

He laughed. "You went to the library to check up on me?"

"Dani and I go every Saturday," she said defensively.

"And what deep dark secrets were you hoping to discover?"

"None really. I wanted to know more about the magazine, and there was nothing, not even about your uncle. What did you do to him anyway?"

"I didn't do anything with him. He's in Europe with some gold digger who thinks he has money. And don't try to turn this around, Jake. You are the one guilty of playing amateur sleuth around here, and very badly, too."

"I've already admitted that." She sliced two portions of cake, a thin one for herself and a more generous one for him.

"Why didn't you simply ask me what you wanted to know?"

"I thought you might think I was more than idly curious."

"Is that what you are?"

She glanced back at him. "Of course." There was that suggestive little half smile again. "If you must know, I was planning on fixing you up with my friend Liza. I thought I should know something about you."

"Were planning? Does that mean you've decided to keep me for yourself?"

"Am planning," she amended, walking around him to open the refrigerator. She retrieved the champagne and handed it to him to open. "I have a feeling you're one of those dreadfully boring one-woman men, and I'm much too fickle for that sort of thing."

"Don't I have any say in whether I'm fixed up or not?"

"Of course not. You're a man."

"Come again?"

"Everyone knows that it's the woman in a relationship who's in control of these things."

"Which things are these?"

Jake got a silver tray from the cabinet and began loading it with the cake and two champagne flutes. "You know. Whether they go out in the first place, how the relationship progresses . . ." He looked at her as if she'd told him the earth was flat.

"For example," she continued. "Bob and Joan are two reasonably attractive people at a party. Bob sees Joan across the crowded room and he likes what he sees, so he decides to go over and talk to her. One of two things can happen. A, Joan is similarly impressed by Bob and they start to talk, or B, Joan thinks he's a jerk and tells him to buzz off. Joan is the one in control of the situation."

"What happens if Bob doesn't go away so easily?"

"Again, one of two things can happen. Joan could be

flattered by his persistence, and again they could talk. If not, Bob becomes one of those obnoxious men that pester all the attractive women at parties and no one invites him to them anymore."

"What if Joan really likes Phil, and Phil hasn't noticed her from across the crowded room or whatever?"

"Then she goes over to him and talks to him, of course."

"I thought that was the man's part."

"Not anymore. It's a new millennium. Women can do anything they want."

"What if Phil's not interested?"

"But he probably is, assuming Joan isn't one of those obnoxious women that pester all the attractive men at parties. Most men are still too flattered by a woman approaching them to say no to anything."

The cork slid from the bottle with a loud pop. Eamon filled each glass, then added the bottle to the tray. Jake led the way into the living room, settling herself on one side of the L-shaped sofa. Eamon claimed the other.

Picking up his glass of champagne, he asked, "And when did you become an expert on the subject?"

"I'm French. And if there's anything the French know about, it's love. We invented it."

"I think biology might have something to do with that."

"I didn't say sex, I said love. You know, courtly love with knights in shining armor and ladies fair and all that. That's what the ideal of contemporary romantic love is based on."

"I thought it was the Spaniards who came up with that."

"That's what they'd like you to believe."

"And you're a believer in the ideal of contemporary romantic love?"

Jake lifted one shoulder in a feminine Gallic shrug. "I think there's a lot to be said for getting to know someone before hopping into bed with them. These days, it's a necessity. And there's nothing wrong with doing special things to please the person you love, as long as you draw the line at cutting off body parts to prove your devotion."

She laughed to herself, wondering how much of this nonsense he was actually taking seriously. She was about as French as a fried potato. Though her mother had done her best to prevent it, Jake considered herself to be American through and through.

"So, what would you do, Ms. Expert, if you happened to see a tall, dark, and handsome stranger across the room, say me, for instance?"

"I'd walk over to you and say, 'Hello, Eamon. How are you?'"

He shook his head in feigned disappointment. "That's the best line you could come up with?"

"I wouldn't need a line. I know you already."

"Suppose you didn't? What would you say?"

He seemed to be daring her to come up with something. "In the first place, I can't suppose things that aren't so. In the second, I'm saving you for Liza, so I'd merely be polite."

"That sounds like a cop-out."

"Now, Eamon, you can't expect me to tell all my secrets when you still haven't told any of yours."

He took a forkful of cake and chewed it slowly. "So, we're back to that again. What do you want to know?"

"Start at the beginning."

He put his plate on the table and sat back, draping his arm along the sofa. "I was born November twelfth, 1965, to James and Peggy Fitzgerald. We lived on Long Island. Four years later my brother Jim came along. We had a dog named Alaskan Rouge and a tree house in the backyard. I went to college in Rhode Island, Brown, then to law school, Harvard. I'd been practicing law in Boston until a couple of months ago when Uncle Eamon decided to retire. Will that do?"

That did explain the plethora of law books in his office, but otherwise the biography was severely lacking. "No. That sounds like one of those dreadful 'sum up your life in twenty-five words or less' essays. There's got to be more than that."

"I don't have any skeletons in my closet, if that's what you're looking for. What you see is what you get."

She doubted that. There was an intensity about him that belied his "I'm just a simple man" front. The waters of Eamon Fitzgerald's psyche surely ran deep.

"How do you like working at the magazine so far?"

Jake pursed her lips. Those ten words could have been substituted by a mere two: CASE CLOSED, in big block letters. "It's interesting." She nibbled on a forkful of cake.

"You see why I asked you to start before my brother did. One interloper per week is enough."

"I hate to tell you this, but most of the staff are not very fond of you."

"Don't be so diplomatic, Jake. Half of them would like to send me on a nice long walk off a very short pier." He took a sip from his cup, apparently unconcerned by the staff's dislike of him.

"Don't you care that they hate you?"

"Not particularly. My uncle Eamon is a sweet old man, but he hasn't got the slightest idea how to handle either money or employees. In most offices, the employees gripe about the heavy workload. I could fire half the staff tomorrow and people still wouldn't have a thing to complain about. No wonder they liked him. No one had to do any work. If they think I'm a sadist for putting an end to that, so be it."

"It isn't just that. You're so distant from everyone. The only time anyone sees you is when you come down on your daily spy missions, and you call everyone by his or her last name. They resent that after being so used to your uncle, who sounds more like a father confessor than an employer."

"Jake, I'm trying to impress on these people that the office is a place of business. It's not a social club where you get paid just for showing up. They're not bad people, or lazy, but you're right, they are used to my uncle's way of doing things.

"And I'm not spying on anyone. I'm ensuring that for at least fifteen minutes a day, everyone is doing what they're supposed to."

"Why don't you give them more time? I'm sure they'll come around."

"I don't have time, Jake."

He spoke so soberly that suddenly she felt sorry for him having to put his life in Boston on hold when his uncle retired. It must be doubly hard since he wasn't a publisher by profession. She wondered why his brother couldn't have handled it, but perhaps being the older of the two he felt more responsible. She might not be the only one with a soft spot for a namesake uncle.

"You know what would be a great idea?" she said. "A company picnic. The weather is warm already, so we could do something outside, maybe the beach. We could do it on a Friday, leave early for wherever we're going and be back by six o'clock when the nursery closes. It would certainly boost morale."

"I'll think about it."

Jake huffed out a sigh. That was hardly the response she'd expected for what she thought was a brilliant idea. "Is that your polite way of saying no?"

"It's the only way to say I'll think about it. Unlike some people, I do not tell fibs to save my skin."

"Oh, no? What about that little stunt in the studio? You knew who I was all along."

"I never said *I* didn't know who you were, I said *they*

didn't know who you were. It was an equivocation at worst."

"What I haven't figured out is whether it was a joke or a punishment for being late."

He shrugged. "Neither. It was an opportunity for a little fun that presented itself."

Eamon Fitzgerald believed in fun? Amazing! "At my expense!"

"You were late for an interview of all things."

"So I deserved what I got?"

"No. But you should have seen your face when Nick said your dress had to go. He only meant he didn't like it. He wasn't going to try to take it from you."

"I didn't know what kind of magazine *Ebony Man* was. I thought I was about to become next month's center-fold."

"Tsk, tsk." He shook his head. "And this from a woman with nude portraits hanging all over her apartment." He gestured to the wall across from him. "That one over the entertainment unit, that is you, isn't it?"

Jake gulped and placed a steadying hand on her cup. In all the years she'd had that painting hanging in one apartment or another, no one, not even Liza, had ever figured out that it was her. She'd done the painting from a photograph for a self-portrait assignment. Though she'd set the timer herself, she'd ended up squinting into the camera when the flash went off. Consequently, the face didn't really look like her, but the rest of it, that was pretty accurate.

"There is nothing wrong with exhibiting the human body," she said.

"Really?"

"I meant that artistically."

"I'm an art lover."

A particularly loud clap of thunder sounded, silencing the retort on Jake's lips. Immediately, it brought a renewed vigor to the rain pelting against the windows. Again she wondered what he was doing there in the middle of such a violent storm.

She leaned her back against the sofa, stretching out her legs on the coffee table. She hadn't realized how closely they'd drawn together while they talked. The top of her head nearly touched his elbow. "Why did you come here tonight, Eamon?"

"I said I would, and I don't like breaking promises, even small ones. And . . ." He tugged on a strand of her hair. "I was curious, too."

She laughed, looking up at him. "About me? I'm incredibly transparent, or hadn't you noticed?"

"I noticed." He seemed to study her for a moment. "I never did tell you happy birthday." He leaned toward her, cupping her shoulder in the palm of his hand. "Happy birthday, Jake."

She assumed he only meant to give her your garden-variety birthday kiss—over the second it had begun. But the instant his lips touched hers, something happened. A jolt of pure pleasure rocketed through her, and a tiny moan escaped her parted lips as his tongue slipped inside to join her own. She didn't think, she just responded, arching closer to him, angling her head to give him better access to her mouth. She inhaled, breathing in the spicy aroma of his cologne, and another masculine scent that was distinctly his own.

When he pulled away, she gazed up at him through the fringe of her lashes. His chest heaved and his hand rested on her waist, gently massaging her skin through the fuzzy fabric of her sweater. He watched her with those enigmatic eyes of his, as if he was waiting for something. But what? Her reaction to their strangely flammable kiss? How about out-and-out shock? She couldn't remember ever being so moved by a single kiss.

Maybe it was the wine, or the fact that she hadn't

slept much in the last couple of days, but her insides were astir with a mixture of awe and delight, and her skin felt flushed all over. Maybe she was coming down with Dani's flu.

He rested his forehead on hers, cupping her face in his palms. "I wasn't expecting this."

So, she wasn't the only one amazed by the unforeseen chemistry between them. "Me either."

She couldn't say who moved first. Honestly, she didn't care. Suddenly, she was in Eamon's arms, her mouth seeking his, her arms winding around his neck to hold him to her. This time, the kiss was longer, deeper, hungrier—as sizzling as the lightning that blazed outside her window.

And all the while, she heard him calling to her softly. That wasn't possible, was it? No matter how marvelously his lips felt on her own, it really would be a marvel if he could talk and kiss at the same time.

"Dani's awake." She pulled away from him and scrambled to her feet, feeling disheveled and quite a bit shaky. She rushed off to Dani's room, not looking back to see Eamon's reaction to her hasty departure.

She got Dani a drink of water and some fresh pajamas. The ones she wore were soaked through with perspiration. But at least her fever had broken. The little girl fell back to sleep almost immediately, but Jake lingered at her bedside trying to figure out what to do.

What just happened between her and Eamon shouldn't have. Heaven only knew why it had. But once it started, she hadn't been able to stop it. Hadn't wanted to stop it. How far would he have taken it, how far would she have let him go, if it hadn't been for Dani's interruption? She didn't have an answer for that, and frankly, she didn't want to know.

Well, they certainly couldn't pick up where they left off. The only thing to do was to tell him that he had to leave because Dani needed her. It was mostly true. She did want to keep an eye on Dani. She leaned over and clicked off the bedside lamp, gathering her courage before heading back down the hall.

Eamon was standing in the dining room when she got back, dressed in his own clothes. She'd forgotten he'd worn them, he'd looked so comfortable in the others.

"I'd better be going," he said, as she came to stand next to him.

She nodded and walked him to the door. She opened it and he stepped outside into the dimly lit hallway.

"Thanks for an interesting evening, Jake." His fingertips caressed the side of her face. She couldn't resist leaning closer to his touch. "You'd better rest up tomorrow. All hell is going to break loose in the office on Monday."

She wondered what he meant by that, but her attention was quickly taken up by Eamon's good-night kiss. Hard and quick and wholly devastating to her senses.

"Good night, Eamon," she whispered, watching him take the stairs rather than the elevator down to the lobby.

Once she'd closed the door, she leaned her back against it and sighed. What on earth had she done? Her lips were slightly swollen and tingly. Her body ached and called her a fool for ever letting him get anywhere near that door.

If she thought about this logically, getting involved with him didn't make sense with her working for him. What would happen if things ended badly? He might fire her, that's what.

She had to consider Dani, whom she wanted to protect from any harm. Introducing another man into Dani's life right now, someone who could be a father figure, might be detrimental to her, especially if things didn't work out.

And then there was Liza. "Oh, to hell with Liza," Jake said aloud. "Let her get her own dates from now on."

Four

All hell came in the form of six-foot-two, brown-haired, brown-eyed James Patrick Fitzgerald. Jake was sitting at her desk, early for a change, reading the paper and drinking coffee from a Styrofoam cup. She'd even worn a sedate pair of black pants with black oxfords and a white silk blouse. Her normally voluminous hair was tied back from her face with a pretty white bow.

Hearing a commotion out in the hallway, she peered out of her office. She knew it couldn't be Eamon. It was too early for his rounds. He rarely appeared before lunchtime. It wasn't the right kind of noise either. When he appeared the sounds were muffled—people scurrying wordlessly back to their desks, papers rustling, then his usual "Good afternoon, Ms. McKenna." This was, well, loud.

Curse the circular hallway! She couldn't see a thing. She only heard a woman laughing. Could that be Dottie? It was her voice, but she sounded so girlish.

She heard a faint rapping sound growing nearer. Then she saw him. Tall, handsome, though not as striking as his older brother, he strutted down the hallway, a briefcase in one hand, a rolled-up copy of the *Times* in the other, tapping it against the wall as he walked. He wore a pale gray suit, a turquoise shirt, and a tie that probably glowed in the dark. His open khaki-colored trench coat flapped behind him from the momentum of his stride.

He stopped in front of her door, comparing her to her nameplate. "You're Jake McKenna?"

She nodded, standing up straight and closing her mouth, which had fallen open in surprise.

"You're the prettiest Jake I've ever seen." He tapped her on the top of the head with the newspaper. "My office in five minutes." He walked the remaining distance to his own office, sauntered inside, and slammed the door.

Curiouser and curiouser, Jake mused, closing her mouth, which once again hung open. *That* was Eamon Fitzgerald's *brother*? How could this man and the one upstairs have been raised in the same household, be born of the same parents, and seemingly be so totally different?

She shook her head, wanting to ponder this further, but her phone was ringing. She sat down and picked up the receiver. "Jake McKenna."

"How was dinner Saturday?"

"Liza, you rat!" Jake jumped up from her chair in indignation. "You didn't call him on purpose."

"I thought if you thought he was so wonderful, you may as well keep him for yourself."

"I don't know what you're talking about."

"I know you and your matchmaking schemes. They're always a disaster. It was time someone turned the tables on you. So, what happened? Did he show up in the first place?"

"He showed up all right. Soaked."

"My, my, a chance to get him out of his clothes early in the evening."

"Liza! It wasn't like that at all, and you know it." Not at first. "I gave him some of Dan's clothes to put on."

"It was only a joke. Don't tell me you of all people are getting serious on me. So?"

"So I made the steaks, except I forgot to grind the peppercorns so it was a little strange, but other than that dinner was okay. The chocolate mousse cake I bought for dessert was delicious though."

"Why do I have the feeling there's something you're not telling me?"

"McKenna!" she heard the younger Fitzgerald bellow.

Under normal circumstances, Jake would have resented being summoned in such a manner. In this case, it gave her a hasty exit.

"Gotta go. The new boss is calling." She hung up and gave a little laugh. Liza wasn't the only one who could deal out some of the other's medicine. It was usually Liza hanging up on her.

"McKenna!"

She glanced at her watch. It was precisely five and a half minutes since he'd sauntered past her into his office. Apparently, he did share his brother's penchant for punctuality.

"Yes, Mr. Fitzgerald," she said, appearing in the doorway.

Of all the nerve! He was talking on the phone, his feet propped up on the desk. Why was he so insistent she go to his office if he wasn't ready to talk to her?

He motioned for her to sit down when he saw her. "Gotta go," he said to whoever was on the other end of the line. "My latest victim is here." He winked at her, and she wondered exactly what sort of victimization he had in mind.

He gave a short laugh, said, "Bye," then hung up the phone, dropping his feet to the floor. Suddenly he was all business, looking very much like Eamon sitting behind that desk.

"Let's get one thing straight. My brother may have hired you without either my knowledge or my consent, but I am the one you are going to have to prove yourself to. This is my department and I will run it as I see fit. Do we understand each other?"

Jake opened her mouth to speak, not that she was sure of what would come out. She was tempted to tell him he was the most arrogant pain in the butt she'd ever met and walk out, but she didn't get the chance to say anything.

"Now that that's settled, what are you doing for lunch today?" A smile broke out across his face.

"I hadn't planned anything."

"Good. I like to get to know the people I work with and I may as well start with you. How does twelve-thirty sound?"

He seemed so sincerely friendly that she wondered what all that bellowing was about. Perhaps because Eamon had gone over his head and done as he pleased without consulting him. He seemed to have no objection to her specifically, so she relaxed.

"That sounds fine."

"Good. I hear big brother already gave you the copy for the October issue. What do you think?"

"There are a lot of interesting possibilities. I've done some sketches."

"Oh? Let's see them."

She went back to her office and snatched them off her drafting table. He looked them over approvingly, suggesting little changes here, more advanced ones there, but overall he liked them.

"You're very talented, Jake," he said when they'd gone through all of them.

"Thank you."

"I've got some things to do before lunch." He glanced at his watch. "Why don't you go take care of whatever you have to and I'll see you at twelve-fifteen?"

"Twelve-fifteen it is."

When she got back to her office, a small box wrapped in gold paper lay on her desk. She unwrapped the gilt ribbon eagerly. Chocolates from her favorite store. She'd finally gotten around to calling her regular freelance clients on Friday to tell them she wouldn't be available for a while. The chocolates were from one of them, wishing her good luck.

She didn't care if Marie Antoinette had sent them. Chocolates were her one dietary vice, and she popped one into her mouth as soon as she got the lid open. Chopped walnuts. Delicious. She pushed the rest to the side of her desk, determined not to be a glutton, then started her work.

Twelve-fifteen came and went, but there was no sign of Jim. He came rushing back to his office twenty minutes later to answer a ringing phone. Jake was already seated in his office when he dashed back in.

After greeting the caller, he put his hand over the mouthpiece. "I changed the reservation to one. I asked Eamon to join us. I think he should see those designs. Go pack them up. I should be through here by the time you're done."

She did as he suggested, slipping the double-page spread-sized sheets into a yellow tube. She wished Jim hadn't pushed back their lunchtime. For one thing, she was starving, not having finished her morning coffee. For another, she was anxious about seeing Eamon again, now that she knew he'd be joining them for lunch.

There was an easy remedy for her growling stomach. She snapped on the plastic cover to the tube and tossed it onto her chair. Sitting on her desk facing the door, she reached for her candy, selecting a gooey one with caramel and nuts.

"Mmm," she sighed, biting into it.

"Didn't Mother ever tell you snacks before mealtime will ruin your appetite?"

Jake looked up to see Eamon leaning against the door frame, smiling sexily.

"This isn't a snack, it's heaven." She licked away the caramel that had dripped on her lip, slowly, sensuously, just to tease him. "It isn't every day a girl gets Godiva chocolates delivered to her office. Want one?"

He shook his head, moving inside the door and closing it behind him. His face took on a serious expression. "About the other night . . ."

"You don't have to explain." She put the chocolates down and got to her feet. That sober look on his face could only mean one thing. He'd thought about it and decided it was best if nothing further happened between them. Everyone was entitled to do something reckless in the heat of the moment—and it had certainly been hot. She couldn't punish him for that.

"I understand," she continued. "Maybe it's best we forgot about that evening."

"Is that what you want?"

No. She looked away from him, trying to conceal her disappointment. "It's better that way. All except the company picnic part. I still think that's a good idea."

Jake was sure of that, at least. It was just what the staff needed to relax around him. It was just what he needed to feel more comfortable around them. And Jake had an innate protective streak that neither being rejected nor being told to mind her own business would quell.

"If it means that much to you, we can have a company picnic. You plan it, I'll pay for it."

There was a knock at the door. A second later, Jim poked his head through the door. "I'm not interrupting anything, am I?"

"No," they both said, but only Jake found it mildly amusing.

"We were discussing the company picnic Jake has agreed to organize."

That wasn't exactly how it happened, but if that's what Eamon wanted to tell his brother, she wouldn't dispute it.

"Who came up with that idea?" Jim opened the door wider, stepping inside.

Jake raised her hand.

"Sketches in one week and a company picnic. What are you going to do next? Part the Red Sea?"

"I thought I'd concentrate on solving the congestion problem on Sixth Avenue. That's a lot tougher."

Jim laughed and Eamon smiled, but the warmth that had been in his eyes when he first came into her office had disappeared.

"Let's go," Eamon said, turning toward the door, "before we have to change the reservation again."

Jim waited for her to retrieve her purse and the tube containing her designs, and put his arm around her shoulder as they stepped into the hallway. "What's eating him?" he whispered.

Jake shrugged. She didn't understand it either. He'd gotten what he wanted, hadn't he? "He's your brother."

"Tell me about it." Jim looked heavenward as if to say this was only one of many inexplicable moods. "He seemed fine when I spoke to him this morning. Are you sure you didn't do anything to him?"

"Not me," Jake said, laughing. "Not unless company picnics make him grouchy."

By then, they'd reached the elevators where Eamon was waiting for them. Jim still had his arm around her and gave her shoulder a squeeze. "So when is this illustrious picnic supposed to take place?" Jim asked.

The elevator came and as they rode down they decided on the weekend after the Fourth of July, a little over a month away. Jim volunteered Eamon's house on Long Island as a location—it was large enough to house everybody and there was a beach nearby. Eamon seemed none too pleased with the idea, but he did agree to it.

Lunch itself was strained at best. The restaurant was too noisy for a business meeting, which was what they were supposed to be having. She and Jim ended up doing most of the talking. He flirted incorrigibly and she responded in kind. It was better than looking over at Eamon, who remained curiously silent during the whole humorous exchange.

"I thought you had something to show me," Eamon said abruptly.

"Lighten up, would you?" Jim took a sip from his coffee cup. "Jake and I were just having a little fun. You weren't taking me seriously, were you?"

"Certainly not. You probably have a whole stable of women chasing after you, and I'm a one-man woman, I'm afraid."

"I thought you were fickle," Eamon said.

Both she and Jim turned to look at Eamon. Somehow she knew he hadn't intended to say that. It had just slipped out.

"That's the problem," she said flippantly. "I can't decide who that one man is going to be." The chilling look he gave her sent a shiver up her spine.

"Take a look at these," Jim said, either missing or ignoring that last exchange. "We might get this thing done sooner than we thought."

Jim winked at her, the last indication either brother gave that she sat at the same table with them. They spent the next fifteen minutes going over her designs, which consisted of a new logo for the magazine, suggested headers and typefaces, and the like. There seemed to be a bond of mutual respect, maybe admiration between the two of them.

"I'm impressed, Jake," Eamon said, rolling up the papers.

"Thank you."

"I've got to go." Eamon stood. "You two stay and finish your coffee." He strode away before either of them had a chance to comment.

Jake shrugged and picked up her coffee cup. She halted, about to take a sip.

"Is there something going on between you and my brother I should know about?"

"Not that I know of." *Not anymore.* "Why?"

"I've never known Eamon not to at least offer to pay for a restaurant bill. I'm trying to figure out why he deliberately stuck me with the check."

When Eamon got back to the office, he blazed past his secretary's desk and slammed the door behind him. He doubted such tactics would stop her, but it might slow her down a bit.

He strode to the opposite corner of his office, behind his desk, and shoved his hands in his trouser pockets. He should have known. He gazed out of his office window, which overlooked the city, seeing nothing. He should have known from the moment she'd told him that the night in her apartment was better off forgotten what, or rather who, had caused her change of heart. All Jim had to do was turn on that magic charm of his and the merry widow McKenna lapped up every drop.

From the time they were kids it had been that way. He was the sober, responsible older brother; Jim was the playboy. He couldn't count the number of women he'd known who'd met Jim and questioned why Eamon couldn't be more like his brother. Why he couldn't loosen up a little bit. The answer never varied: because that wasn't who he was.

And the next thing he'd know, whatever woman it was would have gravitated over to Jim's flavor of the month club, to be tossed aside whenever Jim got tired of them. Then they'd be back to cry on Eamon's shoulder and lament how they should never have fallen for Jim's smooth talk. But by then, whatever initial interest he might have had was long gone. Any woman foolish enough to get involved with his brother was not the woman for him.

It had never bothered him before, and it galled him that it did now. But in that one fateful evening, he'd thought he and Jake had shared something special, something not easily cast aside. Obviously, he'd been mistaken.

The only thing to do was to put her, put them, out of his mind. He turned, intending to press the intercom button on his phone to summon Margot. He started, finding her already sitting in one of the chairs across from his desk.

"Make some noise when you enter a room, would you? You're liable to give someone a heart attack."

"You, perhaps? Lunch not go as planned?"

"Lunch hasn't got anything to do with anything."

"I see."

He knew she didn't believe him, and her calm demeanor annoyed him. So did the prim black dress she wore. Its white lace collar reminded him of something his grandmother would have worn. Or maybe a Puritan. Why couldn't everybody in the office dress that way?

Because not everybody, he supposed, was the indefatigable Margot Spenser. She worked long hours without complaint, possessed the organizational skills of a field general, and with that British accent of hers, exuded enough hauteur to chill the devil himself when she chose to. But if she had a personal life of any sort, he'd be hard pressed to imagine what it could be.

At the moment, he hadn't much of a personal life to speak of, either. It was time to immerse himself in his usual remedy for whatever ailed him.

"Let's get back to work."

* * *

The next few weeks passed quickly in a flurry of activity. Jake not only had her regular work to do, but making plans for the picnic turned into a job unto itself. She'd had to find a caterer, charter a bus, keep track of who among the staff members was coming and who was not.

But she did notice that from the time her first carefully worded memo went out, things around the office started to change. The griping sessions around the water cooler grew shorter and less frequent. The new question was what to wear, what to bring, and what dinner was going to be—a secret Jake guarded zealously.

The editorial department wanted to know why the trip had to end so early since none of them had children in the nursery. So Jake extended the trip to eight o'clock, provided that everyone could make arrangements to pick up their children at six—which they did. Jake herself had had to press her upstairs neighbor into picking up Dani, as Liza would be out of town.

And Eamon seemed to have taken her advice and stopped his daily rounds. The few times he did appear, no one had to scurry to look busy. Everyone was already at their desks. When the staff greeted him, there were more Hi, Eamons than Hello, Mr. Fitzgeralds now, leading her to believe they, not he, were responsible for the level of formality that had existed before. Why hadn't he told her that?

By the Thursday before the picnic, Jake was exhausted, but content. Well, almost content. She couldn't help replaying the incidents of the night of her birthday party in her mind. She'd told him it was best if they forgot about that evening, but now she began to wonder if she hadn't imagined the whole thing.

After that first day when they'd had lunch with Jim, he'd gone back to treating her with the same indifference he'd shown those first few days. True, he called her Jake now instead of Ms. McKenna, but the effect was still the same.

Jake laid her hand on her stomach, giving it a gentle rub. The stomach ache that had started right after lunch had gotten worse. She supposed what people said was true: it wasn't safe to eat the sushi in midtown Manhattan. If it weren't for the mound of corrections she had to make before the weekend she'd go home.

Maybe she just needed to relax for a few minutes. She switched off her computer, turned off the ringer on her phone, and laid her head down on her folded arms. She'd only close her eyes for a moment. She'd feel better in no time.

The next sound Jake heard was the low whirring noise of a vacuum cleaner in the hallway outside her office. The cleaning staff must be awfully early today. She lifted her head and checked her watch. Six-thirty.

Six-thirty. How could she have slept so long? Then she started to panic. The nursery closed at six. She grabbed her purse and her briefcase and ran toward the elevators. Why hadn't anybody called her when she hadn't arrived to pick up Dani on time? She'd turned off the ringer on her phone, that's why.

But that didn't excuse her. She shouldn't have been so careless. What if Dani was alone down there and frightened, thinking Jake had abandoned her? What if Dani wasn't there? What if someone had taken her? On the elevator ride down to the first floor, Jake clutched her stomach. She hurt more than ever, this time probably from nerves more than anything else.

Jake arrived at the nursery door, perspiring and nearly in tears. She could see a light on inside and she could hear Dani talking, so she must be all right. She didn't expect to find Eamon there helping Dani on with her jacket as Dani chatted happily.

"Where the hell have you been?" Eamon demanded, when she entered the room.

"In my office." She didn't bother to explain about the

phone. She went to Dani, scooping her up and hugging her in relief.

"I called your office. There was no answer. I was about to take Dani home with me."

"Obviously, there's no need to," she said, feeling defensive. "What are you doing down here anyway?"

"When the supervisor couldn't reach you, she called me. And don't try to turn this around, Jake. Accusing the accuser is an old lawyer's trick and it won't work with me. Don't you ever leave Dani down here alone, or so help me I'll fire you. I may not be able to do anything about people who neglect their kids, but I damn sure don't have to watch it."

He stormed out, slamming the door with such force that both she and Dani jumped.

"I'm sorry, sweetheart," Jake cooed, stroking Dani's hair.

"It's okay." Dani wriggled out of her arms. "I knew you were coming. 'Sides, I got to play with Uncle Eamon all by myself without the other kids or anything."

"You *like* Uncle Eamon?" Jake helped Dani zip up her jacket.

She nodded. "All the kids do. He comes to see us every day."

Every day? Why on earth would he spend so much time down there? *The plot thickens, or sickens, depending on how you look at it.*

"You know what, Jake?" Dani said in a conspiratorial tone.

"What, sweetheart?"

"Uncle Eamon reminds me of Daddy."

Jake's response was to crumple wordlessly to the nursery floor.

Five

One minute he was standing at the elevators, waiting for a car that would take him back up to his office. The next, Eamon found himself racing back toward the nursery. He'd heard one bloodcurdling, high-pitched scream that could only have come from Dani. As he neared his destination, he heard the little girl imploring, "Help, Uncle Eamon, please help."

Panicked, breathing heavily, he crashed through the nursery door. Immediately, his eyes were riveted to Jake's body lying prone on the floor. Little Dani knelt next to her, holding her hand, urging Jake to wake up. He hadn't known what to expect when he'd heard Dani's scream, but this definitely wasn't it.

He squatted down on the other side of Jake, touching his fingertips to the pulse at the base of her throat. The vein throbbed strong and steady, but a sheen of perspiration coated her skin. He touched the flat of his palm to her forehead. She was burning up. He'd never felt such heat coming from another human being, and instantly he feared for her.

He turned to Dani, who regarded him with tear-filled eyes set in a pale face. Trying to inject a note of calm in his voice, he asked, "What happened, sweetheart?"

"J-Jake and I were getting ready to go and then she just—" Dani broke off, her little bottom lip quivering. "It's all my fault."

He couldn't imagine what made Dani say that, but he sought to reassure her. "Dani, it's not your fault. Jake is sick. We have to get her to the hospital. Can you help me?"

Dani nodded, her chin rising an inch with resolve. "Good girl." He lifted Jake into his arms and rose to his feet. Despite her height, she felt light in his arms. Yet her body generated a level of heat that made sweat break out on his own forehead. "You get your book bag and Jake's purse and let's get out of here."

Within minutes he had the three of them out of the building and out on the sidewalk. Eamon tried to hail a cab, but driver after driver zoomed past him. For a moment there he'd forgotten he was in New York, the black-man-can't-get-a-cab capital of North America. Black man holding a prostrate woman had no shot whatsoever. He'd almost given up hope when a black stretch limousine cut across two lanes of traffic and pulled to a screeching stop directly in front of him.

The front driver's-side window rolled down and the head of a dark-skinned man sporting the black cap universal to all chauffeurs popped out. "Hey, brother, need a ride?"

Eamon could have kissed the man full on the mouth at that moment. "The nearest hospital."

The driver got out and opened the door for them. "Lennox Hill's only a few blocks away."

Somehow Eamon managed to get the three of them inside the car with Jake on his lap and Dani next to him. Dani sat very still, as still as Jake lay in his arms. Not knowing what to say to Dani, he focused his attention on Jake.

He tapped Jake's cheek with his fingertips. "Jake, honey, wake up." Relief washed over him as she started to stir, but his spirits plummeted when she squeezed her eyes tightly shut and moaned. "Do you hurt, sweetheart? Tell me where."

She laid one hand on her stomach. "Hurts so much," she whispered.

To his limited medical knowledge, that could mean almost anything. Still, he wanted to reassure both her and Dani. His hand closed over hers. "Hold on, Jake, we're almost there." *Almost there, but hopelessly stuck in the tail end of rush-hour traffic.*

Eamon swore; then remembering Dani beside him, he glanced at her to see if she'd heard him.

She stared back at him, the barest hint of a smile on her face. "Jake says that word sometimes, too. When she thinks I can't hear her."

"Well, we grown-ups slip up sometimes." He ruffled Dani's hair. "You're very brave though."

"Is—is Jake going to d-die?"

He put an arm around Dani, gathering her closer. "Not if I have anything to say about it."

That seemed to reassure Dani, who laid her head against his side and relaxed a little. He wished there were someone to offer him similar words of comfort. Despite what he'd told Dani, his worry for Jake increased every moment they spent stalled in place.

"Dani, is there anyone I should call to let them know about Jake?"

Dani shook her head. "There's only Liza and she's away."

Great! Jake was alone, and he doubted she had the capacity to make medical decisions for herself at the moment. There was one person Eamon could think of that ought to be told. Jim should be the one worried half to death about Jake's well-being, not he. According to the office grapevine, the two of them were a hot item, eating lunch together most days or closeting themselves in Jim's office to do God knew what while on his time clock. Most of the time, he tried not to think about it. But sometimes, like now, it ate at him that Jake could so easily forget what they'd shared when he could not. He pulled out his cellular phone and dialed Jim's number. Jim answered on the third ring.

"You've got five seconds to tell me why I should care."

Hearing the sound of a feminine giggle in the background, Eamon ground his teeth together. Obviously, Jim was up to his same old tricks. "At the moment, I'm in a car taking Jake to the hospital. Will that do?"

"What's wrong with her?"

"If I knew that, I wouldn't need to take her to the hospital, would I?" He told Jim where they were heading. "Meet us in the emergency room in ten minutes." He disconnected the call before Jim had a chance to respond.

Jim was waiting for them outside the emergency room exit when they pulled up in front of the hospital. By then Jake had perked up a bit. When Jim pulled the car door open, she stepped out into his waiting arms.

"You know, McKenna, there are easier ways of getting attention," Eamon heard Jim tease as he escorted her toward the hospital doors.

Eamon didn't hear what, if anything, her response was to that. He turned his attention away from them, concentrating instead on tipping the driver and getting Dani out of the car. Once inside, he sat Dani next to Jake and went to the desk to inform them of Jake's arrival, a task Jim had obviously neglected to do. He fished Jake's insurance cards out of her purse and gave the information to the clerk.

When he got back to the others, Jake had her head on Jim's shoulder and Dani leaned against Jake's side. Too cozy a scene for him to deal with. Rather than sit, he paced the floor in front of the three others with his hands shoved in his pants pockets.

"When did this start, sweetheart?" he heard Jim ask. "You were fine at lunch."

Eamon paused midstride. "Lunch?"

Jake raised her head. "We went for sushi at the new Japanese restaurant on Lexington."

Eamon ground his teeth together, his temper finally boiling over. Thanks to his irresponsible little brother Jake was probably suffering from a bad case of food poisoning.

Feigning a calm he didn't feel, he said to Jake, "Excuse us a moment."

Without waiting for a response from her, he grabbed Jim by the elbow and strong-armed him over to a spot where they couldn't be seen by Jake or Dani.

"Sushi? Are you out of your mind? It's a wonder the two of you don't have ptomaine poisoning. I would think after all this time you'd have learned to take care of your women a little better than that."

Jim snatched his arm from Eamon's grasp. "For your information, Jake is not 'my woman,' as you so elegantly put it."

"Really, now?"

"Really," Jim answered in the same droll tone. "We work together. We're friends. You might know what those were if you bothered to have any of your own."

"Thanks for the etiquette lesson. I'll have to make sure to write that down."

Jim crossed his arms in front of him, a knowing gleam coming into his eyes. "In fact, the way you're carrying on, I'd swear she was *your* woman."

Eamon wondered if Jake had told Jim about that night in her apartment. He doubted it. What would have been the point of that disclosure? "I am not carrying on."

"Yeah, right. If looks could kill, you'd have fried me on the spot with the one you sent me when she got out of the car."

"I did no such thing," Eamon protested, but there wasn't any conviction in his voice.

"If you want my opinion, it's not such a bad idea. I mean, I wouldn't wish a stick-in-the-mud like you on any woman, but, hey, stranger things have happened."

"You're pushing it."

Jim grinned. "Don't I always? But seriously, I think I ought to take Dani home. She doesn't need to be here. Call me at Jake's when you get some news."

Eamon nodded. "Thanks."

Jim shrugged. "What are brothers for?"

"Damned if I know," Eamon muttered as he followed Jim back to where Jake and Dani waited.

It was another couple of hours before Jake was even seen by a doctor. In that time, her condition had worsened. They'd put her in a small white hospital room, given her a standard hospital gown to change into, and left her alone to her misery.

Half an hour ago, Jake had been examined by an ER doctor, and now a diminutive woman dressed in faded green surgical scrubs was taking her turn. The only thing either doctor had told him was that they doubted it was food poisoning. Even if it was, Jake's stomach had already emptied itself of its contents, California rolls and all.

"What is it?" Eamon asked when the doctor stepped away from the bed.

"The attending and I both believe your wife has appendicitis. We'll do an ultrasound to confirm the diagnosis. If we're proved right, we'll try to do the appendectomy laproscopically, through a few small incisions rather than one large one. We'll need someone to sign the consent papers for both eventualities."

"I'll take care of it."

The surgeon patted his arm. "She's going to be fine, Mr. McKenna." After she left, Eamon sat on the bed next to Jake and took her hand.

She opened her eyes and smiled at him. "Eamon."

"I'm here, sweetheart." He wondered if she'd heard the name the doctor had called him when she left. The staff had assumed he was her husband and therefore shared her last name, and so far he'd done nothing to disabuse them of that notion. "How are you feeling?"

"Dani—"

"Jim took her home."

"I know. Scared."

"You have nothing to worry about. People have their appendixes removed every day."

"Not me, Dani. Father went hos-hospital. Never c-came out."

As much pain as she had to be in, her first concern was for Dani, not her own well-being. In that moment, he admired her more than he could express. "Jim and I will take care of her, okay?"

"No choice."

He smiled. "No, you don't have any choice." He smoothed her hair back from her face. "I won't let you down, Jake." If there was one thing he knew, it was how to be responsible.

"Mr. McKenna, we have to take her upstairs now."

Eamon sighed as two orderlies stepped into the room. He didn't want to let her leave. Even though she'd expressed concern only for Dani, he knew she had to be afraid for herself as well. "You're going to be fine, Jake." He leaned down and placed a soft kiss on her brow. "I'll be here when it's all over."

Tears had pooled in her eyes by the time he pulled back to look at her. "Thank you," she whispered.

He stepped back as the orderlies began wheeling her out of the room. Now all he could do was wait—and wonder. If Jim hadn't been the cause of Jake's change of heart, what had?

Jake awoke in a small white room, completely disoriented. A pain in her right side pulled at her. She inhaled, smelling the unmistakable aroma of industrial cleaner and alcohol. A dull pulse beat in her left hand. She raised her arm, only to find an intravenous inserted into the vein in her hand. She was in a hospital with no recollection of how she'd gotten there or what was wrong with her. She touched her right hand to her abdomen, feeling what seemed like several small strips of utility tape across her stomach. She'd obviously had some kind of surgery, but for what she couldn't imagine.

She opened her eyes wider, finding nothing out of the ordinary in the small room—except for the male form in the chair beside her bed. He sat in the chair, but his head and arms rested on the bed beside her legs. It couldn't be, could it? She had to be having some anesthesia-induced hallucination. She stretched out her hand to confirm that her vision was nothing more than an illusion. She snatched her hand back having encountered a solid, muscular shoulder, not a specter. "Dan?"

The apparition that wasn't an apparition raised its head. "No. It's me, Eamon. How are you feeling?"

"Eamon." Suddenly everything slid into focus: passing out in the nursery, the mad dash to the hospital, being wheeled into an operating room. She remembered all these things as if through a veil of fog. "Dani?" she whispered.

"We've had this conversation before. She's with Jim."

She closed her eyes. "What are you doing here?"

"I couldn't leave you."

Feeling Eamon take her hand, she opened her eyes.

"I'm sorry about the things I said to you this afternoon," he said. "I should have known there had to be a
good reason why you were late."

That's what he worried about, that he'd hurt her feelings? He'd probably saved her life and he thought she'd
hold it against him that he'd lost his temper?

"Don't sweat it. I'd already dismissed it as typical male
bluster. You wouldn't fire me."

"I wouldn't?"

"Of course not. Who else would you get to plan the
company picnics? Oh, God, that's tomorrow, isn't it?"

"Later today, actually."

"Oh, Eamon. Everyone is counting on me."

"Well, everyone is going to have to count on Jim, instead. I've got to go in a little while to get Dani ready
for day care; then Jim is going to head out to Montauk
with the others."

He'd taken care of everything, that both pleased her
and saddened her. With Liza out of town, she had no
one else, no one aside from Dani, who'd miss her if she
disappeared off the face of the earth. She did have one
remaining relative, her uncle Jake, but she hadn't seen
or heard from him in over two years. As much as she
loved him, he had never been a constant in her life, ha-
bitually appearing and disappearing as the mood struck
him. No, there were only Dani and Liza she could count
on, and more often than not it was they who counted on
her.

"Are you sure you know what you're getting yourself
into taking care of Dani? She can be a handful."

He didn't say anything for a moment, and she wondered if she'd offended him with her attempt at humor.
"It might surprise you to know that braiding little girls'
hair is one of my hidden talents. I specialize in one braid
at a ninety-degree angle and the other one sticking
straight up."

She had to press her lips together to keep from laughing. "Don't you dare send my baby to school looking like something the cat dragged in."

"I won't." He stood, took her hand, then sat on the bed beside her. "I'd better go. I'll be back later, after I get Dani to school and get a couple of hours' sleep." She opened her mouth to protest that his return visit wasn't necessary. He laid a finger across her lips before she got a word out of her mouth.

"Don't argue with me, Jake. There's nothing you can do to stop me, anyway." He leaned down, placing a tender kiss on her cheek. "Try to get some sleep yourself."

She nodded, closing her eyes, savoring the lingering effects of the touch of his lips on her skin. "Eamon?"

"Yes."

"Thank you. For everything."

"Quit thanking me," he said, his voice gruff. "Get some sleep."

"Yes, sir," she teased, watching as he exited the room. But her mind refused to quiet enough for her to do as he asked. She worried for Dani in the care of two men she didn't really know very well. She worried for Liza, whom she knew would feel guilty for being on vacation when Jake needed her. In truth, she couldn't imagine how she'd survive the next few days without her.

In the end, it was a long, long time before she finally fell asleep.

Jake spent the next day drifting in and out of sleep. Every time she opened her eyes, Eamon was there, sitting in the chair beside her bed, pacing the room, or standing by the window, staring out at the beautiful sunny day on the other side of the glass.

Wonderful, stubborn, impossible man. He didn't owe her anything, certainly not this devoted concern for her well-being. Hadn't she caused him enough grief already?

He stood by the window now, his hands thrust into his trouser pockets, rocking back on his heels, as though he was impatient, waiting for something. "Eamon?"

He started, clearly surprised to find her awake. He walked toward her, hovering over the bed. "How are you?"

She patted the space on the mattress beside her, but he didn't sit. "I'm fine. How's Dani?"

He smiled. "You were right about her being a handful. I had to comb her hair three times before she was satisfied that she looked presentable. I told the supervisor what happened. She adores Dani."

"It's a mutual thing, I assure you. I can't count the number of times Dani has told me 'Mrs. Freeman says' followed by an explanation of exactly what I'm doing wrong." Jake sighed, unable to keep up the pretense that she wasn't worried sick any longer.

"How is she really, Eamon?"

He sat down on the bed and took her hand. "She woke up crying in the middle of the night. She told Jim she dreamed about you going up to heaven with her father."

Jake squeezed her eyes shut, fighting back the tears that suddenly welled in her eyes. Poor Dani. She'd been through so much in her young life. Jake hated to be the cause of more strife. A solitary tear slipped down her cheek.

Eamon brushed it away with the pad of his thumb. "Dani will be fine, Jake. I promise you. Have I ever let you down?"

She thought of the time he'd come to her birthday party in the pouring rain, the way he'd agreed to her picnic, his treatment of her in the last two days. No, he'd never let her down. But it frightened her to realize she trusted him completely. "I've only known you a month and a half."

He cupped the side of her face in his palm, stroking her cheek with his thumb. "And you haven't learned anything about me in that time?"

Those eyes of his bored into her, those eyes that seemed to see into her very soul. She inhaled, filling her lungs with the scent of pure male and the lingering aroma of his cologne. She'd learned that he was a man of honor, that he kept his word. She'd learned that she wanted him, that her body came alive at his simplest touch.

So, again she wondered, why had he withdrawn from her after those white-hot kisses they'd shared in her apartment? She thought to ask him that, then figured maybe she was better off not knowing. The last time she'd questioned a man about his feelings for her, she'd gotten her heart stomped but good.

Suddenly, the door flew open and a young nurse came in pulling a cart behind her.

"Sorry to intrude, Mr. McKenna, but I've got to take your wife's temperature."

Jake's eyebrows arched up, nearly to her hairline. *Mr. who?* His *what?* She glared at Eamon, who stood abruptly, clearing out of the nurse's way. Now that she thought about it, she had a dim recollection of other nurses taking her temperature or removing her IV or examining her incision, calling her Mrs. McKenna. She'd been too drowsy to pay much attention to that distinction.

"I'll wait outside."

Jake started to tell him not to dare step out that door, when the nurse promptly popped a thermometer in her mouth.

"There's no need. I'll be finished in a minute." She fastened a blood pressure cuff around Jake's arm and began pumping the bulb. "Hmm," she said after a moment.

"What is it?" Eamon asked.

"Your wife's blood pressure is a little high."

No kidding. She stared mutely at Eamon, who appeared to be making a detailed study of his fingernails. The minute the nurse walked out of the door, he had some serious explaining to do.

The nurse removed the thermometer. She wrote something on Jake's chart, then smiled at her devilishly. "I guess you two can pick up where you left off." She wheeled the cart out of the room, closing the door behind her.

Jake watched her departure, then turned to Eamon. "Why did you tell them we were married?"

"I didn't exactly, they just assumed. I didn't correct the misunderstanding."

"Why not?"

"Hospitals are not in the habit of letting people's employers make medical decisions for them. The state you were in, you would have agreed to coronary bypass surgery as long as they'd give you anesthesia."

"Was I that bad?"

Eamon nodded. "You were pretty out of it."

Jake sighed. After all he'd done for her, she couldn't fault him for that little white lie. "Did they tell you how long I'd have to be in here?"

"Two more days."

"Two more *days*?" She'd been thinking in terms of hours. Whatever happened to all those complaints about hospitals kicking people out before they were actually ready to go? "I can't stay here that long. Dani needs me."

"I can take care of Dani."

"That's not what I meant. She needs to see me, to know I'm all right. I don't want her having any more bad dreams worrying that I'm going to die like her father."

"There's nothing you can do about that, Jake. I'm sorry. Look, I've got to leave to pick up Dani anyway. We'll call you when we get back to your apartment."

"It's not the same thing."

"It's the best I can do."

Jake bit her lip, trying to hide her disappointment. "I know. At the risk of repeating myself yet again, thank you."

"I'll call you in an hour." Eamon leaned down and kissed her cheek. "And I thought I told you to quit thanking me."

Jake grinned. "Thanks for reminding me."

The floor was deathly quiet when Eamon arrived at the offices of *Ebony Man* twenty minutes later. For some reason, he was drawn to Jake's office. He didn't bother to question his motivation, but instead merely gave in to the impulse.

He sat in her chair, leaned back, and folded his hands in front of him. Unlike her home, her office was immaculate, not so much as a marker out of place. And no personal items, save for a coffee mug with the slogan *Artists do it with color* emblazoned in rainbow colors over white ceramic. If it weren't for the glimpse of her personal life he'd gotten when he'd been in her apartment, he'd know nothing about her.

In truth, he still didn't know anything about her, not even why she still wore her husband's ring. But now more than ever, he wanted to know. He wanted to protect her, to save her from being alone in the world, as alone as he felt. He wanted more than that, but for the present, he'd have to settle for making sure she recovered, both for Dani's sake and for his own.

Hearing a noise out in the hallway, Eamon glanced toward the open door.

Jim appeared a moment later, dressed in shorts and a T-shirt. He leaned against the door frame. "What are you doing here?"

"I could ask you the same question. Aren't you supposed to be out on Montauk?"

"We came home early. No one was in a partying mood knowing Jake was in the hospital. So what are you doing here instead of being with her?"

"I came back to get Dani."

"Where are you hiding her?" Jim made a show of looking around the room and behind the open door.

"I haven't gotten her yet."

"Okay, spit it out. What's eating you?"

"Nothing. I've come to a decision."

"Oh, Lord. Look out. A decision about what?"

"Jake."

"So you have decided to take my advice, for a change. But your timing stinks. I don't think she'll be ready to play 'storm the bastille' for a while."

Eamon folded his arms across his chest and narrowed his eyes at his brother. "Your lack of couth is truly astounding. Who raised you?"

"You did, brother dear, so you have no one to blame but yourself."

"I refuse to take full credit for that fiasco. Could you try to be serious for one moment?"

Jim sat in the chair facing Jake's desk. "All right. What's up?"

"I was thinking that Jake isn't going to be in any condition to take care of herself, let alone Dani, when she gets out of the hospital. She's going to need someone to look after her."

"I'd love to help, but I'm leaving in the morning to head back to Florida for a few days."

Eamon groaned. "I'd forgotten about that, but I wasn't thinking about you."

"Then who?"

"Me. Jake doesn't know it yet, but when she leaves the hospital, she's going to be staying with me."

Six

Two hours later, Jake wasn't in the mood to thank any-body. Eamon hadn't called as he said he would, and Jake feared something had happened to prevent him from keeping his promise.

Pacing around the room in the hospital's gown and green foam slippers was only making her incisions hurt. She got back into bed just as a knock sounded on her door.

"Who is it?" she called. Lord knew it couldn't be a member of the hospital staff. They barged in whenever they pleased.

"Special delivery for Jake McKenna," came a high-pitched nasal voice from the other side of the door. The door opened and Dani rushed in. She wore a tiny pair of surgical scrubs.

"Dani," Jake cried, holding out her arms for her niece.

"Jake!"

Before she could take a step, Eamon appeared in the doorway and scooped her up. "Easy, Dani," he said, then placed her on Jake's bed in a sitting position. Jim entered last, closing the door behind him.

"Can I touch you?" Dani asked.

"Of course." Jake scootched over so Dani could sit comfortably next to her. "Just don't lean on my stomach, okay?" Jake ran her hand over Dani's hair, which for once had stayed in two pigtails. Jake put her arm around the little girl and hugged her. "I missed you."

"I missed you too, Jake. I was so worried about you."

"I know, sweetie. But you can see I'm fine."

"What did they do to you?"

"They took out my appendix."

"Do you have a big scar?"

"No, only three little ones."

"Oh."

Jake shook her head. Dani actually sounded disappointed. She turned her attention to the two men standing by her bed. Jim wore scrubs identical to Dani's; Eamon wore a jet-black suit with a white shirt and subdued tie. "What are you guys doing here? Jim, I thought you were supposed to be up on Montauk."

"We came back right after lunch. No one was in a partying mood knowing you were here."

She let her gaze travel over to Eamon. Words of gratitude formed in her mind. He'd known how worried she was about Dani and smuggled her up for Jake to see her. She was sure the hospital would never give permission for a six-year-old to visit on an adult ward. But she knew he wouldn't appreciate hearing them, so instead she teased, "And you, Eamon. Just like a man. You promise you'll call and then nothing."

He ignored her gibe. "How are you feeling?"

"Okay."

He gave her a skeptical look but didn't comment on that. "We'd better be going. Dani's already fallen asleep."

Jake looked down at Dani. Her little chest rose and fell slowly and regularly. "I guess so." Jake placed a soft kiss on Dani's cheek, then leaned back for Eamon to pick her up.

"I'm going to take Dani home; then I'll be back."

"There's no need. I'll probably be asleep in five minutes."

"See you later, Jake," Eamon said. "Are you coming, Jim?"

"You go on ahead. I'll meet you at the car in a minute."

For a moment, Eamon looked as if he might say something, but he turned and left the room carrying Dani in his arms. After the door closed, she focused her gaze on Jim. "What's up?"

Jim slouched into the chair by the bed. "How are you, really?"

"Ever heard the expression rode hard and put away wet?"

Jim grinned. "Happened to me a few times, but I'm not complaining."

She laughed as deeply as the pain in her stomach allowed. "You could make a sexual innuendo out of a ball of lint."

"Probably." Jim leaned forward, a sober expression on his face. "Listen, I'm going out of town for a few days and I want you to promise me something before I go."

Jake lifted a hand as if being sworn in. "I promise I won't tell Eamon I caught you and the copy editor in the supply closet."

"I appreciate your discretion, but that's not what I had in mind." The sober expression returned. "Eamon's going to ask you to stay with him until you get better. Promise me you'll agree."

For a moment Jake stared at him dumbfounded. "Why on earth would he do that?"

"He feels responsible for you."

"Nonsense. He feels guilty for yelling at me when I was sick."

Jim shook his head. "I know my brother, Jake. He doesn't go out of his way for too many people. He only does that for people he's made up his mind to care about."

"Made up his mind to care about? You make it sound as if caring for someone were a decision, not an emotion."

"For Eamon it is. And my guess is something went on between the two of you, maybe even before I got here, that neither one of you has been kind enough to share with me."

"Jim—" she warned. If Eamon hadn't told his brother about the night in her apartment, neither would she. Besides, he was wrong about Eamon. If anything, he'd made the decision *not* to care for her.

Jim held up his hand. "I'm not fishing for information. I just don't want you to let anything that happened between you color your decision when it comes to staying with him. You know you can't manage Dani on your own in your condition."

Jake sighed. She could barely manage Dani when she was in the pink of health. "I'll think about it."

Jim stood. "I suppose that's the best I'm going to get out of you. I'd better go before Eamon sends the National Guard to look for me." He bent and kissed her forehead. "Take care of yourself, McKenna. I need you back at the office. Who else is going to eat uncooked eel with me?"

She swatted him on the shoulder. "That's probably what got me in here in the first place."

He winked at her. "See you in a few days."

After Jim left, Jake leaned back against her pillows. She couldn't take Dani home alone and she had nowhere besides Eamon's to go. She contemplated calling Liza, but Liza had her own problems to deal with. As with everything else in the past few days, life wasn't offering her many choices.

Undoubtedly, when Eamon returned he intended to pop the question. Now all she had to figure out was what she was going to tell him.

* * *

Having the care and feeding of a woman's child could provide unexpected bonuses, Eamon mused as Dani took her turn moving the dog around the New York City version of Monopoly she'd conned him into purchasing on their way home. He wasn't concentrating on the game, and therefore she was whipping his butt with hotels on Trump Tower and Tiffany & Co. Fortunately, he'd be bankrupt soon and his ersatz financial misery would be at an end.

Fortunately, too, Dani was in a talkative mood, probably because she missed Jake. In the hour they had been playing, he discovered that Jake had a secret passion for ballroom dancing, that she completed the *Times* crossword puzzle every Sunday without fail, and, most importantly, that she wasn't seeing anyone, not even Jim.

As they sorted the fake money to put it back in the box, Dani glanced up at him, a sober expression on her face. "When is Jake going to get out of the hospital?"

"Tomorrow."

"Then we'll go home?"

"I don't know, Dani. I don't know if Jake will be able to take care of you by herself. I'd rather you stayed with me. Would you like that?"

Dani nodded. "Did you ask her yet?"

"No."

Dani nodded. "Ask her when she's asleep. When she's asleep she'll say yes to anything."

Eamon stifled a laugh. Obviously Dani knew Jake's weakness and had used it to her advantage. In some ways, Dani struck him as a very old soul housed in a tiny body. He ruffled her hair. "I'll have to remember that."

Eamon supposed the Fates were with him when he walked into Jake's hospital room to find her asleep. He pulled the chair up to her bedside, sat down, and leaned toward her. She lay facing him. The dim light of the room softened her features. The angelic smile on her face made him wonder what she was dreaming.

He edged closer and took her hand in both of his. "Jake, sweetheart, listen to me. When you get out of here tomorrow, I want you and Dani to stay with me until you get better. Say yes." He waited, expecting her sleepy acquiescence.

Instead she opened both eyes and stared at him and her smile deepened. "I see you've been taking lessons from Dani on how to get what you want from me."

"I thought you were asleep."

"Obviously." She pulled her hand from his grasp and sat up. "What Dani doesn't realize is that she makes enough noise to rouse Rip Van Winkle. And since Dani rarely asks for anything unreasonable, it's easy to say yes."

"But you aren't going to say yes to me?"

"No. I know that for some reason I can't fathom, you feel responsible for Dani and me, but I can't allow us to be a further burden for you."

"Why don't you let me decide if and when you and Dani become a burden to me? I wouldn't make the offer if I didn't want to."

"That's just it, Eamon. Why do you want to? I certainly can't pay you anything for your troubles. In the shape I'm in, you couldn't even take it out in trade. Unless you're vying for the title of Father Teresa, why would you bother?"

He couldn't fault her for suspecting his true motives, not that he intended to share them with her. Doing that would only guarantee she'd steer as far away from him as living in New York would allow. As free-spirited as he'd first thought her to be, he'd noticed the wariness in her these past few days, the reticence to allow him too far into her life, even if she was grateful for his presence.

"Look, Jake, I'm not being completely altruistic here. I'm simply protecting my interest now that you've been working at the magazine long enough for the health plan to kick in."

She gave him a droll look and folded her arms across her chest.

He sat back in his chair and sighed. "What do you want me to do, Jake? Stand by and do nothing while someone I know needs help and I can provide it? I can't do that."

"So I should do what you want to salve your conscience?"

Despite the contrariness of her words, he could tell she was weakening and he went in for the kill. "No, but think of Dani. You may not realize it, but she feels responsible for you, too. She thinks your getting sick is her fault. How do you think she will feel if the two of you go home and something happens?"

She threw up her hands. "Oh, all right already. I'll stay with you. But only until Liza gets back to New York."

She sounded so dejected that he wanted to laugh. "Why does it bother you so much?"

She shook her head. "You wouldn't understand."

Maybe not. Though he wished she would confide in him, he didn't press her. He stood and rebuttoned his jacket. "I should get going. Jim needs to get to the airport." He brushed his lips across Jake's brow. "Thank you."

As he pulled away he noticed the impish expression on her face. "Quit thanking me," she teased.

"I'll pick you up tomorrow at ten."

"I'll be here."

At a quarter to ten the next morning, Jake's surgeon opened the door and poked her head through. "How are we doing this morning?"

Jake sat up straighter in bed as her surgeon entered the room. "I don't know about you, but I'm getting cabin fever."

The diminutive doctor grinned. "Sorry about that. The imperial 'we.' They have a course on it at medical school."

"So, do I get out of here today?"

"If I had your husband waiting for me at home, I'd be anxious to get out of here, too. Let's take a look at your incisions."

Jake held her breath as the doctor pulled on a pair of gloves before lifting her gown to poke and probe her abdomen. "How does it look?"

"Good. You're healing nicely. How do you feel?"

"A little tired. The hospital is no place to stay if you actually expect to get some rest."

The doctor snapped off her gloves. "I want you to take it easy for a while. And drink lots of fluids. You were a bit dehydrated when you came in. No lifting, no clothes with elastic waists, no strenuous exercise, no showers until the Steri-Strips come off. They should fall off on their own within a week."

The doctor paused, settling an assessing gaze on Jake. "Anything else?" Jake asked.

"No sex. For at least six weeks."

Jake was about to say that wasn't a concern when she remembered that Eamon had allowed the staff to believe he was her husband. "I'll try to hold out."

The doctor leaned back on her heels and shoved her hands into the pockets of her white coat. "He's not your husband, is he?"

Seeing no point in continuing the deception, Jake asked, "How did you know?"

"No wedding band." The doctor shrugged. "Hey, I'm single, too. I looked. And any woman who managed to get a guy like that hitched would be a fool not to put her tag on him. You don't strike me as being particularly stupid."

Jake laughed. "Actually, he's my boss."

"Lucky you. My boss is older than dirt, has a belly like Buddha, and plays with his dentures when he thinks no one's looking." The doctor went to the foot of the bed, took Jake's chart from the holder, and scribbled something on the first page. "Someone will come by in a few minutes with some papers for you to sign. Then you're free to go."

Jake beamed her gratitude at the doctor. "Thank you."

The doctor winked. "All in a day's work."

As she opened the door to leave, Eamon entered. For a moment the two of them exchanged pleasantries. Jake remained silent until the doctor left and Eamon moved farther into the room. Nodding toward the gym bag he carried, she asked, "What's that?"

"Going-home clothes."

Jake eyed the bag again. Although she was grateful for something to wear, she wasn't sure how she felt knowing Eamon had snooped around in her underwear drawer.

He tossed the bag onto the chair. "Don't worry. Dani picked out everything, including another bag of clothes I already brought to my house."

"By the way, where is Dani?"

"At my place with Margot."

Jake covered her open mouth with her hand. "You didn't, Eamon. Dani is probably giving that poor woman a fit."

"Why don't you get dressed and we'll find out?"

Jake did as he suggested, taking the bag to the tiny bathroom by the door. After brushing her teeth and sponging off her body as best she could without touching the sterile tape, Jake unzipped the bag. Eamon had brought not only her clothes, but her skin-care regimen, her brushes, and an assortment of cosmetics. "Thank you, Dani," Jake whispered. No man would have thought of including those few simple amenities. Maybe there was some hope for her little tomboy, yet.

In fifteen minutes, Jake had made herself as presentable as possible with jeans that were a size too big and hair that was just on the other side of being totally unmanageable. She stepped out of the bathroom to stand before Eamon. "So what's the verdict?"

Eamon took the bag from her, then stepped back, tilting his head to one side, apparently studying her. "Guilty by reason of temporary lack of personal hygiene."

She smiled. She didn't suppose now was the time to develop a sense of vanity. "So, what happened to my chariot?" she asked, referring to the customary wheelchair ride discharged patients were subjected to.

"I checked. They're sending someone, along with some papers for you to sign."

"As long as it's not the bill for this place. I want to recuperate a little more before they give me a heart attack."

"If they bill you for anything, I'll handle it."

Sighing, Jake said nothing. Arguing with him would only be a waste of her breath, since even if they charged her fifty cents she'd be hard pressed to come up with it. But as they drove from the hospital on the East Side to Eamon's condo on Central Park West, she wondered what she had gotten herself and Dani into.

Eamon's apartment was everything Jake expected it would be: large, tastefully decorated, and immaculate. The front door opened onto a small foyer. On the other side of the foyer was a large rectangular living room. Floor-to-ceiling windows looked out onto the park. Margot sat on the black leather sofa reading a copy of Dr. Spock's *Baby and Child Care*. Dani was nowhere in sight. As they approached, Margot dropped the book to the sofa and stood. "Ah, you're back." Margot fastened her amber gaze on Jake. "I'm glad to see you looking so well. How do you feel?"

"Much better, thank you." Jake glanced right and left, first toward a corridor that led deeper into the apartment, then to a small hallway that led to the kitchen. The apartment was eerily quiet considering it was supposed to contain a small child. "Where's Dani?"

Before Margot could answer, Dani bounded into the room. She drew up short after Margot shot her a disapproving glance.

"Good morning, Jake. It is good to see you." Dani extended her hand toward Eamon. "Good morning, Uncle Eamon."

For a second, she and Eamon shared a glance; then Eamon took Dani's small hand in his and bent way down to kiss the back of her hand. "The pleasure is all ours."

Dani giggled and danced away from him toward Margot. "Did I do it right?"

"Passably. And the question is, 'Did I do it correctly?'"

"Yeah, yeah, correctly," Dani echoed. "Is it time then?"

Margot pulled an old-fashioned pocket watch from her jacket. "I believe it is." She returned the watch. "You finished all your chores?"

"Yes."

"Well then, you go get the telly ready and I'll get the popcorn."

Dani bounded off, then seemed to catch herself. She walked the rest of the way, her posture an imitation of Margot's straight-backed carriage.

Having watched the exchange between her niece and Eamon's assistant, Jake shook her head. "Dani did chores?"

Margot fastened a gaze on her that said, "Don't all children?" Margot cleared her throat. "She made her bed, straightened her clothes, and tidied up her toys."

"I see."

"If you'll excuse me, I have some corn to pop."

Jake shook her head again as Margot exited the room in the direction of the kitchen. Feeling Eamon's gaze on her, she glanced up at him. "Do you suppose she'd come and live in my spare bedroom?"

"The black Mary Poppins. As Margot would say, the very idea gives me a fright."

Eamon grinned down at her. She smiled back, realizing how few times she'd seen him genuinely smile. For an instant, their gazes locked. Jake would have sworn she saw something else in his expression beside humor, interest maybe, or worse yet, desire. She looked away, knowing she would only get herself in trouble trying to read more into Eamon's intentions than there really was. Just because his patient concern and largesse in letting them stay here had touched her profoundly, it didn't mean that his lack of interest in her as a woman had changed.

She forced a plastic smile to her face. "So do I get a tour of the place, or what?"

His smile receded, too, perhaps in response to the shift in her mood. "Let's start with the kitchen."

He led her in the same direction Margot had gone, to a large black-and-white kitchen. Brilliant sunshine poured in through sheer white curtains that hung at the windows. Every conceivable appliance and amenity was displayed on counters or hung from a ceiling rack. The stove was the double oven model she'd spent years pining over in Macy's basement housewares section.

"Cool," Jake said, glancing around. The microwave beeped and Margot pulled out the popcorn bag and emptied it into a large bowl, apparently oblivious of the intense temperature of the snack.

"I'll be in Dani's room watching *Spy Kids 2* if anyone is looking for me."

Jake thought she detected a hint of a smile on Margot's face, but she marched off before Jake could be sure. Dismissing the woman from her mind, Jake said, "Where next?"

Eamon led her through the rest of the apartment, first to a formal dining room that housed an antique dining table and matching sideboard, then to his home office, and on to the two bedrooms, a smaller one that Dani and Margot occupied and a larger one dominated by a large sleigh bed with a slotted headboard.

They had obviously reached the end of the tour. Eamon set her bag down by the bed. "So, what do you think?"

"Your apartment is lovely. Dani is the first child you've had here, isn't she?"

"What makes you ask that?"

"Too much breakable stuff too low down."

"You're right on both counts."

Jake eyed the king-size bed. "About the sleeping arrangement . . ." She trailed off, looking for a way to voice her concerns delicately.

Eamon chuckled. "Dani will stay in the other room, you'll sleep here, and I'll be on the sofa in my office." He nodded toward the one door on the hall he hadn't opened. "It pulls out."

"Eamon, I can't put you out of your bed. I can share the room with Dani."

"And what if she rolls over in her sleep and injures you? You need a bed of your own."

"Then I'll sleep on the sofa. I—"

Eamon placed a finger on her lips, silencing her protests. "Don't fight me on this, Jake. I'm bigger than you."

Jake sighed. How did you argue with a man who only seemed to have your best interests at heart? If it were anybody else, she would suspect their motives, but despite what made sense, she trusted Eamon. "You're sure you don't mind?"

"I wouldn't have offered if I minded. And speaking of sleeping, I think it's time you took a nap."

Jake waved her hand dismissively. "I spent so much time in bed in the hospital, I've started to grow mold."

Eamon cupped his palm around her shoulder. "What did I tell you about arguing with me?"

Jake sighed. Was she ever going to win an argument with him? "All right. But make sure to wake me if Dani needs me."

"I promise." He bent and placed a soft kiss on her forehead. "Sweet dreams." With a wink he let himself out of the room and closed the door behind him.

Jake sat down on the bed. She did feel as wrung out as an old rag. She'd only put her head down for a minute though. She couldn't leave either Eamon or Margot with the care of Dani too long. Dani was her responsibility.

Jake shrugged out of her jeans and shirt, leaving only her underwear and T-shirt. She got under the covers and rested her head on the mound of pillows at the head of the bed. She yawned, closed her eyes, and reminded herself that she only planned to sleep a few minutes. But the next time she opened her eyes, the night and the room were dark.

Seven

Eamon stood at the open door to his bedroom watching Jake. Despite her claim that she'd rested enough in the hospital, she'd fallen asleep within minutes of his leaving her here. If it weren't for Dani getting antsy to see her and his own concern that she would be up all night if he let her sleep, he wouldn't bother to wake her. And there was also the fact that if he left her alone, he wouldn't have the opportunity to look at her as he did now.

Awash in the dim hallway light, she appeared soft and peaceful in slumber, angelic. Yet there was nothing pure about the thoughts that circled in his head, all of which entailed joining her in that bed. His groin tightened and his nostrils flared, even as he tried to focus his mind elsewhere.

"Eamon?"

He cleared his throat. "Yes?" He hadn't realized she was awake. How long had she been aware of him standing there?

"What time is it?"

"Almost eight-thirty."

"Why didn't you wake me?" He heard the rustle of covers. The bedside lamp flicked on a second later. "Where's Dani?"

"Waiting to kiss you good night. Do you feel up to it?" She brushed her hair from her face. "Of course."

"I'll go get her."

Eamon went to the room next door and leaned against the doorjamb. Dani was sitting cross-legged, her nose buried in a Dr. Seuss book. "Jake's awake."

Dani looked up, a hopeful expression on her face. "Can I see her?"

Eamon nodded and the little girl scampered off the bed and out the door. By the time he joined them in his bedroom, Dani was snuggled up under the covers next to Jake. Jake had her arm around the little girl holding her close.

For a moment, as he watched the two chat happily, bile rose in his throat and an acute feeling of regret sliced through him. In that instant he knew why he'd hired her, and wondered why it hadn't occurred to him before. She'd told him she had a small child to raise alone, and the information had hit him like a sucker punch even though he hadn't admitted it to himself at the time.

"Uncle Eamon?"

Hearing Dani's voice, he refocused his eyes and realized they were both staring at him. "What can I do for you, short stuff?"

"Do I really have to go to bed right now?" Both Dani and Jake looked at him plaintively.

"Ten more minutes." He fastened his gaze on Jake. He appreciated her not countermanding what he'd said out of hand. Although he had no right to dictate Dani's bedtime or anything else, he understood the cardinal rule of dealing with children: the adults had to stick together. "Are you hungry?"

Jake patted her stomach. "Famished. What do you have in mind?"

"I've got a jar of soup with your name on it."

Jake made a face but didn't protest.

Eamon had to fight to keep a smile from his face. "I'll be right back."

He went to the kitchen and heated a jar of Campbell's chicken and rice in the microwave, scattered some Ritz crackers on a tray, and brewed a cup of the herbal tea Margot claimed promoted healing. When all was ready, Eamon carried the tray back to the room and, after scooting Dani out of the way, set it before Jake.

"Come on, Dani," Eamon urged. "I'll read you a story."

"Good night, sweetheart," Jake said, leaning over to kiss Dani's cheek. "I'll see you in the morning."

"Good night, Jake."

Dani bounded off the bed and came to stand beside him. She slid her tiny hand into his. Was there anything more precious than the trust of a child? Eamon didn't think so.

After Dani had fallen asleep he returned to Jake. She'd finished the soup and crackers and was sipping the tea. He sat at the foot of the bed and braced one hand on the mattress. "How do you feel?"

"I'd feel a lot better if you'd stop asking me that." She leaned back against the pillows and stretched. "Actually, I do feel much better. What's next on the agenda?"

"I rented some grown-up movies, too. Want to come pick one?"

"Popcorn?"

He nodded.

"You've got yourself a date. Give me a few minutes to get ready."

"Your toothbrush is in the bathroom and your clothes are in the top drawer." Eamon lifted the tray from her lap. "Meet you in the living room in ten minutes."

After Eamon left, Jake threw off her covers and padded to the bathroom. From the outside, she assumed it to be a small room, but once she'd stepped over the threshold, its spaciousness surprised her. Tiled in royal blue and white, it boasted a large sunken tub and a shower stall bigger than her entire bathroom at home. What she wouldn't give to be able to step inside and, if nothing else, wash her hair.

She sponged off, brushed her teeth, ran a brush through her hair, and finding her one pair of lounging pajamas among the items in the top dresser drawer, praised Dani once again. She dressed, tried to run a brush through her hair, but ended up braiding it and tying it off with a rubber band.

Eamon was waiting for her when she got to the living room. He sat comfortably on the black leather sofa across from the wide-screen TV, wearing a pair of jeans and a neatly pressed short-sleeved shirt. Was this man ever less than perfect physically? Even the sports socks on his feet looked like they had just come out of the package. Jake suppressed a smile. All that neatness fueled in her a desire to muss him up just a little.

"What's so funny?" Eamon stood as she neared him and moved over to give her room to sit down.

No way was she going to answer that question. "The smell of popcorn is making me giddy." She sat and Eamon sat beside her, draping his arm along the back of the sofa cushion. Noticing the three DVD boxes on the glass coffee table in front of them, she asked, "What's on the marquee tonight?"

He leaned forward and picked up the boxes and fanned them out between two hands. "You have a choice. We've got *The Sixth Sense*, *Terms of Endearment*, and *The Matrix*. As it's a Saturday night, pickin's were slim at Blockbuster."

It didn't elude her that he'd picked one basic action movie, one horror flick, and a first-class tearjerker. Was this some sort of test? To be perverse, she pointed to the one she'd be least likely to pick under normal circumstances.

"The Matrix it is," he said, but he looked at her closely. "Somehow I didn't expect that."

So it had been a test. "I wouldn't dream of making you sit through a chick flick, and I get scared silly just watching *Ghost.* Besides, who in their right mind would pass up seeing a woman kick four men's butts in the first five minutes of a movie?"

She wasn't sure he bought her explanation, but he rose from the sofa and loaded the DVD into the player. He returned to his seat beside her with a remote. He clicked one button and the movie began to play; he clicked another and sound issued from several small speakers situated around the room.

"Just like in the movies," Jake commented as Eamon adjusted the decibel level.

"Not quite." Eamon clicked another button and the two torch lamps that illuminated the room dimmed to a faint glow. "Better?"

"What else can you do with that thing?"

Eamon turned to her. Ignoring her gibe he asked, "Are you comfortable?"

Jake brought one of the pillows from behind her back onto her lap and nodded. "Some of that popcorn you've got there wouldn't hurt me."

He handed her the bucket of freshly popped corn, which she rested on top of her pillow.

"Thanks."

Jake munched some of the corn, but about a half hour into the film she started to flag. She felt Eamon's hand come to rest on her kneecap. "Are you all right?"

She nodded, though she felt like a dishrag someone had forgotten to wring out. "This may sound crazy, but I want to lie down on the floor."

If he doubted her mental status, his expression didn't show it. He got up and pushed the coffee table toward the TV, leaving more than enough room to accommodate her. He disappeared into the bedroom for a minute. When he came back he carried a pillow and a light blanket that he spread on the floor. He helped her to her feet and eased her to a sitting position on the floor. Jake lay back and rested her head on the pillow as Eamon tucked one edge of the blanket around her.

Jake closed her eyes and snuggled farther beneath her warm cocoon. When she opened her eyes, she was surprised to find Eamon lying beside her, his head propped up on his hand as he watched her.

Jake brushed her hair from her face with her left hand and rested it on the pillow. "Thank you."

That sexy half smile of his lifted his lips. "I thought I told you to stop thanking me."

"I can't help it. I'd thought you'd think I was nuts for wanting to make a bed out of your carpet."

"Sometimes the floor is the most comfortable place to be when you are in pain."

Jake closed her eyes. She thought she'd kept that from him, but in truth, not only her stomach but also her back hurt as well. She opened her eyes. "I guess I've got that transparency thing working again."

He smiled, but not a smile of humor. His gaze held hers, and the intensity in his eyes surprised her. "Are you still in love with him?"

Jake blinked. "Him who?"

He took her hand in his and rubbed her thumb over her wedding band. "The real Mr. McKenna. You still wear his ring."

"My lucky ring? I found it on the subway."

"Then who was the Mr. McKenna in the photograph with you and Dani?"

Merriment danced in her eyes. "The only Mr. McKennas in my life were my stepfather and my stepbrother, Dan, and, of course, you at the hospital. Dani isn't my daughter, she's my brother's. That's why I told you she couldn't possibly have my eyes." She shook her head as if contemplating the impossible. "You thought I was married? Who on earth would marry me?"

"I figured someone would have managed to lasso you."

She shrugged. "I was engaged once, but it didn't work out. It turns out he was more interested in my supposed inheritance than he was in marrying me. When he discovered *Grandmere* had left all her earthly goods to the Louvre, he said toodle-oo."

"He was a fool."

She shook her head. "He saved us both from a disaster. It would never have worked anyway. Even if money weren't an issue, he never wanted me, he wanted what he thought I should be."

"What was that?"

"Have you ever heard of Jessamyn Troubat?"

"Of course. She was born in America and married some French businessman. One of her paintings hangs in my study."

"She was also my grandmother."

Eamon's breath whistled out through his teeth. "I had no idea. What was it like having a famous artist as a grandmother?"

"I wouldn't know. She never acknowledged me."

"Why not?"

Jake looked away, focusing her gaze on the action sequence playing out on the TV. She didn't think of her grandmother often, but when she did it was always with regret. Although Jessamyn Troubat had achieved fame capturing the joy of children on canvas, in reality she was a bitter old woman, disappointed by life, by her marriage, by what her children had become. As a young woman, she'd fled to France, escaping a life of poverty and illegitimacy and racism in the Deep South, hoping to gain the status abroad she could never achieve at home. Within a year, she'd met and married a wealthy French businessman. Because of her work, French society welcomed her, but never let her forget that she was not only black but of the wrong class to truly be one of them. Just like in America, the lowliness of her birth dictated her status in life.

Eamon stroked her cheek with his knuckles. "Why not?" he repeated.

Jake turned her head to focus on his face. Those ice-blue eyes of his bored into her. Maybe it was drowsiness pulling at her, but her head swam and a dull, pleasant ache came alive in her belly. She focused on a safe place, his chest, before she spoke.

"More than anything, I think my grandmother wanted the world's respect. More than love or acceptance or even caring. For her troubles, she got a son whom she considered a wastrel and a daughter, my mother, who got pregnant by a man she barely knew—an American. My grandmother kicked her out of the house, and having nowhere else to go, she came here. I only saw my grandmother once."

"What happened?"

Jake sighed. Did she really want to tell him about her humiliation at her grandmother's hands? Consciously, her answer was no, but her mouth was functioning faster than her brain. She'd never told anyone, not even Liza, what had happened on that trip. But words spilled from her mouth, telling how her uncle Jake had taken her and Dan to France after her mother's death, hoping that finally there could be a reconciliation between them.

"My grandmother was at the summer house in Nice, which my grandfather left me in his will. It's a beautiful old house with a fabulous garden. My grandmother was entertaining guests there. We show up at the door, me in this frilly white dress Uncle Jake had picked out for me. I was so nervous my knees were trembling underneath all that crinoline."

Jake paused to lick her dry lips. "A butler answered the door and informed us that Madame Troubat was otherwise occupied and couldn't see us. Dan and I wanted to go, but Uncle Jake refused to leave until he spoke to her. When she finally came to the door, she looked Uncle Jake in the eye and said she had no son. She barely spared me a glance before she slammed the door in our faces."

She glanced up at Eamon. The intense expression in his eyes and the grim set of his jaw made her wonder what he was thinking. "What's the matter?"

"Was your grandfather alive at the time?"

She shook her head, not knowing what he was leading to. "No."

"So let me get this straight—she barred you from coming into your own home. A home from which you could have had her evicted?"

"That about sums it up, yes. But I never wanted that house. I never wanted anything from her."

She looked away from him. Her humor had fled and instead melancholy sought to claim her. She had never cared what the old crone thought of her, but his mother's approval had meant everything to Uncle Jake. That long-ago day, an old woman's rancor had crushed something precious in her uncle. In some indefinable way, he'd been different, more withdrawn after that.

"What do *you* want, Jake?"

He stroked her cheek with the backs of his fingers. Jake closed her eyes to steel herself against the tenderness of his touch. His breath fanned her cheek. The embers of desire flared to life in her belly. There was no way she would answer honestly such a loaded question while any part of him was touching her.

"Sorry to disappoint you, counselor, but the deposition is over for tonight."

"Considering you probably can't even stand without my help, the deposition isn't over until I say it is."

"Is this what you do to people when you get them on the witness stand—badger them until they tell you what you want to know?"

"Sometimes. Now answer my question."

She opened her eyes and looked at him. It was on the tip of her tongue to say, "You," but even in her sleepy and aroused state, she had better sense than that. "I want to make a good home for Dani. I want to be able to provide her with a decent future."

"What about you, Jake? Don't you want anything for yourself?"

Biting her lip, she shook her head. If her grandmother had taught her anything it was that wanting got people in trouble. "I want never to want anything so badly that I am willing to hurt someone else to get it. I never want to want anything so badly that I deliberately destroy someone else's life."

He seemed to digest that a moment; then he stroked an errant hair from her face. "You know what I want right now?"

"No. What?"

"To get you into bed."

Her tongue darted out to swipe her dry lips. "That was blunt of you."

"I meant putting you in bed. Alone."

"Oh." Mortified, she looked away from him. "Thanks for leaving me even the faintest hope you found me attractive."

Eamon cupped her chin in his palm and turned her face toward him. "What are you talking about?"

"Aren't you the one who said we should forget the night in my apartment ever happened?"

"As I remember it, that would be you."

Jake replayed the scene in her mind and couldn't fault his memory. "You would have said it. I just beat you to the punch line."

"I wasn't going to say that. I was going to say it would be best if we exercised a little discretion in the office. A subject you obviously know nothing about."

In a very small voice Jake said, "Oh. Then why did you agree to not seeing each other anymore?"

Eamon's breath fanned across her cheek as he exhaled heavily. "I thought maybe you had changed your mind after meeting Jim."

"Your brother?" He couldn't possibly believe she'd prefer Jim over him. "He's like a big puppy dog that will drink out of whatever dish someone lets him."

He smiled down at her, laying his index finger against her chest. "You're the one who said you were fickle."

"Fickle, not crazy. Jim and I are friends, that's all."

His hand trailed upward to caress her cheek. "So where does that leave us, Jake?"

A week ago, she wouldn't have hesitated to lean up and kiss him, which is what she wanted to do. With her and Dani living in his house, if only for a few days, the dynamics had shifted. Besides, when all this started, she'd envisioned at most a casual relationship developing between them. She couldn't speak for Eamon, but considering his patient care of her, a fling no longer held the appeal it once had. She answered him honestly. "I don't know."

A rueful smile tilted his lips. "Then I guess my first instinct to put you in bed was correct. Come on."

As he stood, he pulled her to her feet with one hand around her waist and held her in his arms until she was steady. "Can you walk?"

Though his touch made her dizzier than the sudden rise from the floor, she nodded. "I'm fine."

He led her back to the bedroom with a hand on her arm and tucked her in bed. "Good night, Jake," he whispered, though he doubted she heard him. If he wasn't mistaken, Jake had already fallen asleep.

He went back to the living room, righted the furniture, and threw away the trash. Afterward he settled on the sofa with a fresh beer and propped his feet on the coffee table, something he rarely did. Sighing, he brought the bottle to his lips and for a moment drank deeply.

"What am I going to do with you, Jake McKenna?" he asked aloud. She'd truly surprised him when she'd told him that the only reason she'd put a halt to things between them was that she'd expected him to do the same. Until that moment, he'd still harbored the suspicion that Jim or some other man, most likely her nonexistent dead husband, was really to blame. While it relieved him to know that no other man living or dead laid claim to her, the fact remained that with very little provocation, she'd been willing to walk away.

He also had to face the fact that Jake was more complex than he had given her credit for at first. Without complaint, she'd taken over the care of her stepbrother's child, which spoke volumes in her favor. If anything, that knowledge deepened his respect for her and honed his desire for her to a fine point.

Yet after listening to her recount that event from her past, anger on her behalf had risen in him. He understood her reticence to demand much of life for herself. But the question remained: how did you get a woman determined not to want anything to want you?

Jake woke the next morning to the smell of bacon sizzling in the pan. She checked the clock at her bedside. Barely six o'clock. Why did that not surprise her? No matter what time she put Dani to bed, she rose, like a rooster, before the sun. But poor Eamon. After last night, the man probably needed his sleep.

After brushing her teeth and lamenting the sad state of her hair, she padded out to the kitchen. Eamon stood at that gorgeous stove flipping crispy strips of bacon on the built-in grill. Dani sat on a tall stool beside him, mixing something in a large blue bowl. Both of them seemed to notice her at once.

"What are you doing up so early?" Eamon asked.

Jake couldn't help it. Her eyes drank in Eamon's tall physique clad in a T-shirt that stretched across his chest in an appealing way and a pair of tight jeans that molded to everywhere else. She swallowed and realized her mouth had gone suddenly dry. "I smelled food."

"Why don't you have a seat? My assistant and I will have breakfast ready in a few minutes."

"Hi, Jake," Dani said, making an imperfect circle with a whisk. "I'm in charge of the eggs."

Jake smiled. "I see." Since her presence was not required, she turned her attention back to Eamon. "I guess I'll retire to the living room with that copy of the *Times* I saw on the coffee table."

Eamon winked at her. "See you in a few minutes."

Jake sat on the sofa, rifled through the paper until she found the magazine section, and opened it to the weekly crossword puzzle. She studied the clues, and although she knew several answers she didn't fill them in. For one thing, she lacked anything to write with; for another, her thoughts were scattered, flitting back and forth between the paper in front of her and the tableau in the kitchen that she could hear but not see. Eamon and Dani chatted while the eggs cooked.

She hadn't heard such animation in Dani's voice since her father was alive. While that pleased her, it scared her as well. Dani had said herself that Eamon reminded her of her father. While she didn't mind Dani basking in the attention of a male father figure in the short term, she wondered what effect it would have on Dani if this situation went on too long.

And what about Eamon? She'd heard of men who endeared themselves to a woman's children hoping to make time with the mother, but Eamon seemed to genuinely enjoy being with Dani. And last night, when she'd confessed she hadn't wanted to put a stop to whatever had been brewing between them, he hadn't so much as tried to kiss her. She didn't know what to make of him. Maybe after getting to know her better, he'd changed his mind about getting involved with her. Whatever the reason, maybe it was best if neither one of them got too attached to Uncle Eamon.

Eight

Eamon lowered his coffee cup, sat back in his chair, and focused his gaze on Jake's plate. She'd barely eaten a thing, though her nose had woken her when it smelled food. She seemed more subdued now, too. She'd barely spoken two words while Dani had talked both their ears off. She didn't look at him now either, even though Dani had scampered off minutes ago leaving the two of them alone. He'd swear that either the china pattern fascinated her or she was about to fall asleep.

"Can I ask you a question?" Eamon said, breaking the silence that stretched between them.

Jake's head snapped up. "Sure."

She answered without hesitation, but he saw the wariness in her eyes. "Why does Dani insist on being called Dani, not Danielle?"

Jake's shoulders lowered in obvious relief. "For one thing, she thinks Danielle sounds too girly."

"Not suitable for the tomboy of today?"

"Definitely not. For another, she read in a kids' biography of Houdini how he came up with his stage name. He believed that if you took someone else's name and added an I to the end of it, that meant you were like that person. He admired another magician Houdin. I forget his first name."

"Robert, a Frenchman. Hence, Houdin, add an I to get Houdini."

"Hence, Dan, Dani's father, add an I and get Dani. But how did you know about Houdin?"

He took a sip from his cup, taking his time before answering. "It might or might not impress you to know I wanted to be a magician when I was a kid."

She stared at him wide-eyed. "You? You wanted to be a magician?"

He almost laughed at the incredulous look on her face. "Why does that surprise you so much?"

"Somehow I can't imagine you pulling a rabbit from your hat."

"Why not?"

"Too messy. Rabbits have no respect for personal property."

"I was more into close-up—cards, coins, sleight of hand."

She rested her elbows on the table and leaned in. "I bet you made an absolute nuisance of yourself pulling coins out of people's orifices."

"Pretty much. How did you know?"

"My brother was an amateur magician also. He had Dani doing tricks with nickels by the time she was three. Her hands were too small to palm quarters."

"Hence the fascination with Houdini?"

Jake nodded, but the light went out of her eyes. "Or used to be. Dani hasn't pulled a coin out of my ear since her father died."

"What about Dani's mother? When did she die?"

"She didn't. Dani's mother doesn't want her. Dani was barely a week old when her mother abandoned her and my brother. If she wants to stay gone that's all right with me." She sighed and her shoulders drooped. "You did it again."

"Did what?"

"Got me talking about myself without divulging anything about yourself."

"That wasn't my intention. Force of habit, I guess. In my line of work, the ability to ferret out personal information is a job requirement."

"Then you must be a very good lawyer."

"I do all right."

She cocked her head to one side. "Modesty. An almost forgotten commodity. Do you miss it? Your law practice, I mean."

He answered without hesitation or thought to dissemble. "Yes." Though mostly he missed the feeling of knowing what he was doing. She was right about him—modesty aside, he was a damn good lawyer. How he rated as a publisher? The jury was still out on that.

She licked her lips, drawing his attention to her mouth. "Can I ask you another question? Something more personal?"

He folded his arms in front of him. He should have known giving her a taste of openness would be a mistake. "Go ahead."

"How is it you have reached the advanced age of— how old are you?"

"Thirty-six."

"Thirty-six without some woman lassoing you?"

Eamon swallowed. He didn't know why it hadn't occurred to him that his marital status would be the first thing she would inquire about. "One did. I was married for almost four years."

"It didn't work out?"

"She died."

"H-how?"

Dani chose that minute to bound into the room, offering him a reprieve, if only a temporary one. She laid her cheek on Jake's shoulder like a kitten waiting to be petted. Jake slipped an arm around her and scrubbed her hand up and down the little girl's arm. "What's up?"

"Commercial. The one with the kissing."

Jake's lips stretched wide in an apparent attempt not to laugh. "I see."

"It should be over now." Dani extracted herself from Jake and skipped out of the room.

They both watched Dani's exit. When Jake turned back to him, she shrugged. "Who knew it would take me getting sick to turn Dani into an affectionate child? Usually I have to sit on her just to get a hug."

"She's worried about you."

Jake sighed. "I know, but there's not much I can do to prove to her that I'm all right. Only time can do that."

They lapsed into silence. Jake toyed with the food on her plate, but didn't eat any of it. He wished he could offer both her and Dani some reassurance that things would be all right. An idea came to him, and he strove to keep the excitement from his face so she wouldn't question him and ruin his surprise.

"I have to go downtown for a little while. Would you mind if I took Dani with me?"

"Eamon," she started to protest. "You've done more than enough. If you have to go out, Dani and I will be fine here together."

"Nonsense. As my mother would say, you look like the last rose of summer still hanging on the vine. We'll only be gone a couple of hours and you can get a nap."

Jake's shoulders slumped. "I don't suppose it would do me much good to argue."

Grasping their plates, one in each hand, he stood. "Nope." As he moved past her she tugged on his pant leg.

"Don't think this is over. One of these days you're going to have to answer my questions."

One of these days, but not now. "Don't be so eager to delve into my past, Jake. You might not like what you find."

* * *

Three hours later, Jake was awakened by the sound of Dani calling her name. She sat up in bed and brushed the few stray hairs out of her eyes. Afternoon sunshine streamed into the room, making artificial light unnecessary.

"Jake, we're baaack." A second later Dani burst into the room. "Look what Uncle Eamon bought me."

Judging from the grin on Eamon's face, she wouldn't be surprised if it was a Shetland pony, but Jake doubted the animal would fit in the bag Dani carried. She dropped the bag on the floor beside Jake's bed.

"What is it, sweetheart?" She focused on the tiny box in Dani's hand.

"If you have a quarter, I'll show you."

Jake patted her sides. "I'm afraid I'm tapped out."

"Here." From his position at the doorway, Eamon tossed her a coin.

Jake caught it in one hand and presented it to Dani. "All set."

Dani held the little box up for Jake to view. "This is a Magical Money Eater. You want to see how it works?"

"Sure."

Dani pulled out a little drawer in the box. "Put the quarter in the slot."

"Okay." Jake laid the coin flat in the little indentation in the drawer.

"Now we slide the drawer back in and the Money Eater will eat it." Dani pushed the drawer closed and made exaggerated chewing sounds and ended with an authentic-sounding burp.

"Dani," Jake exclaimed.

"It's not me," Dani protested. "It's the box. Watch." She pulled out the drawer again to reveal the empty slot. "See, the box ate it."

Jake laughed and hugged Dani to her. "Okay, the box ate it. But that quarter is coming out of your allowance."

"It's really supposed to be a money changer, but I haven't figured out the changing part yet."

"Why don't you go practice?" Eamon suggested.

"Okay."

Dani scampered off as Eamon stepped forward, coming to sit beside her on the bed. He touched his fingertips to her cheek. "You seem much better."

"I feel much better. Where did you two go off to today?"

"I had intended to take Dani to Tannen's but I forgot they're closed on Sunday, so we moseyed down to Abra Cadabra in the Village. That little box I bought her you can get in any Chinese store down on Canal Street—"

Jake silenced him with a finger across his lips. "Don't try to belittle what you've done. It isn't exactly pulling a coin out of my ear, but I thought for sure Dani's interest in magic had died with her father, and that would have been a shame."

He chuckled. "I am properly chastened. I bought you something, too."

Jake tilted her head to one side. "What?"

He reached into the bag at his feet and withdrew a bottle each of shampoo and conditioner, the brand she used. "Ready to have your hair washed?"

She looked at those bottles and her scalp started to tingle. "More than ready. I feel like I've got a dead skunk growing out of my head. But I can't get into the shower."

"I think we can work something out if you're game."

She pushed back the covers. "Lead on, McDuff."

"In a minute. Wait here."

He rose from the bed and left the room. While he was gone, she undid the rubber band at the end of her braid and unplaited the thick mass. She was about to rise from the bed when she heard Eamon call, "Close your eyes."

"Why?"

"Because I asked you to."

"This is juvenile."

"Maybe. Are your eyes closed?"

Jake let her eyelids drift shut. "Yes."

She heard Eamon come into the room and the clink of something metallic bumping together as he carried it across the room.

"Can I open my eyes now?"

"Yes."

She opened her eyes and regarded him. He leaned against the door frame watching her, whatever he'd brought in gone from sight. "You might consider changing into something that handles water a little better. I don't think that silk will survive getting wet."

She narrowed her eyes and tilted her head to the side. "Are you sure this isn't simply a ploy to get me out of my clothes?"

"If I wanted to get you out of your clothes, I wouldn't need a ploy."

Jake swallowed. No, he wouldn't need a ploy to undress her. All he'd need to do would be to keep looking at her like that. "I'll be there in a minute."

After Eamon disappeared into the bathroom, Jake stripped out of her pajamas, put on a T-shirt and the pair of jeans she'd worn home from the hospital, and followed him. She posed in the doorway with her arms aloft. "Will this do?"

"We'll manage." She eyed the setup he'd arranged and almost laughed. "Where'd you get the chair?"

"I rented it from the hair salon around the corner. The owner told me where I could get the hose and the lip for the sink. Do the accommodations meet with your approval?"

Jake nodded, not trusting what sort of voice would come out of her constricted throat. She inhaled and let her breath out slowly. She couldn't believe he'd gone to so much trouble simply to fulfill her desire to wash her hair. How had he known in the first place? She couldn't remember mentioning her desire for personal cleanliness to anyone, not even Dani. Perhaps the only real magic that occurred today was that he'd learned to read her mind.

She'd also thought he'd found a way for her to wash her own hair, but obviously he intended to do it himself. "Are you sure you know what you're getting yourself into?" She tugged on a lock of her hair. "My hairdresser charges me extra just to sit in her chair."

He patted the top of the chair. "Sit."

He helped her sit and adjust her neck in the plastic cutout that covered the rim of the sink. "Comfy?"

She closed her eyes. "I'll manage."

She heard the turn of the faucet and moments later warm, soothing water ran along her scalp. In absolute bliss, she moaned.

"How does that feel?"

"Mmm, you have to ask?"

"Not really." She heard the smile in his voice though she couldn't see his face. "Ready for some shampoo?"

"Ready as I'll ever be."

His hands, sure and gentle, massaged her scalp, setting off tiny electrical sparks wherever he touched. She sighed and dragged air into her lungs through her mouth. For a moment, she imagined those same hands, that same gentle touch roaming lower to touch all the heated places on her body.

"What's the matter?"

Jake's eyes flew open to view Eamon's face. In this odd position reading his expression proved impossible. "Nothing. Why?"

"You were breathing funny."

No kidding. She shut her eyes, wondering if he didn't know exactly what effect his touch had on her. "I think it's time to rinse, don't you?"

"If you say so."

The warm water felt heavenly, but so did Eamon's fingers as they helped remove the shampoo from her hair. She couldn't help the sigh that escaped from her lips.

"You sure there's nothing wrong?"

"Positive, you egotist. You want me to say it? You put the shampoo girl at my hair salon to shame."

"I haven't got an egotistical bone in my body. I just wanted to make sure your incisions weren't hurting."

They were, but not enough to ask him to stop. "I'm fine."

He shampooed her hair again, then applied conditioner. As he gave her hair a final rinse, she asked the question that had been plaguing her since she sat down in the chair. "How many other women have you treated to your hair-washing technique?"

He turned off the water and attempted to wrap her hair in a towel. "Actually, you're the first."

"I suppose you'll be wanting a tip now."

"Not at all." He helped her sit up, then stand. "Knowing that I'll no longer be sharing my dinner table with Medusa's younger sister is all the compensation I need."

She smacked him on the arm. "You're all heart."

He winked at her. "If you can take over from here, I'm going to check on Dani and start dinner."

"I'll be fine." He started to leave, but she called to him. He turned, an expectant look on his face. Words of gratitude formed on her lips, but knowing he wouldn't appreciate them, she bit them back. "Never mind."

"Dinner should be ready in about half an hour."

She watched Eamon leave, then went to retrieve her comb and brush from the other room. Because of the French quarter of her heritage, left to its own devices, her hair dried in waves and curls rather than kinks. She brushed her tresses out as best she could, then tied them back with a hair scrunchie.

Afterward, she surveyed herself in the mirror. Some of the postoperative pallor had left her face, for which she was grateful. Eamon had seen to it that her hair looked presentable. She'd never been overly concerned with her looks, but hadn't wanted to fall completely apart either, not only for her sake but for Dani's. The little girl would never believe she was getting better if she looked sickly.

Although he was uncomfortable accepting her thanks, the fact was, she was indebted to him. Jake sighed. He didn't seem to want anything from her besides her recovery. But how much would she owe him by the time she got back on her feet?

After a sumptuous dinner of beans and franks and a rousing game of Go Fish, Eamon declared the evening at an end. Jake looked exhausted and Dani had to go to camp the next day, and he hadn't done one drop of the work he'd brought home to tackle this weekend.

Dani protested at first until Jake fixed her with the only stern look he'd ever seen on Jake's face. "Dani McKenna, you will not give Uncle Eamon a hard time."

"Do I *have* to take a bath?"

"No. We can always send you to Stinky Children's Day Camp tomorrow."

Dani grumbled. "All right."

As she stalked off, head downcast, Eamon turned to Jake. "I didn't realize she had a problem with cleanliness."

Jake rolled her eyes and shook her head. "She doesn't. She thinks baths are for babies. She'd rather take a shower, but she's too young for that unsupervised and heaven forbid anyone should be in the bathroom with her."

Eamon grinned. "I did notice that part. After I ran her bath she pushed me out of the room and slammed the door in my face."

Jake giggled. "*She* pushed *you* out of the room?"

"I admit I didn't put up much of a struggle."

Jake laughed "That's my Dani."

"I guess I'd better go see to Her Majesty's ablutions." For no other reason than that he liked touching her, Eamon ran his finger down the slope of Jake's nose. "See you in a few."

Twenty minutes later, with Dani washed and dressed in Elmo pajamas, Jake sat on the edge of her bed reading the tail end of the third chapter of *Charlotte's Web*. When the chapter ended Jake closed the book and looked down at a sleepy Dani. "Good night, sweetheart." She leaned down to receive Dani's hug and kiss.

"Good night, Jake."

"Who's got a good-night kiss for Uncle Eamon?"

Jake pulled back and glanced over her shoulder to see Eamon standing in the doorway. How long had he been watching them without her being aware of his presence?

"I do," Dani called. She held out her arms as Eamon bent way down to receive her kiss.

"All right, you," Jake chided. "Go to sleep."

Without protest Dani settled underneath the covers and closed her eyes. "Night."

Jake smoothed the covers over her small body. "See you in the morning."

She didn't protest as Eamon grasped her elbow and helped her to her feet. "Now it's your turn," he said.

Jake wasn't going to protest an early bedtime either. She felt ready to drop. "Do I get a bedtime story, too?" she teased.

Eamon clicked off Dani's bedroom light and slung his arm around her shoulders. "Sure. Goldilocks and the Three Attorneys. They're representing her on that trespassing charge."

Jake giggled. "I thought they'd have gotten her on breaking and entering, although technically she entered, then broke."

By then they'd reached the door to Eamon's bedroom. He dropped his arm from around her shoulders. "Good night, Jake."

"Aren't you going to tuck me in?" The minute the words were out of her mouth, she regretted them. Hadn't she made up her mind only that morning to distance both herself and Dani from him? She tried to tell herself she simply had gotten caught up in their teasing banter, but she knew that wasn't true. Despite what she'd told herself and what made sense, she wanted the time alone with him. She wanted the opportunity to see if something would happen between them.

Without waiting for a response from him, she walked past him and slid under the covers to lean her back against the headboard. She patted the spot beside her on the bed.

With seeming reluctance, he walked toward her, but he remained standing. "You seem pretty tucked in to me."

"Seriously, Eamon, what are we going to do about tomorrow?"

"What do you mean?" He did sit then, his tall frame crowding her more than she thought he would.

"Dani's got camp tomorrow. You get into your office at the crack of dawn—"

"Why don't you let me worry about that? I'll drop Dani off and I'll bring her home when I come in. I've already found someone to come and stay with you during the day. So there is nothing to worry about."

"You asked someone to stay with me?"

"Of course. You expected me to leave you here alone?"

Honestly, she hadn't expected anything. She hadn't

thought about how she would spend the time that he and Dani were out of the house.

"Now it's time for you to go to sleep. Who's got a good-night kiss for Uncle Eamon?"

He was teasing her, echoing the words he'd spoken to Dani. But humor didn't rise in her; desire did. The desire to feel his lips on hers. She cradled his face in her hands. His skin radiated with warmth and his five o'clock shadow tickled her fingertips. But she chickened out. She leaned forward and touched her lips to his cheek. She pulled back enough to see his eyes, which had darkened to a deep blue. Their mouths were only inches apart. "How was that?"

In answer, he gave her what she wanted. One of his hands lifted to pull her closer and his mouth found hers. She moaned as his tongue traveled along the seam of her lips, begging entry. Eagerly she parted her lips for him and when his tongue delved inside she suckled it and pressed herself closer to him. A deep groan rumbled up through him as his other arm closed around her, crushing her to him. She whimpered, not in pain, but from the sheer pleasure of his embrace.

Slowly he pulled away from her. Her eyes flickered open to focus on his intense ice-blue ones. He stroked an errant strand of hair away from her face. "How was that?"

"Do the words 'whoa, baby' mean anything to you?"

He chuckled. "Go to sleep, Jake. I'll see you in the morning."

After he left, Jake settled back against her pillows with a smile on her face. Her lips tingled and her breasts felt heavy and aroused. The ache of desire in her belly still flamed, though its heat had receded a little. How could he expect her to sleep when every pore of her had been brought to full awareness by that one wild kiss?

Jake sighed. How could she have allowed herself to get

so stirred up by him, when only that morning she'd vowed not to let herself or Dani get too close to him? Having a man's tongue in your mouth definitely qualified as getting close. So maybe he wasn't as uninterested in her as she'd supposed last night. That still didn't make getting involved with him any better of an idea. Leaving Dani's well-being entirely out of the equation, she'd still be begging for trouble.

Hadn't she been through roughly the same scenario with her former fiancé, Stan? A successful businessman, educated in the Ivy League, perfectly proper Stan had surprised her with his interest in her. She imagined him, like she imagined Eamon, more at ease with some brittle, ultrafashionable woman afraid to let herself go for fear of mussing her hair or breaking a fingernail. Then again, Stan had never kissed her with one-eighth the passion Eamon had, not even when they made love. Stan considered her exuberance unseemly for the granddaughter of a woman whose paintings hung in the Museum of Modern Art.

Obviously Stan hadn't heard of French libertarianism or realized that Jake was a product of that upbringing. What Stan saw as loose behavior, Jake viewed as expressing her sexuality with the man she thought she loved.

Jake sighed. To please him, Jake had tamped down her naturally ebullient personality, trying to become what he wanted. In the end it hadn't really mattered what she did, because his main goal in wooing her was to get his hands on her grandmother's fortune. She'd promised herself then that she would never again remake herself to make some man happy, but she knew it was in her character to want to smooth things over, to fit the round hole in the square peg to make everything all right. An altruistic impulse for sure, but sometimes a girl had to look out for her own interests.

It might help if she knew what Eamon wanted from

her. In any scenario that made rational sense, she couldn't imagine him wanting more than a casual fling and a few good rolls in the hay. Not only wasn't she his type, but sooner or later he'd be heading back to his life in Boston. Judging from his haste in getting the new designs in place, his exit would probably be on the sooner end of things. If that's all he wanted from her, boy, did his timing stink!

While she could understand and even appreciate a brief physical liaison, Dani could not. Dani would see them spending time together and assume more existed to the relationship, even root for it. Perhaps Dani was too attached to him already.

Jake turned out the light and laid her head on the pillow. Maybe she was jumping the gun to start with. A couple of kisses didn't exactly make an affair. If she were smart, she'd make sure that nothing further happened between them.

But remembering the passion of Eamon's lips on hers and the heat of his embrace, she wished that she were free to discover where things might lead if left to follow their own course.

Nine

Eamon sat as his desk, his nose resting against his steepled fingers. The cursor on his computer screen winked at him, but he ignored it. Thoughts of the previous day crowded his consciousness, pushing out other, more prosaic matters. Jake McKenna—the only topic his brain seemed to want to accept that morning. Jake who was staying in his house, sleeping in his bed, haunting his dreams, and otherwise wreaking havoc on his nervous system.

And he'd done it to himself. He'd invited her into his home and without much effort she'd turned him and his world upside down. Or rather he'd turned his world upside down for her. He couldn't even sleep in his own bed. He doubted he ever would again without thinking of her.

He'd washed her hair not only because Dani had told him Jake wanted it, but because he'd missed seeing that wild mane around her face. His thoughts and his libido skimmed over an image of Jake sitting in that beauty shop chair, her eyes closed, the sultriest purrs of contentment wafting up to him over the sound of the water and the scent of shampoo. If any noise she made during lovemaking sounded half that sexy, she could drive a man, any man, over the brink in no time flat. As it was, he'd ended up with an almost painful erection for his troubles. Thanks to the gods of foresight he'd wrapped a towel around his waist before he began, so she hadn't noticed.

Then she'd kissed him good night, and the heat from her embrace had damn near singed his eyebrows. Did she have any idea of the effect she had on him? He doubted it, if she could blithely roll over and go to sleep after that. When he left her, he'd gone to his den-cum-home office to try to get some work done. Instead he'd sat in front of his computer, much as he did now, and accomplished nothing.

He thought of Jim, who was undoubtedly reinventing the word *party* down in Florida about now. Jim would probably hemorrhage his internal organs laughing if he knew some woman, any woman, had turned his stoic older brother to mush.

Eamon sighed. Sometimes he worried about Jim and his party-animal lifestyle. Aside from the threat of disease and irate husbands, he knew that underneath the happy-go-lucky exterior lurked a well of bitterness and anger Jim had never addressed and refused to acknowledge.

Eamon had told Jake that Jim had come along when he was four years old. He'd deliberately left out the fact that Jim had been adopted as an infant. Jim's mother had left him on the front steps of a church with the proverbial note attached to his blanket.

Eamon suspected Jim's love-'em-and-leave-'em ways had less to do with having a good time than punishing the fairer sex for his mother's abandonment. Every time a woman began to genuinely care for Jim, she found herself cut out of his life, excommunicated, as if she had never existed.

In all likelihood, Jim's mother had been a young girl unable to care for her child. But in society's eyes and Jim's as well, a man who abandoned his children was merely a deadbeat, but a woman who did the same was a monster. Jim used to joke that at least she hadn't left him in the trash on garbage pickup day, but there had never been any humor in his eyes when he'd said it.

He heard a soft knock at the door and a second later Jim poked his head in. "Guess who?"

"I was just thinking about you."

Jim walk toward him and sprawled into one of the chairs facing the desk. "Nothing good, I'm sure."

Eamon's eyebrows lifted as he studied his brother. The indolent pose was old hat, the scowl on his face was new. Eamon crossed his arms. "How was your trip?"

"I met a girl."

Eamon snorted. Jim saying he met a girl was like other people saying they read the morning paper. "Who is she and how much money does her family want?" Jim fastened a glare on him that told him his humor was not appreciated. "All right. Go on."

"I went to check on Paul's place. She was in the pool. Stark naked."

Eamon's eyebrows lifted. "I'd think that would be a bonus for you."

"It would have been if she hadn't called the police and tried to have me arrested. I'm just lucky I knew one of the guys who showed up."

Only Jim could get himself in a fix like that and live to tell about it from outside of a jail cell. "I still don't see the problem."

Jim sighed. "The problem is, dear brother, that I ended up taking her out to dinner and somehow we ended up in flagrante delicto on the living room sofa. You'd know how adventurous that was if you'd ever tried to make love on wicker furniture."

"You're a regular Evel Knievel." Eamon studied his brother's face. For the first time he noticed the dark shading under his left eye. "You were so bad she hit you?"

Unconsciously, Jim's fingertips wandered to the bruise beneath his eye. "That was my reward for a bit of ungentlemanly conduct. At first I thought she was a trespasser." Jim offered him a tight smile. "I guess you had to be there."

"I guess so."

"My real problem is that I don't know who she is. She said she was a friend of Paul's, but I'm positive she gave me a fake name. And when I woke up in the morning she was gone."

Eamon rested his elbows on the desk and steepled his fingers. If he'd doubted the girl's story, why hadn't he checked her purse? That's what any rational person would have done. Then again, a rational person wouldn't have slept with a girl he barely knew in the first place. "You spent all night on a wicker sofa?"

"No, we eventually made it to the bed. That isn't the point. She could have been anyone."

Eamon's brow furrowed. "Tell me you used a condom. Please tell me you used a condom."

"Of course. I'm not that stupid."

Partially relieved, Eamon sat back in his chair. The realization that it didn't matter who she was unless Jim wanted to find her kept his relief from being absolute. In Eamon's estimation, involvement with a woman who blackened your eye one minute and made love to you the next could only lead to trouble. So he shrugged nonchalantly. "The one that got away."

Jim shrugged too, but without the same degree of nonchalance. "I guess. How's Jake?"

Eamon accepted his brother's shift of topic without comment. "She's recuperating."

"At your place?"

Eamon nodded. "She and Dani are fine." He didn't know why he felt compelled to bring the little girl into the picture, as if Jake weren't the main focus of his concern.

"I see." The grin on Jim's face told him that he hadn't fooled anybody. "And how is sleeping on the sofa agreeing with you?"

"It isn't. I'm thinking of taking the two of them out to Montauk for the weekend if Jake can stand the ride. At least there I can have a bedroom with a real bed to myself. Unless you want to join us."

"The enthusiasm of your offer is completely underwhelming." Jim shifted in his seat to a more upright position. "You can have the lovely ladies McKenna all to yourself this weekend, though I would like to visit Jake if you don't mind."

Eamon cleared his throat. "Why would I mind?"

"Then I just imagined you nearly wrenching my arm from its socket at the hospital when you thought I wasn't treating Jake right."

"Has anyone ever told you that you have an unfortunate overreliance on hyperbole?"

"Come again?"

"You exaggerate too much."

Jim grinned. "That's what I thought you said." He stood, pushing back his chair. "I'm going to see how deep the mess is on my desk; then I'm going over to see Jake."

If Jim was giving him one last chance to protest, he was wasting his effort. "Have a good time."

With a shrug, Jim left. Eamon straightened in his chair. He was definitely going to get his mind in gear and get some work done. He'd start with something simple, like signing the stack of correspondence Margot had left on his desk that morning.

He whacked the side of the ancient desk that had once belonged to his uncle Eamon. The drawers stuck and the surface looked as if it had been through a world war, but he hadn't the heart to put it on the junk heap where it belonged. He tugged on the drawer until it opened. The contents shifted forward and the pack of cigarettes he'd kept in one desk or another came to rest beside his fingers. His willpower pack. He'd given up the short-lived habit twelve years ago, cold turkey. The pack in his desk was the last one he'd bought but never smoked.

For the first time in a long time, he was tempted to open them. But he reminded himself of his mantra where cigarettes were concerned—part "Invictus" part common sense: he was the master of his fate, he was the captain of his soul. Twenty little cancer sticks didn't rule him. He ruled himself. Besides, if he ever managed to get the smashed, mangled pack open, all he'd probably find were some whisps of decomposing paper and tobacco.

He found the pen he wanted and shut the drawer with a little more force than necessary.

The sound of the doorbell ringing woke Jake from her afternoon nap. Lana, Eamon's downstairs neighbor, the woman Eamon had gotten to stay with her, would undoubtedly answer it, though Jake wondered who would be visiting at this time of day. She sat up, brushed the hair from her eyes, and turned on the lamp beside her bed.

A few seconds later, Liza's appearance in the bedroom doorway answered her question. Liza rushed over, sat on the side of the bed next to Jake, and embraced her.

"Oh, God, Jake. I'm so sorry I wasn't here. How are you?"

Liza released her enough that she could sit back. "I was a lot better before you smushed my innards."

Liza brushed her hair over her shoulder. "I can't believe you wait until I take the one lousy vacation I've had in years to nearly do yourself in."

"I didn't plan it that way." Neither had Liza gone on a simple vacation. "How did it go?"

Liza pressed her lips together and lowered her head. Jake supposed she had the answer as to how Liza's meeting with the man who'd fathered her had gone. "He wouldn't see you?"

"He wasn't there." Liza stood, wrapping her arms around herself. "It took me four days to muster up the nerve to drive out to his house. Then when I got there I found out he was in San Francisco of all places."

Liza turned plaintive eyes to her, but Jake didn't know what to say. She'd never thought Liza's pursuit of her birth father was a good idea. What could she accomplish by dropping in on a man who had forsaken his right to be in her life before she was old enough to remember him? But ever since they were girls together, Liza had been obsessed with who her father might be and hadn't understood Jake's lack of interest concerning her own. When Liza's mother died a year ago, Liza found his name among her mother's papers. It took Liza six months to track him down and another six months to work up the nerve to try to see him. And now all that waiting, worrying, frayed nerves, and expense had been for nothing.

"I'm so sorry," Jake said finally. And she was. Liza didn't deserve any more disappointment than she'd experienced already. "Are you going to try to see him again?"

"Yes. No. I don't know." Liza turned and began to pace.

Jake watched her, unsure of what to make of her friend's uncharacteristically anxious behavior. Usually, the more upset Liza was, the more detached she became. Aside from that, she noticed that though Liza was usually very put-together, her suit was wrinkled and her legs were surprisingly bare. Liza normally wore panty hose with pants. "Is there something you're not telling me?"

Liza froze and turned plaintive eyes to Jake. "I have just done the stupidest thing in my entire life."

Since heretofore the "stupidest" thing Liza laid claim to doing was getting a "Rachel" haircut a few years ago when the TV show *Friends* was popular, Jake couldn't imagine what sort of transgression Liza might have committed to make her say that. "What happened?"

"I met a man."

That statement could presage all kinds of trouble. "And . . ." Jake prompted.

"Well, I didn't exactly meet him." Liza shook her head. "Let me start from the beginning."

That would be nice, Jake thought, but said nothing. She crossed her arms, wondering where Liza's story might lead.

"My father's house is out on the edge of nowhere. The air conditioning in my rental car died and by the time I got there I was sweaty and exhausted. No one answered the doorbell, but the door pushed open and I went inside. I was thinking maybe he hadn't heard me, or maybe that's what I wanted to think because I didn't want to come home without meeting him."

Jake nodded. "And this man was there instead?"

"Not at first. I looked through the house and found no one. There was a pool out back, my last hope, but when I got out there, it was empty. I stood there for a long time just staring at that water. I don't know what made me do this, maybe I wanted to drown myself at that moment, but I stripped down to my birthday suit and threw myself in the pool."

Liza started to pace again. Jake wondered if Liza worried about how low her mental state had sunk. "I don't think you were suicidal. People don't kill themselves in the nude. That's why they thought Marilyn Monroe must have been the victim of foul play because she was dressed only in her birthday suit when they found her."

Liza stopped. "I didn't mean drown that way. I meant I felt so dirty, so tired, so disappointed, I wanted to wash it all away. Then he showed up."

Liza sighed. "One minute I was minding my own

business floating in the pool, the next he was standing over me. He startled me and made some lewd comments about the state in which he'd found me. I panicked. I thought he was some sort of pervert. He thought I was a trespasser—"

"Which you were."

"Anyway." Liza fastened her with a harsh look for interrupting. "I tried to hightail it out the front door wrapped only in a towel. I mean I wasn't going to stay there with some psycho. He tried to stop me and we ended up in a heap on the floor, the towel had fallen heaven knew where. It was like something out of one of those old romantic comedies."

"But Jane Russell always managed to hang on to her clothes."

"Yeah, well, he gave me my towel back and we told each other who we were, except I gave him a fake name."

Jake's mouth dropped open. "Liza, you didn't." It had been years since they had pretended to be Anastasia and Scheherezade respectively. Jake had been Anastasia, the missing empress with a grandmother who lived in France. Liza had been Scheherezade, the teller of a thousand tales, most of which revolved around the secret whereabouts of her father, the sheik.

"I did."

"And he believed that?"

"I told him he could call me Sherry, but no, I don't think he believed me considering he claimed his name was James Brown, but I could call him 'the Godfather of Soul' if I wanted to."

Jake laughed. So far this sounded like a nearly harmless flirtation. "So where does the 'stupidest thing I've ever done' part came in?"

Liza wrapped her arms around her waist and huffed out a breath. "I slept with him, Jake. He offered to buy me dinner as sort of a peace offering for acting like a jerk and scaring me half to death. I was starving and tired, so I said yes. I don't know what got into me, but when he brought me back, I kissed him. The next thing I knew we were on the sofa and our clothes were in a pile on the floor."

Jake stared at her friend in amazement. "Are you trying to tell me that you, Liza Morrow, slept with a complete stranger?" Jake tried to hide her shock behind humor, but everything Liza described was so completely out of character for her that Jake was worried now, too. "Tell me the sex was at least worth the trouble."

"Oh, God, Jake, it wasn't just sex, it was a transcendental experience. It was hot, sweat-running-down-your-back, scream-your-lungs-out sex. It was like nothing I'd ever experienced before, never let myself feel before. You know what I mean?"

Jake swallowed, not quite able to meet Liza's dreamy-eyed gaze. A twinge of the green-eyed monster churned in her stomach. Jake had never lost herself in any man, not even Stan. If she were honest with herself, part of her envied her friend's experience. "So you are feeling guilty for indulging in a night of wild, passionate sex?"

"Hell no. It happened and I'm not going to beat myself up about it. But when I woke up this morning, I felt so embarrassed to be lying next to a man whose name I didn't even know. I ran out of there without so much as leaving him a note."

Liza sighed. "He didn't deserve that, Jake, for me to steal out of there as if what we shared meant nothing. In fact, the opposite is true. He was very sweet to me, and I needed that. Once we finally made it to the bed, he held me until I fell asleep. I don't know how to explain what I mean. Despite the pretense, there was also a connection between us." Liza scuffed the carpet with the toe of her shoe. "With all my complaining about what idiots men can be, you'd think I'd latch on to the first one that showed a little sensitivity."

"You'd think." Jake smiled sympathetically, hoping Liza would say more.

Instead Liza flopped on the bed beside her. "Enough about me. Tell me what happened to you. I called your office from my cab from the airport. They told me you were out of the office and gave me this address. I detoured here rather than going home, not that here is a bad place to be."

"It's Eamon's apartment."

"Eamon, your boss, Eamon?"

"That's the one." Jake relayed everything that had happened since her collapse on the nursery floor. Everything except her burgeoning feelings for Eamon. Despite her intentions, she found herself growing more and more attached and attracted to him. She couldn't trust Liza in her present mood not to encourage her.

As Jake spoke, Liza swung her leg in an anxious fashion. When Jake drew to a halt, she said, "Let me get this straight—this paragon of virtue rushes you to the hospital, saves your life, pays your bills, and takes you *and* Dani in, yet he wants absolutely nothing from you? Maybe someone ought to tell Superman another guy is encroaching on his territory."

"I didn't say that." He wanted her, she knew that, though his timing stank. He felt sorry for her. But beyond that, she didn't understand his motivation any better than Liza did. "He feels responsible for me."

"So when do I get to meet this paragon of masculine virtue?"

"Tonight if you want. He and Dani should be home about six."

"It's a date." Liza stood. "In the meantime, I'm going to go home and change. I've been in this outfit since yesterday. After I left my father's house, I went straight to the airport. By the way, who was that amazon that let me in?"

"Eamon's downstairs neighbor," Jake said with more rancor than she intended. When Eamon had said Mrs. Appelby would be up to check on her, Jake had expected a little old bespectacled lady. What she'd gotten was a near-six-foot-tall, buxom beauty with jet-black hair and exotic amber eyes.

Liza arched her brows but didn't comment. "Try to stay out of trouble until I get back."

When the doorbell rang again not ten minutes later, Jake assumed Liza must have forgotten something and come back. Fully awake now, she ventured into the living room to meet her. She got there in time to witness Lana Appelby hugging the stuffings out of Jim.

When she released him, Jim swayed a bit, but grinned. "Hey, McKenna, how's tricks?"

She smiled back. "How was Florida?"

He flopped down next to her on the sofa. "Interesting." He tucked a stray hair behind her ear. "You're looking well. Has Eamon been behaving himself?"

"He's been very good to me, a perfect gentleman."

Mischief twinkled in his brown eyes as Jim shook his head. "Haven't I taught that man anything?"

She laughed and hugged him to her. She'd missed his humor and his friendship in the past few days. She set him away from her and studied his face. "There's something different about you."

"You noticed." He touched his fingers to his eye, drawing her attention to the bruise there. "I don't usually sport a Monday afternoon shiner."

No, he didn't, but that didn't have anything to do with the difference she noticed. She cocked her head to one side. "What trouble did you get yourself into now?"

He grinned. "If you think this is bad, you should have seen the other guy."

"Yeah, right. I hope you didn't hurt his fist too much with your face."

"You wound me, Jake. Truly."

"You're not going to tell me what really happened, are you?"

"Nope." He stood. "Unfortunately I've got to get back to the office. One of us has got to keep the wheels of the art department moving."

"I'm sorry to leave you in the lurch like this."

He chucked her under her chin. "You just worry about getting back on your feet. I'll see you around, kid."

After Jim left, Jake pulled one of the sofa pillows onto her lap. Despite the fact that Jim was three years older than she, she still looked on him as an errant younger brother. So now she had two people to worry about besides herself and Dani.

And she'd learned one valuable lesson: stay the hell out of Florida.

Ten

Rather than sit at his desk getting nothing accomplished, Eamon picked up Dani from the nursery at five o'clock and headed home. He opened the door to his apartment to the sound of feminine laughter. He recognized Jake's effervescent laugh, but didn't recognize the throatier voice he heard.

"Jake," he called, to let the women know he was in the house.

"We're in here," she called back.

He helped Dani take off her jacket and hung it and her book bag in the hall closet; then the two of them made their way to the kitchen. Jake sat at the kitchen table. Another woman, tall, with shoulder-length black hair and incredible whiskey-colored eyes, stood at the stove, stirring something in a frying pan. Both stared back at him. He would gladly have paid a million dollars for the look of smiling welcome on Jake's face.

"Hi, you two," Jake said as Dani ran toward her. The little girl threw herself into Jake's embrace. Jake stroked the little girl's hair. "How was camp?"

While Jake tended to Dani, the other woman drew his attention. "I'm Liza," she announced, extending her hand. She withdrew it, removed the pot holder covering it, then stuck it out again. He advanced toward her and shook it. "I'm Eamon."

"So Jake tells me. You have a lovely home."

"Thank you."

She released his hand, but she continued a thorough head-to-toe examination with her eyes. She didn't strike him as a flirt, and her appraisal seemed too impersonal to signal interest. She was here to give him the thumbs-up or down on Jake's behalf.

Her gaze returned to his face. He lifted one eyebrow. "Do I pass muster?"

She smiled. "You'll do."

"What are you two talking about?" Jake asked.

Liza turned back to her skillet, leaving him to answer. "Just getting acquainted. If you'll excuse me, I'm going to go change."

In his bedroom, Eamon stripped out of his suit and changed into a pair of khaki pants and a polo shirt. For good measure, he brushed his teeth and splashed on a dash of cologne. He stopped outside the kitchen, listening for a moment to the women's conversation.

"I still can't believe you wanted to fix me up with him. I've had it with dating men who are prettier than I am. They spend more time in front of the mirror than I do."

He couldn't hear Jake's response, but a moment later the two of them laughed in that low-pitched way women do when they are discussing a man they find attractive.

Deciding to quit eavesdropping before they discovered him, Eamon stepped through the entranceway to the kitchen. Immediately both women turned to look at him. "I suppose I should take over as host of the evening. Can I get either of you ladies something to drink?"

"We've started without you." Jake held up a glass half full of a red fruity liquid. She took a dainty sip before setting the glass on the table. "Liza made sangria."

"I'll get you a glass," Liza volunteered.

He took a sip and set his glass beside Jake's. "You ladies are going to spoil me. I hope I'm not pressing my luck by asking, but what's for dinner?"

"Tacos."

Jake added, "Liza promised to make them for Dani. Dani says mine taste like Tac oh, nos."

Both women laughed, but his eyes were on Jake.

Liza cleared her throat. "If you two will excuse me, I'm going to freshen up; then I'll get everything on the table."

After Liza left, he slid into the chair across from Jake. "How are you feeling?"

"Good." She sipped from her glass. Her gaze wandered over him, then returned to his face. "I hope you don't mind that I invited Liza to stay for dinner."

"Not at all, considering that she's cooking it." Until that moment it hadn't occurred to him to ask what had happened to his neighbor, who had volunteered to act as his cook for as long as Eamon needed her. "By the way, what happened to Lana?"

Her brow arched and she folded her arms in front of her. "You mean Ms. Universe 2003?"

Eamon fought to contain the smile that wanted to break free hearing the jealousy in Jake's voice. With a look of innocence he asked, "Who?"

"Oh, please, Eamon. You know exactly what I mean. That woman looks like she could bench press more than you. She left when she realized Liza was staying."

Although her possessiveness pleased him, he sought to put her at ease. "Believe it or not, her husband makes Woody Allen look like Arnold Schwarzenegger."

"Get out!"

"Honestly. And she dotes on him as if he were Louis the Fourteenth."

Jake giggled. "I guess there's no accounting for taste."

"Guess not." Looking into her smiling eyes, he couldn't think of a single rational thing to say. Her tongue darted out to trace a path along her lower lip. He watched it, riveted, until Dani came bounding into the kitchen with Liza right behind her.

"Hate to interrupt, folks," Liza said, "but somebody's hungry."

Eamon blinked and sat back. "What can I do to help?"

"Not a thing. My assistant and I have everything under control."

Forty-five minutes later, all the tacos had been devoured. The two women sat at the table while Eamon finished up the dishes he insisted on loading into the dishwasher. Eamon wiped his hands on a dish towel and turned to face the women. "Well, ladies, this has been an enjoyable evening, but I've got to get some work done. Thanks for dinner, Liza, and for keeping Jake company today."

"It was my pleasure."

He turned to her and winked. "Don't stay up too late."

"I won't."

He turned and left the kitchen, leaving her alone with Liza. Jake turned to her friend. Liza sat with her elbows on the table, her chin propped on her folded hands. "Do you want the verdict now, or should we wait until later?"

"Now would be fine."

"I like him, Jake. Well mannered, well groomed, and he cleans up after himself. We already gave him a thumbs-up in the looks department. What more could a girl want?"

Not much, Jake agreed. "But can you honestly imagine me with a man like that? He just ate tacos without getting a drop of sauce on his chin."

Liza's brows furrowed. "What has that got to do with anything?"

"Liza, he's the neatest, most organized, most controlled man I've ever met. I barely manage to get to work on time."

Liza wagged her finger at her. "I see the problem. You can understand your attraction to him. You can't fathom his attraction to you."

"Bingo. I can't see his interest going beyond the sexual, and I'm not even good for that right now. He probably looks at me and thinks I'll be wild in bed and wants to find out firsthand."

"Maybe, but I saw the way he looked at you. Sure, there was desire in his gaze, but caring, too."

Jake sighed. "Even if there was, sooner or later, he's going to be going back to Boston. And I have no intention of getting left here in New York with a broken heart."

Liza nodded. "Then be careful, Jake."

Jake agreed, but suspected that bit of advice came a little too late.

Over the next few days, they set a pattern. Every morning Jake rose just as Eamon and Dani were about to walk out the door. She offered a motherly kiss to Dani, but Eamon noticed with some regret, she offered him only a perfunctory touch of her lips, one given because she thought she should, not because she wanted to. Ever since the night her friend came to dinner, she'd withdrawn from him. He had no idea what Jake and Liza had talked about, but if he'd suspected it would lead to this detachment on her part he'd have camped out in the kitchen.

He didn't know what to do about this shift in attitude, but he refused to let it throw him. When Jake got a clean bill of health from her doctor on Thursday, it made him more determined to take her and Dani away from the city to his house on Long Island. Maybe there he could get her to open up to him.

Jake had fallen asleep during the two-hour ride. When he pulled into the driveway at the side of the house, a large Cape Cod painted white with yellow shutters, she didn't stir. He shook her shoulder gently. "Jake, we're here."

She turned sexy, sleep-darkened eyes to him. "That was quick."

He brushed a strand of hair from her cheek. "That's because you slept the whole way."

She sat up and checked the backseat. "How are you doing back there?"

Dani looked up from the book she'd been reading. "I'm fine."

Eamon smiled. No matter what, her first concern was for Dani. "Ready to get out?"

Jake nodded and stretched within the confines of the car. Eamon got out, walked around the car to open her door, and held out his hand to her. Her warm palm slid against his as she took his hand and stood. He opened the door for Dani, then refocused his gaze on Jake. "What do you think?"

She gave the house a once-over, then grinned up at him. "The house suits you."

"What do you mean?"

"Even the hedges don't have a leaf out of place."

He chuckled. "You haven't seen the inside yet." He motioned toward the front door. "I'll come back and get the bags later."

They started up the white stone walkway that led to the door. Before they got halfway there, the door opened and Starr darted out. Before he could warn them, Jake shrieked and Dani nearly climbed the side of the house to get out of her way. As usual, she launched herself at him and, this time, succeeded in knocking him to the ground. Between swipes of her tongue he saw both Jake and Dani staring at him with the same wide-eyed shocked expression.

He'd told them that he had a dog, but he supposed neither of them was expecting this much dog. "Enough," he told the dog, pushing her massive paws from his chest. He rose and straightened his clothes. "Jake, Dani, this is Starr." He rubbed the massive dog's coat. "You be-have yourself," he warned. The dog looked up at him, her pink tongue bobbing in her mouth and a glint of challenge in her eye. She barked once and turned in Jake and Dani's direction.

"Wh-what is that thing?" Jake asked, clutching Dani to her.

"It's a wolf," Dani said with interest.

Laughter bubbled up in Eamon, but he tamped it down. He suspected neither of them would forgive him for his humor at this moment. He had planned a more sedate introduction, but that was blown to hell now. He held on to the dog's collar to give the two of them time to acclimate themselves to the dog. "*She* is an Alaskan malamute. Her name is Eskimo Starr." He patted her back. "She's very friendly and she likes children."

"She does?" Dani took a step forward, out of Jake's grasp.

Atta girl, Eamon thought as Dani inched closer.

Dani held out her hand, then quickly withdrew it. "Does she bite?"

"Only her food—and me on occasion."

That seemed to mollify Dani. She held out her hand for the dog to smell. After a moment, the dog nudged Dani's hand with the top of her head, an invitation to pet her. Dani looked back at Jake, an excited expression on her face. "She likes me."

"Of course she does, sweetheart."

Eamon's gaze traveled to Jake and beyond to his next-door neighbor's oldest son, who ambled toward them leaving the front door open. Tall, lanky, and almost four-teen, the kid moved as if he'd borrowed his limbs from someone else and wasn't quite sure how to use them. When he reached where Jake stood he stopped and shrugged. "She knew you were here and I thought she'd scratch a hole in the door, so I let her out."

Eamon ruffled the fur behind the dog's right ear. "It's all right. Please tell your mother I say thank you."

"I will." With a wave at the dog, he turned, tripped over his own foot, and took off at a run toward his own house.

Eamon winced watching the unathletic boy jog home. He remembered that awkward stage when his body had grown faster than his mind's ability to control it. Thankfully it had been a very short stage.

He turned to Jake, who stood rooted in the same spot. "Ready for the grand tour?"

She nodded. "Does she always greet you like that?"

Eamon put his arm around Jake's shoulders and led her toward the house. Starr ran ahead and Dani ran after her. "Not always, but I suspect she's still mad at me for the mating debacle."

"What happened?"

"The breeder I bought her from wanted to pair her with a male from another champion line and I agreed. But the mating didn't go as planned. First of all, when she was a puppy, the vet told me that a lot of malamutes suffer from hip dysplasia when they get older and to avoid it I should give her a special kind of vitamin. I had no idea one of the side effects would be that she would grow larger than most any other of the breed I've seen. Needless to say, she was a little intimidating to her much smaller, prospective mate."

Jake grinned up at him. "So it was no love match like your friend the Amazon and her husband?"

"Not at all. *She* actually mounted *him*. I guess she wanted to show him how it was done. After that, he slunk off to a corner, a broken man. So, I brought her home. In retribution, she tore to shreds my second favorite pair of shoes, which happened to be on my feet at the time."

They reached the front door. Eamon stepped aside to let Jake pass first. "I should warn you the place isn't completely furnished."

She eyed him over her shoulder. "If that's anything like the warning you gave us that you had a dog, I am truly terrified."

The front hallway led to a large living room on the right. The large open space contained a fireplace, a love seat, and little else. Starr had taken up residence underneath the front window. Dani sat cross-legged on the floor with the dog's head in her lap. The two were deep in private conversation.

Jake stepped into the carpeted room, then turned to face him. "Okay, so you didn't lie."

"I bought this place about three years ago, but I haven't been here enough to worry about decorating down here. The bedrooms are habitable, though. All that's lacking are some fresh sheets."

"I see." She looked him up and down; then, with her hands clasped behind her back, she strolled through the room. Facing the back of the house, she asked, "What's through there?"

"The kitchen on the left, a small solarium on the right. Farther than that is the beach." He came up behind her. "I thought after a little unpacking you'd like to hit the sand before it gets too late."

"Sounds like a plan."

Eamon swallowed. His body relished the prospect of seeing Jake in some skimpy bikini. "Come on, I'll show you to your room."

She started to call Dani to join them, but he forestalled her. "She'll be fine." He inched Jake toward the stairs at the left of the house.

"I'm sorry if I'm being paranoid, but I'm a city girl. We never had dogs. A large breed is too big to keep in an apartment and small ones get on everybody's nerves."

They reached the steps. As much as Jake had healed in the last week, she couldn't make it up the first step. "I guess I'd better put you in the bedroom down here."

Grasping his arm for balance, she nodded. "The spirit is willing, but the flesh says no way."

Chuckling, he led her to the back bedroom, the one he used when he stayed here. He flicked on the light to reveal a king-size bed and matching dresser, both stained a deep mahogany. A small desk sat in one corner of the room. "What do you think?" he asked.

She turned her head, scanning the four walls. "This is your bedroom, isn't it?"

"Yes."

She turned troubled eyes to him. "I'm putting you out of your room again."

A lock of her hair floated around her face. He indulged his whim and tucked it behind her ear. "Don't worry about that. I want you to be comfortable here. I want—" He stopped, partly because the words to express his emotions deserted him, partly because he knew how she felt about wanting. He forced a smile to his face. "I want you to hurry up and get ready before the sun sets."

She studied his face for a moment, making him wonder if he hadn't done a good enough job of concealing his feelings. A slow smile crept across her face. "I can't oblige you as long as my bag is still in the car."

He smiled genuinely this time. "I'll be right back."

Once Eamon left her suitcase on her bed, Jake took another look around the room. Definitely a masculine space that fit its owner. Once again, she invaded his territory and he gave it up without complaint. She didn't understand him, but she wanted to. Maybe it was like Jim said, he'd decided to care about her. But for the life of her she couldn't figure out why he would. They were too different in every way that mattered.

Jake sighed. And then there were her feelings for him. What woman wouldn't fall for a man who looked like a

Greek god, kissed like Rudolf Valentino's understudy, and saved your life on top of it? Her mother used to say that love had no rhyme or reason. When it hit you, all you could do was hang on for the ride. But what she felt, besides gratitude, was lust, not love. Unrequited lust, since she was incapable of acting on her impulses. That's what she tried to convince herself of, until she heard Dani calling her name.

Dani skipped into the room carrying her bathing suit and plastic beach sandals. The dog trailed behind her. When Dani halted, the dog sat by her feet.

"Looks like you have a new friend there," Jake said to Dani.

"She does tricks, too." Dani turned to face the animal. "Shake hands," she commanded. The dog lifted one paw and placed it in Dani's hand. "Good girl," Dani said in her best dog-trainer voice. She let go of the dog's paw and turned to Jake. "See?"

"Brava!" Jake clapped for Dani, then for her canine companion. "Now let's get changed."

Jake helped Dani on with her suit, a one-piece blue number with green piping. Then she put on her own suit, one she'd borrowed from Liza. It fit snugly considering the difference in the two women's builds, but the one-piece garment did conceal the scars from her surgery that one of her own bathing suits would not.

As Jake slipped on her sandals, a knock sounded on the door. "Are you ladies ready in there?"

"Just about." Jake pulled an oversize T-shirt over her head as a cover-up before she opened the door.

Eamon looked the three of them over, woman, child, and dog. "I suppose you'll do," he said in his best impression of his assistant Margot.

Jake laughed. "Which way to the beach?"

Fifteen minutes later, Jake and Eamon reclined in beach chairs watching Dani play by the shoreline. The dog chased after the incoming waves, barking and biting at them as if they were invaders threatening to attack.

Eamon drew her attention by running his index finger along her forearm. "You're not going to wear that T-shirt the whole time, are you?"

She focused on his face and the teasing smile that broadened his lips. "Are you familiar with how they do laproscopic surgery?"

"Not intimately."

"First they cut holes in you; then they fill your stomach with air until it's the size of a nine-month-pregnant woman's so they can see what they are doing on a monitor. Then they slice off the bad stuff and pull it through one of the holes they cut."

"Your point being?"

"I still look like I'm about four months along. I figured I ought to spare the world that sight."

"There's nobody here but us."

Jake scanned the little inlet. She counted three other houses on the curving strip of sand before her, all of which appeared uninhabited at the moment. "Point taken."

He sat up, placing his feet in the sand. "I'm going to go in for a while, so I leave the decision up to you."

As she watched him walk down to the beach, her breath eased out on a long sigh. Dressed only in a pair of navy blue swim trunks, he provided her with a visual feast of muscle and sinew if only from behind. She'd wondered at what sort of physique lurked beneath his spotless suits and neat sport clothes. He met her expectations and then some. She wiped away a spot of moisture that collected at the corner of her mouth. Admiration was one thing; out-and-out drooling was another.

Jake lifted her novel from her lap and tried to focus on the words before her. After ten minutes, she gave

COULD IT BE MAGIC?

it up, pulled off her T-shirt, and went to the water's edge to join Dani. They worked at building a sand castle until Eamon came out of the water and joined them. He shook himself like a mongrel, spraying water all over them. When both she and Dani glared up at him, he laughed. He squatted beside Jake. "What are you doing?"

"Making a sand castle," Dani answered. "Want to help?"

He glanced at Jake, who'd shed her T-shirt to bare a disgustingly modest swimsuit. Even so, she looked undeniably sexy sitting in the sand with her legs tucked up beneath her. "I'm going to take Starr for a run; then I'll be back."

He struck off down the beach with the dog on his heels. Starr always loved their runs along the sand. Today he needed one himself, to work off the sexual frustration Jake inspired in him. He turned his head to check on her in time to catch her watching him. She immediately turned away.

Eamon focused on the path in front of him. Maybe she wasn't as immune to him as she wanted him to believe. When he got back from his run, he'd find out.

Jake and Dani finished their sand castle, complete with moat, just in time for a large wave to come in and wash half of it away. Dani looked so put out that Jake hugged the little girl to her. "Not fair," Dani protested against Jake's shoulder.

"No, it wasn't." She scrubbed her hands over Dani's back.

"Why the long faces?"

Jake craned her neck around to see Eamon standing above them. "Our sand castle got washed away."

Eamon ruffled Dani's hair. "If you promise to cheer up, I'll let you bury me in the sand."

"Oh, boy!"

Jake laughed as Dani shot off her lap. She grabbed the bucket and took Eamon's hand, leading him over to where the chairs stood. Jake brushed the sand from her body and followed. Within minutes, Dani had half of his body covered. The dog took this as an opportunity to make nice with her master, lying beside him and licking his face.

Sitting back in her lounge chair, Jake laughed. "You volunteered for this."

"What was I thinking?"

When Dani got him fully covered, she sat back on her heels. "Now you have to stay like that."

"No way," Eamon protested. "I think you buried a sand crab in here with me. Ouch!" He rose from the sand like a ghoul rising from the grave. Sand stuck to him just about everywhere. He stretched out his arms like Frankenstein and chased Dani. Dani giggled and threw herself on Jake's lap for protection. The dog barked and snapped at Eamon's heels.

Eamon relaxed his arms to his sides and stared at the dog. "Excuse me, but who buys your dog food, you traitor." He ruffled Starr's fur. "I wasn't going to hurt Dani."

Jake closed her open mouth and stared at the dog, who had turned on her own master to protect Dani.

"Don't look so surprised," Eamon said. "I told you she likes kids. Someone could come up here and bash you and me in the head and she probably wouldn't say boo as long as he didn't touch Dani."

Jake shook her head watching the animal, who practically purred from Eamon's attention. Such a dog could come in handy. No wonder Eamon had felt confident leaving Dani and the dog alone together.

"Can you swim?"

Jake blinked and focused on Eamon. "Passably well. I don't drown at the deep end of the pool."

"I meant is it okay for you to swim. After your surgery."

The Steri Strips had done their job and fallen off at the beginning of the week. Still she wasn't sure if she should risk it. "I have no idea."

"Then how about a walk along the beach?"

Having no handy reason to refuse, she took Eamon's hand and let him help her from her seat. "A short one."

Eamon lifted his hand as if being sworn in. "I promise."

She left Dani with the admonition to behave herself, then walked with Eamon to the edge of the water. The waning afternoon sun stole most of the heat of the day. The water that lapped at her toes was frigid, but she waded in a little anyway.

Eamon laced his fingers with hers as they walked along in ankle high water. "How are you doing?" he asked.

"This water is freezing."

He glanced down her body to her breasts. "I've noticed."

Surprised, she stopped and tugged on his arm until he turned to face her. Such earthy sexual innuendo she didn't expect from him.

"Was I not supposed to notice? I'm sorry. Just do me a favor and don't sneeze. You'll pop right out of that bathing suit and I'll have to kill myself pretending I don't see anything."

She hit him again. "You beast." His response was to grab her wrist and pull her closer. As if it were the most natural thing in the world, she went to him and tucked her nose into the juncture between his neck and shoulder. Despite the icy temperature of the water, the warmth of his body heated her. She couldn't help the small sigh of contentment that escaped her lips.

"Ah, Jake," he whispered against her ear. His fingers tangled in her hair, tilting her head back. His eyes had darkened to a deep blue made fluid by the reflection of sunlight on the water. No man had ever looked at her as he did, with such raw hunger in his gaze. Deep within her, she felt it, too, that intense need, like an ache in her belly.

She swallowed, but her mouth seemed devoid of moisture. She ran her tongue along the seam of her suddenly dry lips. Before she could put it back where it belonged, his mouth was on hers, claiming her tongue, suckling it, drawing an immediate response from her. Her arms wound around his neck, holding him to her. His hands roved lower, to grasp her hips. A groan rumbled up through his chest as his fingers dug into her derriere, molding the soft flesh in his palms.

That sound reverberated through her like an alarm. She pushed away from him as the realization of what she'd allowed to happen dawned on her. Despite her promises to herself, all he'd had to do was touch her and she'd melted like a Popsicle in the noonday sun.

"W-we should get back," she stammered. Without waiting for a response from him, she turned and started back to where Dani sat playing with the dog. By the time she got to the sand, her stomach ached and her brain swam with the residual effect of Eamon's kisses. She grabbed her towel from the beach chair and wrapped it around herself. All the while she knew Dani watched her with a puzzled expression on her face.

"What's the matter, Jake?"

"Nothing. I'm hungry I guess." It was as plausible a lie as any. She certainly couldn't explain sexual chemistry to a six year old, or women who couldn't keep their hands to themselves.

"I'll get the grill started."

Jake hadn't heard Eamon come up beside her. The expression on his face gave away nothing of what he felt, but she suspected her bolting from the water had surprised him at the very least.

"Then Dani and I will get changed."

He nodded, but said nothing. Jake had no choice but to lead Dani back to the house.

After a dinner of grilled hamburgers, Eamon built a fire in the fireplace. Without too much effort he let Jake beat him at the only game kept in the house: Scrabble. During the game, they'd opened a bottle of wine. He couldn't speak for Jake, but he was feeling pretty mellow. Dani fell asleep curled around the dog. Starr slept too, making yipping noises in her sleep.

Jake set her wineglass on the TV tray they'd used as a table. "That's not a dog," Jake said, "it's a wookie."

Eamon nodded toward Dani. "Maybe I should put Sleeping Beauty in bed."

"Her and me, too." She stifled a delicate yawn behind her hand. "I'm beat."

Eamon cupped her chin in his palm and stroked his thumb over her cheek. "I wore you out today, did I?"

She caught her lower lip between her teeth. "A little."

"And I didn't even trot out any of my good stuff."

She tilted her head to one side and regarded him with narrowed eyes. "Oh, really? What good stuff would that be?"

She'd spoken those words as a challenge. He didn't mind turning it back on her. His thumb traced the curve of her lower lip. "Don't tempt me, Jake, or I might be inclined to show you."

For a moment, he saw interest in the depths of her brown eyes. Then she turned her face from him, dislodging his hand. "Maybe you'd better put Dani into bed."

He sighed. "All right." He rose from the sofa and squatted beside Dani. Both Dani and the dog groused when he picked her up. Thankfully, Dani had already changed into her pajamas, so all he had to do was lay her on the narrow bed in her room.

When he got back to the living room, he wasn't completely surprised to find it empty and quiet save for the snoring of his sleeping dog. Eamon flopped onto the sofa in the same spot he'd occupied when Jake sat beside him. Staring into the fire, he stretched out his legs and crossed them. He picked up his wineglass, drained its contents, and refilled it.

Out on the water, he'd pushed her too far. He'd known that as he did it, but hadn't been able to help himself. Maybe if it hadn't been so long since he'd been with a woman he might have a modicum of control, but he doubted it. It was her, her presence, the sweet scent of her, her tinkling laugh, that got to him and pushed him over the edge.

It galled him that she had no trouble pulling back, holding him to the line she'd drawn for their relationship. She didn't step past it and didn't allow him to, either. While he admired her ability to stick to her own convictions, he recognized he was getting nowhere with her, nowhere fast.

Fatigue and frustration pulled at him, making him tired beyond the day's activities. He closed his eyes and after a moment, he dozed off.

He started awake in the middle of the night, still on the sofa, his neck cramped and his head fuzzy. He'd been dreaming about Jake, something vague and unsettling. Usually when he dreamed of her, she was smiling and accommodating. This dream was . . . different.

He rose from the sofa and went to his room. He stopped in the doorway noticing the large form on his bed. The dog was in his bed again. That was nothing new, but how had she managed to make it under the covers this time? Sometimes he thought Starr had more brainpower than he did. He stripped and lay down on top of the bed. He should push the dog onto the floor where she belonged, but he lacked the will or the energy to do so. He closed his eyes, pulled the edge of the blanket over his nude body, and slept.

Eleven

Jake awoke the next morning, an unfamiliar buzzing in her ears and something equally unfamiliar and heavy draped across her waist and thighs. Unable to move without pain, she popped one eye open and looked straight into the face of Eamon Fitzgerald. She popped open her other eye, lifted her head, and surveyed his sleeping form. Not only was Eamon in bed with her, he was stark, staring naked besides. He lay on his side facing her, his arm and leg covering her. The buzzing she'd heard was the light, insistent sound of Eamon's snoring.

Jake closed her eyes, feeling a bit like a voyeur. But the image was still there, Eamon in all his glory. Only the bunching of the covers between their bodies prevented her from seeing every inch of him. She wasn't sure whether to be grateful or curse whoever had organized the first quilting bee.

And then there was the question of what he was doing in bed with her in the first place. When he'd offered her this room, he'd made no mention of sharing it with her. No wonder he hadn't bothered to come after her last night after she'd made a beeline out of the room when he put Dani to bed. That mad escape had been cowardly and unworthy of her, but she couldn't have sat there another moment enduring the heat of his body, the challenge in his eyes, and the fire in her own belly, urging her to forget about reason and accept the passion he offered.

Slowly, so as not to wake him, she disentangled herself from him and rose from the bed. She'd never get back to sleep with Eamon draped all over her. Besides, her body was unaccustomed to the amount of rest she'd gotten in the last few days. She stretched, and her body protested. She needed a hot shower and to find something to occupy her time until a decent hour of the morning. Then she would deal with Eamon Fitzgerald, Esq., later.

The sound of seabirds squawking woke Eamon an hour later. His lashes fluttered open, once, twice. He squeezed his eyes shut and shook his head. He could swear he'd seen Jake sitting in a chair in the corner of the room. He opened his eyes again, and the image remained—Jake sitting cross-legged with a sketch pad on her lap. He snuck a quick look at his own body. The bedspread covered him from waist to toes. "Hi," he said.

"Welcome to the land of the living. The way you snore I thought you'd choke on something in your sleep."

"I do not snore." Still unconvinced of his wakefulness, he tried to lower his right hand to rub the sleep from his eyes. His arm moved only so much and no more. A metallic clink accompanied each movement. "Why can't I move my arm?"

"It's handcuffed to the headboard."

Eamon snorted. At this point, that sounded like as reasonable an explanation as any. "May I ask why my hand is handcuffed to the headboard?"

She grinned at him, obviously trying not to laugh. "I was sketching you. You kept getting it in the way."

He shifted so he could see the handcuff. "Would you mind taking it off now?"

She rose from the chair and walked toward him.
"Spoilsport. I wasn't finished."

He waited until she stood only inches away from him.
He sprung the lock on the handcuffs. He grabbed Jake
and laid her gently on the bed beside him so as not to
hurt her. In two seconds, he had both her hands shack-
led to the slats of the brass headboard. He rested his
cheek on his upturned palm and looked down at her.
She stared up at him with wide eyes and a mouth
rounded with surprise.

She snapped her mouth closed and her eyes narrowed. "How did you do that?"

"Trick handcuffs. I found them in my closet but didn't
want to give them to Dani until I'd asked you first."

"I bet you can guess what my answer is. Take these
things off."

He glanced down her body. Her T-shirt had ridden
up, exposing her long legs and a hint of black panties.
"Well, well, well, Jake McKenna. It looks like I have you
at my mercy now."

"No kidding. But why do you? Why were you in my
bed last night?"

He had to think about that a minute. "Force of habit,
I guess. I fell asleep on the sofa, got up, and went to my
room. Why? Did I take advantage of you in my sleep?"

He knew he hadn't. He would have remembered that.
"No, but you did nearly crush me with your arm across
my stomach."

Instantly contrite, he stroked his knuckles over her
cheek. "Did I hurt you?"

"Actually, no."

She tried to look away from him, but he wouldn't
allow it. Tired of playing guessing games, he figured he
needed a more direct approach. "What is it, Jake? In the
last couple of days I've felt you withdraw from me. Have
I done something to upset you?"

She bit her lower lip, a nervous habit she seemed to have acquired last night. "You have been very good to Dani and me."

"Then what?"

"Has it occurred to you that I'm worried about Dani?"

His eyebrows knitted together. "In what way? You have to know I adore Dani. I would never do anything to hurt her."

"Except leave. Eamon, she's very attached to you. Do you know what she said to me a moment before I collapsed in the nursery? That you reminded her of her father. How is she going to feel when you walk out of her life to go back to Boston?"

"Jake, I'm not going back to Boston."

She shook her head, her eyes narrowed. "But you said you didn't have time to give the staff. I thought you meant you—"

He placed a silencing finger over her lips. "I meant that if I didn't turn things around soon, I'd be broke. Have you got any idea how much money it takes to pay twenty salaries, rent office space, pay the printer and the distributor? All this while pulling in subsistent revenue from the few advertisers we do have. I'm in debt up to my eyeballs. I don't know yet exactly what I intend to do, but I have no intention of going back to Boston."

She seemed to digest that for a moment. "I'm not sure that changes anything."

He screwed his courage to the sticking place. "Who are you really worried about, Dani or yourself?"

"Both."

There was honesty. But since he'd never done anything to his knowledge to inspire a lack of trust in him, he wondered what had. "Did he hurt you?"

"He who?"

"Your former fiancé."

She shrugged. "At first, maybe. It hurt my pride to know that he wasn't really interested in me at all."

She succeeded in turning away from him. "Don't shut me out, Jake. I'm not him. Give me a chance to prove that to you."

She turned to him, studying his face. "Why?"

He didn't pretend not to know what she meant. Why did he want a relationship with her? Because everything about her charmed him from her big brown eyes to her tinkling laugh to the way she cared for Dani, who needed her protection, and Jim and Liza, who shouldn't. He didn't tell her any of those things, though. If she was ready to bolt when she thought he didn't care enough, he wondered what she'd do if he exposed the true depth of his feelings.

Instead, he ran a finger down the bridge of her nose. "Because if you don't, my only choice will be to go through with your original plan and date Liza. I'll have to force myself to monopolize the mirror just to live up to her expectations."

She'd been watching him with a wary, narrow-eyed stare. At his mention of mirrors her eyes flew open and she hit him on the arm. "You were eavesdropping!"

"Just a little."

She pushed at his shoulder with the heel of her hand. "You rat."

He lifted her hand. One cuff encircled that wrist. The other cuff, open and empty, swayed from the connecting chain.

When he looked at her she shrugged. "Did you think *I* didn't know how to get out of a pair of trick handcuffs?"

Laughing, he buried his nose in her hair. Rather than share his humor she remained perfectly still. He pulled away, looking down into her troubled brown eyes. "What's the matter, sweetheart?"

She shook her head and made a helpless gesture with

her hands. "If you're going to break my heart, tell me now. I want to have my crying towel handy."

In an odd way the despair in her voice heartened him. If she worried he'd break her heart, that meant it was in jeopardy. It meant she felt something for him. "Is that what you think I'm going to do?"

"Not intentionally."

"What do you want from me, Jake? A guarantee that nothing bad will happen? Life doesn't offer us any guarantees except death."

"You're a bundle of cheer, aren't you?" She let out her breath in one large huff. "I don't know what to say."

"Then kiss me."

He held his breath, wondering if he'd pressed her too hard again. She cradled his face in her palms and ran her thumb along his bottom lip. "If you hurt Dani, I'll kill you." Then she drew him down to her. Their mouths met and something akin to electricity thrummed through him. Her tongue rubbed against his, not gentle but demanding, erotic. For a moment he let himself get lost in the wildness of the kiss. Eventually, he pulled back and looked at her. She hadn't opened her eyes. A dreamy smile turned up her lips. "That wasn't so bad, was it?"

Teasingly she pushed at his thigh with her foot. "I wouldn't kick you out of bed because of it." He ran his hand up her leg, from her calf to her hip, pressing her back against the mattress.

"What are you doing?"

Her voice sounded breathy, sexy, and he chuckled knowing he'd done that to her. "Relax, sweetheart." He brushed aside her shirt to reveal three one-inch healing scars. He bent and kissed one of them, feeling her stomach contract beneath his lips.

"Eamon," she said, her voice more a moan than a protest.

"Yes?" His own voice sounded husky and strange, but that was the effect she had on him. He kissed the scar just below her belly button and she jerked. Only one scar remained, the one slightly above her pubic bone. Before he could lower his head a third time, he heard a small voice from the other side of the door. "Jake, Uncle Eamon, where are you?"

"Damn," Eamon muttered, pulling away. For a moment he and Jake shared a panicked look. He rolled off the bed to find the pants and shirt he'd worn the night before.

"Just a minute, sweetheart," Jake called. She detached the cuff from her wrist, sat up, and tried to fluff her hair into some sort of order.

He pulled his shirt over his head, just as she turned to check if he was ready. She waited for him to smooth it into place before calling to Dani. "Come on in, sweetheart."

Dani rushed in with the dog trailing behind her. Jake opened her arms to the little girl, who laid her head on Jake's shoulder. "I had a bad dream."

There seemed to be a lot of that going around, Eamon mused. Not wanting to intrude on the moment, he left the room and went to his room upstairs and indulged in a very chilly shower.

Hugging Dani to her, Jake rocked back and forth in a soothing manner. Dani needed reassurance, and it filled Jake's heart to know she could provide it. She wished she had someone to offer her reassurance that she had done the right thing with Eamon, but there was no one. The one voice she'd trusted had been silenced in a car accident nine months ago. She missed her brother in a way she hadn't in a long while, and without him she felt oddly vulnerable and alone.

He wanted what she wanted: to see where their relationship would take them, without her putting a damper on things. The prospect terrified her because, so far, he'd given her everything and nothing. He'd taken care of her, opened up his homes to her, given her his beds, taken care of Dani. Sometimes she thought he did these things, not out of obligation or caring, but to cover up the fact that he'd denied her the one thing that would help her understand him: information. He'd told her not to nose around in his past, that she wouldn't like what she found. But if he cared for her, didn't that present its own obligation to tell her—before she hit bottom in this mad fall into being in love with him? Didn't he owe her his honesty as well as his passion?

Jake sighed. Maybe the rules of his profession made it difficult for him to let anyone in: lawyers found out your secrets, they didn't confess theirs. He'd told her he'd been married. Maybe his wife's death had shut off something inside him he didn't want to reveal. Maybe he'd been guarded so long he didn't know how to open up. She didn't know if any of those scenarios were true, but she did know one thing. They would never get anywhere if he couldn't tell her the truth.

Riding in the car on the long way home, Eamon snuck a glance at Jake's profile as she rode beside him. They had swum in the morning, but the afternoon had turned windy. Jake had sat in her chair sketching while he and Dani flew kites by the shore. None of them had wanted to leave their little idyll until night had begun to fall, which was why they now headed back to the city in complete darkness. Thankfully, Dani had fallen asleep ten minutes after they'd gotten in the car. One more round of "Ninety-nine Bottles of Beer on the Wall" and he'd have gladly thrown himself from the vehicle.

The present silence would have been welcomed if it weren't for the anxious expression on Jake's face. He lifted his right hand from the steering wheel and took her hand in his. "You're pretty quiet over there."

"I'm basking in the silence since Dani fell asleep."

"Is that all?"

"It occurs to me that despite everything, I really know very little about you."

He should have known Jake's natural inquisitiveness would never allow her to accept the no-trespassing sign he'd placed on his past. "What do you want to know?"

"What's your favorite color?"

Considering he'd expected a more intimate question, he hesitated before he answered. "Blue."

"How old were you when you lost your virginity?"

"Nineteen."

"Why so late?"

"I was an honors student and worked two jobs. I didn't have time for girls. Besides, Jim more than made up for both of us when it came to seducing the fairer sex. How about you?" The question popped out before he realized he didn't really want to know.

"Sixteen."

"Why so early?"

"The neighborhood Lothario took an interest in me. I was curious so I didn't put up too much of a struggle. The experience was quite a bit less than expected."

"You know what's ironic? If our experiences were reversed, there would have been no need to question it."

"I'd have plenty of questions if you'd been seduced by Donnie Braithwaite." She laughed in that way he loved. "But I know what you mean. It's more expected for a guy to lose his virginity early. A girl is a slut. Unless, of course, you have my mother for a parent. She was of the opinion that no woman should remain a virgin until she was married. Then her husband could be as lousy a lover as he wanted and the poor girl would never know the difference."

Eamon swallowed. At the moment, he wouldn't mind hunting down Donnie whatever-his-name-was and any other man who'd disappointed Jake. But now that the can of worms had been opened, he couldn't resist poking around in it. "So, was he the first of many?"

"Not at all. If anything, I realized I'd probably be better off postponing any future occurrences. But, we were talking about you, not me."

He let a smile tilt the corners of his mouth. "I wondered when you were going to notice that."

"Okay then, why did you want to become a lawyer? Saw *To Kill a Mockingbird* too many times? Or was it *Inherit the Wind*?"

"Neither. It was *Twelve Angry Men*. I figured if a jury could pick apart the prosecution's case so easily, the defense attorney hadn't done his job. I thought I could do better."

"Have you?"

He lifted one shoulder. Movie lawyers almost invariably defended the innocent, not those whose defense consisted of having damning testimony or evidence excluded. Or those who might not have committed the crime with which they are charged, but guilty of enough else that no one but a lawyer would seek to defend them. A truly innocent client: that was a scary prospect, because there was actually something at stake besides his reputation if the trial went poorly. A lifetime in fact, as he'd made his claim to fame defending Boston's most notorious accused murderers. When he'd been young and starry-eyed he'd thought it was the area in which he could make the most difference.

He answered finally, "I guess so."

"What is your worst fear?"

"This is beginning to sound like one of those *Cosmo*

quizzes—'how well do you know your man?' or some nonsense." He watched her in the periphery of his vision, wondering if she'd object to him characterizing himself as her man. Or maybe if it would distract her from seeking an answer to her question. It did neither.

"Answer the question."

He sighed and adjusted his grip on the steering wheel. "I've never really thought about it." He stole a glance at her. She'd already told him hers—turning into a bitter old woman like her grandmother. He couldn't be any less honest with her. "If I had to name something, I'd be afraid to have someone depend on me and for me to fail them." He stole a glance at her, wondering what she thought of his answer.

She held his gaze for a second. "Why did you get married?"

He knew she would get to this subject sooner or later. As much as he felt the inevitability of answering the question, he dreaded what she, Ms. Expert on Love, would think of his answer. "Because she asked me."

"*She* asked *you?*"

"Why does that surprise you so much? Don't you think I'd make some woman a nice catch?"

"It's not that." She shrugged. "I can't see you not making the first move. Did she buy you a ring, too?"

"No." He inhaled and let his breath out in several short puffs. "It wasn't a love match, Jake. Claudia and I had been friends since law school. Boston is a very conservative town and the firm she worked for made the Moral Majority look like the ACLU. When she found herself pregnant and unwed, she knew it would jeopardize her quest for partnership."

"So she asked you to help her out."

"We were friends. For a brief while we had been more than friends. I was a known quantity to her family and they would accept me without too many questions."

"I can see her asking, but why did you accept?"

"It made sense. I wanted a family, and I wasn't arrogant enough to believe that only the fruit of my own loins would do. I didn't want to see Claudia taken advantage of by someone who had fewer scruples than I did." He huffed out a harsh breath. "I was up for partnership, too."

"What happened to the baby?"

Eamon swallowed over the catch in his throat. "Paula was the light of my life. She died three years ago in the same car crash that killed her mother."

"I'm so sorry." Jake twisted her hands in her lap.

With one hand he covered both of hers. "Actually, it felt good to talk about it." And it did. Then again, he hadn't told her everything.

Twelve

Within minutes of Eamon's getting into work Monday morning, Jim ambushed him in his office. He slid into one of the seats facing him and leaned forward. "How was the weekend in the country?"

Eamon made a show of checking his watch. "Isn't it a bit early for you to be up and about? The sun rose only about an hour ago."

"You forget, with Jake out of the office, I'm doing two people's work."

"There isn't enough work to keep either of you busy, never mind both."

"That won't be the case much longer, though. But I didn't come here to talk about work."

"No, you came to pick apart my social life."

"Social life. An arcane term implying one has no sex life to speak of." Jim sat back and sighed. "At least you have a social life to pick apart."

Eamon surveyed his brother. His post-Florida black eye had healed, but there were circles under both eyes that suggested a lack of sleep. "Don't tell me you are still pining away over your mystery woman."

"Okay, then I won't tell you. But I have to admit I'm a bit jealous of your relationship with Jake."

"Do my ears deceive me? Jim the nomad wants to settle down?"

"I don't know if settle down is the exact term I'd use.

The joys of playing the field have always been overrated. I wouldn't mind if one special woman kept me on the sidelines for a little while."

"I must need to lie down. I think I saw a pig fly by the window."

Jim rolled his eyes. "I don't know why I tell you anything."

"Because I'm your older brother and you love and respect me?"

"That's still up for debate." Jim leaned back, laying one ankle across the opposite knee. "I just came in to check on how things are going with you and Jake. I've already decided I want her for my new sister-in-law, so don't screw up."

"Yes, sir. But what makes you so convinced you want Jake as a sister-in-law?"

"Aside from anyone being preferable to that manipulative, grasping shrew you married the first time? She made Leona Helmsley look like Mother Teresa."

He couldn't argue with Jim's assessment. When they'd married, Eamon hadn't suspected that the one thing he and Claudia had in common—their ambition—would turn into the thing he hated the most about her. Paula's entrance into their lives had transformed him, but left Claudia unmoved.

Eamon let a grin slide across his face. "Yes, aside from that."

Jim shook his head. "If you are expecting some logical, thought-out answer like you would give me, you're going to be disappointed. I only know she's good for you. By the way, are you aware you are wearing a brown tie with a blue suit?"

Eamon glanced down, surprised to find that his tie, striped with several shades of brown, clashed miserably with blue pinstripes. Oddly, he couldn't remember putting on any tie at all. "What is that supposed to prove?"

Jim shrugged. "Nothing, really." He stood. "Just know that I'm happy for you, brother."

"Thank you."

Eamon watched his brother leave, wishing he could do something to cure Jim's malaise. For one thing, on the rare occasions when Jim got down on himself, he usually ended up doing something remarkably stupid to mess up his life. For another, he truly wanted to see his brother happy, or barring that, content with his life, settled, not wandering from place to place, looking for heaven only knew what to satisfy him.

He thought of Jake's friend, Liza, with the smoky voice and bedroom eyes. Exactly the sort of woman to tempt his brother. Although Jim loved beautiful women, he wasn't averse to a functioning brain cell or two. But given Jim's present mood and Liza's no-nonsense personality, the two of them would probably kill each other.

Eamon shifted in his seat. He was probably the last person who should consider playing matchmaker, considering he'd settled very little with Jake. He couldn't get her off his mind, though—neither the sexy way she'd moaned his name the previous morning when he'd kissed her scars nor the compassion in her voice when he'd told her about Paula.

Although it was barely nine o'clock in the morning, he wished this day would hurry up and be over with so he could get back to her.

Jake knew the instant Eamon and Dani were at the door. She was in the kitchen putting the final touches on dinner. The dog had wedged herself under the kitchen table when Jake had started to prepare dinner, obviously waiting to pounce on any scrap that fell her way. All of a sudden the dog began to bark at her, as if to say,

"They're home." Starr lumbered out of the room. A second later she heard Eamon's key turn in the lock.

Dani appeared in the kitchen doorway first. The summer sun had tanned her skin and streaked her hair a lighter shade of brown. One of her knees sported a *Lord of the Rings* Band-Aid and both of her socks were missing. She ran to Jake and hugged her.

Jake returned her hug, then tried without success to smooth down Dani's tangled hair. "How was camp?"

"Great! We went swimming."

"I can see that. Are you hungry?"

Dani nodded.

Jake patted her back. "Then go get washed up and you can help me set the table." Jake watched Dani skip from the room, until her gaze snagged on Eamon standing in the doorway, watching her with a peculiar expression on his face. She narrowed her eyes. "Why are you looking at me like that?"

Eamon shook his head as if trying to fight off a vision. "She always hugs you as if she hasn't seen you in ten years."

Jake swallowed. She had noticed that, too, since she'd come out of the hospital. "She didn't use to."

Eamon strode toward her and enfolded her in his arms. She leaned into him, wrapping her arms around his back. Her nose rested in the crook of his neck. She inhaled the vestiges of his cologne mingled with his own masculine scent.

He pulled her tighter, as if he wouldn't let go for ten years. "I missed you, too."

A smile formed on her lips, until his fingers tangled in her hair, pulling her head back. His gaze was hot, his kiss even hotter. Jake closed her eyes and let the heady sensations wash over her—the softness of his lips, the heat of his body, the erotic motions of his hands on her back, and the feel of his hands cradling her hips. His erection pressed against her belly. She couldn't seem to help herself. She moved against him, reveling in the masculine groan that rumbled through his chest at her boldness.

At the sound of Dani coughing, they sprang away from each other. Jake looked past Eamon to see Dani standing in the doorway with her arms crossed over her chest. "Little kids aren't supposed to see that kind of stuff."

Jake glanced at Eamon, who was doing his best not to laugh. She looked back at Dani. "We'll keep that in mind. Are you ready to set the table?"

"As long as there isn't going to be any more kissing."

"No more kissing, I promise."

"Since I'm not needed anymore," Eamon interjected, "I'm going to wash up; then I'll take Starr for a walk."

He winked at her before heading out of the room. Jake handed Dani the napkins to start setting the table. Jake turned back to the task of buttering a loaf of French bread. After a moment she noticed how quiet Dani was. She glanced at the little girl over her shoulder. She had arranged the napkins on the table and had started on the silverware. Still, Jake felt something wasn't right.

"Why are you so quiet over there?"

Dani looked back at her. "You like Uncle Eamon, right?"

"Of course I like him." Jake wasn't being obtuse, but she had learned the hard way to answer the simplest version of any question children asked and answer only as much as they seemed to want to know. A couple of months ago, Jake had taken care of a neighbor's infant. Dani had asked her where the baby came from. Jake had launched into a diatribe on basic human procreation when all Dani wanted to know was whom the baby belonged to.

"I mean you like him, like him. Like kissing and stuff."

"Why?"

"Are you going to get married?"

"I don't know, Dani. Would that bother you?"

Dani shrugged. "It wouldn't be so bad. Then Starr could be my dog, too."

Jake laughed. The tension that had gripped her since Dani started this line of questioning eased out of her. The prospect of her and Eamon being together must not worry Dani if she was already calculating what was in it for her. "You never told me you wanted a dog."

Dani shrugged. "I just started wanting one."

"Is there anything else you want to tell me?"

"Not really." Dani finished laying the silverware on the table.

Jake shook her head, praying for strength. "Why don't you see if Uncle Eamon is back yet, so we can have dinner?"

Later, after she'd tucked Dani in bed with Starr asleep by her bed, she went to rejoin Eamon in the living room. She sat facing him with her bent knee resting on the sofa cushion, her other foot on the floor. She rested her elbow on the sofa back and cradled her cheek against her palm. For the first time that night they were alone together.

Eamon turned to face her, mimicking her posture. He rubbed his thumb against her cheek. "How are you doing?"

"I'm fine. Just a little tired, I guess."

His eyes scanned her face while his finger brushed her hair behind her ear. "I'm not surprised. It's only been a couple of weeks since the surgery."

Jake exhaled. It seemed like a year ago, and she was tired of not being herself. "I suppose."

"You're not upset about Dani walking in on us before?"

She shook her head. Dani was a perceptive child. She would have come to Jake with her questions sooner or later.

"I admit I get a little crazy when I'm around you." His

thumb traced the outline of her lower lip. He lowered his head and traced the same path with his tongue. Jake thrilled to the contact, and to the idea of making the very staid Eamon Fitzgerald lose control. Staid wasn't the right adjective either, but she'd be damned if she started looking for a thesaurus now.

Eamon groaned, as she drew his tongue into her mouth and suckled it. It was what he wanted, but the sheer pleasure of her touch overwhelmed him. He shifted and he drew her closer, so that she lay half on top of him. Her breasts crushed against his chest, drawing another groan from him. He knew he should stop. Even if she wanted to make love to him, it was too soon for her. But he couldn't seem to help himself. He shifted again, this time to give him better access to her breasts. He let his hand rove upward, over her waist, her rib cage, and finally to capture her breast in his hand. He molded her sweet flesh in his palm, rubbing his thumb against her nipple. A surge of satisfaction coursed through him when her back arched and she moaned into his mouth.

He should stop now, before he drove them both insane for something they could not have. But what little control he had seemed to have deserted him. His hand slid beneath her shirt, roving over one full breast and then the other. But it wasn't enough. He broke the kiss and set her away from him enough so that he could see her face. Her breathing was ragged and perspiration dotted her forehead. She looked at him with darkened half-closed eyes. "Eamon," she whispered.

"I want to see you," he whispered back.

He lifted her shirt over her head and tossed it on the floor. His gaze roamed over her, drinking in the beauty of her full, bare breasts, tipped with large, dark areolas. He cupped one breast in his hand, lifting it so that he could bring her nipple into his mouth. The taste of her drove him crazy and the scent of her made him wild. He laved one breast and then the other with his tongue, then suckled her. She whimpered and clung to him, her nails digging into the flesh of his shoulders. Her hips moved against his, bringing him painfully erect. He knew he'd better stop now, while he still could.

He shifted and pulled her down to him so that she lay on top of him. She trembled against him and her heartbeat was as rapid as his own. He stroked his hands over her back as he tried to concentrate on breathing properly. "I'm sorry, sweetheart."

She lifted her head to look down on him. "For what?"

"For getting us both all stirred up with no place to go."

"If I recall correctly, I wasn't complaining."

He laughed and hugged her to him. For a moment, he contented himself with simply holding her. After a minute he noticed her breathing had evened out. Jake had fallen asleep. He scrubbed his hands up and down her back. "It's time I got you into bed."

"Promises, promises," Jake said in a sleepy voice.

Eamon picked her up and carried her to her room. With a little effort he managed to lay her down underneath the covers. "Good night, Jake," he whispered, placed a gentle kiss on her forehead, and went to his office and the sofa awaiting him there.

Friday at noon, Jake opened the door to find Liza on the other side carrying a shopping bag from their favorite midtown Chinese restaurant. She and Liza had talked on the phone during the week, but this was the first time they'd seen each other since last week. "What are you doing here?"

"You know how dead my office is this time of year. Nobody hires during the summer unless they're absolutely desperate. But if you want me to go." Liza raised her arm to gesture back the way she'd come.

Jake grabbed her arm and pulled her inside the apartment. "Don't you dare. I haven't eaten lunch yet and there are only so many hours of *Jerry Springer* you can watch before strangling half the human race seems like a good idea."

"Getting a little stir-crazy?"

Jake closed the front door, then turned to lead the way toward the kitchen. "Raging cabin fever." As they approached, Starr emerged from her spot under the table.

Liza stopped in her tracks and stared. "What is that?"

"Believe it or not, it's Eamon's dog." Starr barked and wagged her tail. "She likes you."

"Thank goodness for that." After a few sniffs of Liza's hand, Starr settled underneath the table again.

Liza set the bagful of Chinese food on the table. Jake poked inside. "Peking duck?"

Liza leaned one hand on a chair back and canted her hips to one side. "I know how much you love it. You wouldn't believe the wrangling I had to go through to get them to wrap it up to go."

After they spread out the meal on the table, Jake filled one of the flat pancakes with slices of duck, cucumber, and celery. She sampled a bite, leaned back in her chair, and sighed. "This is heaven."

Liza dabbed her mouth with her napkin. "Speaking of celestial places, how was Montauk?"

"Fabulous. Dani and I had a great time."

Liza narrowed her eyes. "You know very well that's not what I meant."

Jake sipped from her water glass. "Informative. He told me he's not going back to Boston, and some other things. Personal things."

Liza's eyebrows lifted. "I don't believe it. Jake McKenna can keep a secret!"

"I've always managed to keep other people's secrets. It's my own I have no problem divulging."

"True enough. Whatever he told you, I hope it didn't ruin things."

On the contrary, his opening up to her had endeared him to her all the more. Telling her couldn't have been easy. She had the feeling he'd never told anyone some of the things he'd disclosed to her. And still, she suspected, more existed to the story that he hadn't.

Jake met Liza's probing gaze. "Not at all."

Liza scrutinized her. "Mmm-hmm. What have you been up to since you've been back?"

"You'd swear you walked in on the all-black cast of *Leave it to Beaver*. I've had the house clean and dinner on the table every night when they get home." Jake lifted one shoulder. And when he kissed her—She was not going to venture in that direction. Although they had both been careful not to get as carried away as they had the first night, she still melted every time he touched her.

"So what's the problem?"

"The problem is we aren't the Cleavers. I have to go home. I have to go back to work."

"Then why don't you?"

Jake sat back and sighed. "Because part of me wants the illusion. If we were really living together, we would have had to settle some issues between us, if nothing other than who sleeps on what side of the bed. Right now, it's easy, because both of us realize it isn't real."

"Bull, it's easy because neither one of you has been brave enough to do more than scratch the surface." Liza grinned. "Lord knows you've got issues. If he's anything like you, maybe you ought to sign up for couples therapy now and save yourselves the messy divorce later."

"Not funny."

"Well then, maybe you ought to ask yourself why you are content to play house rather than reaching for something more substantial. And why is he?"

She couldn't speak for Eamon, but her own motivations were a no-brainer. If you didn't ask for something, you couldn't be disappointed if you didn't get it. Because every time she cared for someone, life snatched that person away. Her mother and stepfather, Dan, Uncle Jake, even Stan—all gone or missing in action. When Liza went to Florida to find her father, Jake had been secretly terrified that the two would reconnect and she would lose the only friend, the only person, who had been a constant in her life since childhood.

Better to be like her uncle Jake, who never settled anywhere long enough to get attached to anyone. Never allow yourself to care so much that you couldn't walk away. But she'd never been able to carry that off either. So she lived in this limbo where she shut people out for fear of caring too much. Eamon was the first man she'd let herself care about in a long time, maybe since Stan flew the coop five years ago.

If Liza was right, that they'd only scratched the surface, what would she find if she dug deeper?

Later, as the three of them relaxed around the kitchen table, Jake noticed the bandage on Dani's leg. "What happened to your knee?" Jake asked. Dani lowered her head and gripped her hands together. Immediately Jake knew she'd gotten into another fight. "Dani," Jake said in a patient voice, "haven't we talked about fighting before? You know I don't approve."

"He started it. He called me shrimpie. If he didn't want me to hit him, he shouldn't have called me names."

Jake sighed. How did you argue with logic like that? The boy, whoever he was, had obviously wanted to bait Dani. Her temper wasn't exactly a well-kept secret.

"That isn't the point, Dani," Eamon said before Jake

had a chance to say anything. "Tell me something, who got in trouble for fighting, you or him?"

"I did. I couldn't go in the water for ten minutes. He just laughed and called me a loser."

"That's because you gave him exactly what he wanted. He wanted to get you in trouble and he succeeded."

"Well, what am I supposed to do? Let him call me names?"

"Yup. Pretend you don't hear him. It will drive him crazy."

A slow, devious smile spread across Dani's face. "I could do that. He hates when when people don't pay attention to him." Dani slid out of her chair and launched herself at Eamon. She hugged him, a reverent expression on her face. "Thanks."

Eamon returned her embrace, then ruffled her already disordered hair. "Why don't you go wash up and we can open the magic set?"

"Okay."

Jake watched Eamon watch Dani skip from the room. Although she appreciated his wisdom, his taking over the situation rankled her. For the last few minutes she might as well have been a fly on the wall or the dog lying under the table for all her presence had mattered to either of them. Added to that, Eamon had sent Dani from the room, promising her he'd spend time with her. It seemed to her that only a couple of days ago, he would have sought her opinion first before promising Dani anything.

Eamon turned his head to focus on her. "That's okay with you, isn't it? I went down to Tannens at lunchtime and bought her a little magic set—nothing special. A set of cup and balls and a few other baby tricks."

Jake crossed her arms in front of her. Why ask what she thought now when all had been decided? "It's fine. I'll join you guys after I straighten up the kitchen."

"Leave it. I'll take care of it later, but surely you know we magicians can't have a layperson finding out our secrets."

He'd meant to tease her, but he also intended to exclude her. She knew her brother had adhered to the magician's credo of not disclosing how tricks were done and had taught the same to Dani. It didn't make it sting any less that neither of them wanted her around. "So I've been told."

Eamon looked at her closely, but said nothing. He stood. "Maybe after Dani goes to sleep we can catch the tail end of *Chocolat?*"

They'd started watching the movie the night before, but Jake had fallen asleep against Eamon's shoulder before it ended. "Maybe."

A pensive smile spread across his face. "Dani's a wonderful little girl, Jake."

"Thank you." She acknowledged his compliment, but a feeling of unease gripped her.

"You know, Paula would have been her age now. Dani reminds me of her in some ways." He lifted one shoulder in a shrug. "Maybe that's why we got along so well before I realized her connection to you."

"Uncle Eamon," Dani called from the other room, "I'm ready."

"I'd better go." Eamon rose and kissed Jake's forehead. "See you in a few."

Jake stared at Eamon's retreating back, wondering if he'd heard the words that had just come out of his own mouth. Finally it made sense—his frequent trips to the nursery, his devotion to Dani. She could have misinterpreted the meaning of Eamon's words, but she didn't think so. He'd found in Dani the daughter he'd lost.

How could she have been so stupid—again? At least with Stan, he had tried to deceive her, to keep his motives hidden until he had his hands on her nonexistent money. With Eamon, her eyes had been wide open. Why hadn't she seen that his interest lay more in Dani than in her? Maybe because he'd hidden his past from her until he'd had no choice but to divulge it. Maybe because he didn't realize it himself.

And how could she fault Dani for looking to Eamon as a father figure? Even so, Dani's defection stung. Maybe she ought to be ashamed to admit it, but she envied the way Eamon reached Dani, in ways she'd never been able to. But if the two of them had found what they were looking for, where did that leave her?

She'd told Liza she wanted the illusion, but like all illusions it was ultimately unsatisfying. A wife without the joys of sex, a mother without the pain of birth—everything she had was hers by default. And she'd been lying to herself. She did want something for herself. She wanted a man to love her for who she was, not what she could bring to him.

She knew Eamon desired her, he cared for her. At one time she might have been satisfied with that, but no more. She needed Eamon to love her back, just as much as she loved him. To accept anything less would be emotional suicide. And she knew what she had to do.

At nine o'clock, Eamon checked his watch. "Time for bed, Dani."

"Already?" Dani protested.

"Already. I don't want Jake getting mad at us for not following the rules. Go brush your teeth and put on your pajamas and we'll be back to tuck you in."

"Only if you promise you'll help me practice again tomorrow."

Eamon ruffled her hair. "Has anybody ever told you you would make one heck of a lawyer? Always bargaining."

"No."

"Well, they should. Make sure to put everything back where it belongs."

"I will."

He stood on legs that were half asleep from sitting on the floor too long and went to find Jake. He expected to find her on the sofa or maybe already in bed. He found her instead in the kitchen, washing the dishes he'd told her to leave alone.

For a moment he leaned against the door frame watching her scrub a saucepan with a wire brush. She seemed tired, or maybe upset. For the second time that night he had the urge to ask her what was bothering her. As if she'd felt his presence she turned her head to look at him. Their gazes met, but she looked away returning her attention to her task.

"I told you I'd take care of the kitchen."

"I figured I ought to find something useful to do with myself."

He didn't know what to make of that comment, so he let it slide. For the moment. "Dani's getting ready for bed."

"I'm surprised she didn't beg for more time, like she usually does."

"I promised her we could practice some more tomorrow, if that's okay with you."

She pressed her lips together and scrubbed harder, saying nothing.

He didn't know what had gotten into Jake, but he didn't like it. Before dinner she'd been her usual charming self, so he couldn't imagine what had caused this change in her. He opened his mouth to question her about it when Dani called from her bedroom.

"Uncle Eamon, I'm ready to be tucked in."

"Shall we?" Eamon asked, trying to lighten Jake's mood with humor.

Jake lifted her soap-covered, glove-wearing hands. "Will you tell Dani I'll come in a few minutes?"

"Sure." Feeling uneasy, Eamon went to Dani's room and sat on the edge of her bed. She clutched a stuffed bunny that she liked to sleep with but generally ignored the rest of the day. "Ready for bed, sweetheart?"

Dani nodded sleepily. "Where's Jake?"

"She'll be in in a minute." He bent and kissed her forehead. "Good night, Dani."

"Good night, Uncle Eamon. I love you."

Emotion clogged his throat, roughening his voice. "I love you, too, sweetheart."

Dani closed her eyes and Eamon went back to the kitchen. Jake had finished the dishes and had started wiping down the table. She had her back to him. He came up behind her and wrapped his arms around her waist. She stiffened in his arms.

"Don't, Eamon, please." He released her and she went to the sink to deposit the sponge and rinse her hands.

He rocked back on his heels and shoved his hands in his pockets. "What is with you tonight, Jake?"

She shut off the water and turned to face him, leaning her hip against the sink. "We need to talk."

At least they were in agreement on one thing. "Go ahead."

"I need to go home."

"That's not a problem. We can stop by tomorrow if you want to pick something up." Even as he spoke the words he realized that's not what she meant. His heartbeat accelerated, and dread, like icy fingers, crept through him.

Jake shook her head. "I mean I need to go home to stay."

"I see. And what made you come to this conclusion?"

"Let's face it, Eamon. We can't stay here forever. I'm well enough to take care of Dani by myself. We've imposed on you long enough."

"I wasn't aware you were imposing on me. I thought

you were allowing me to help you and Dani. I wouldn't have asked to do that if I didn't want to."

"I know, but still, it's time."

He wondered about the timing of her decision. She hadn't seemed in any rush to go anywhere earlier. He reached for the only crumb of an answer he could think of. "Does this have anything to do with what I said before?"

"Our staying here is confusing to Dani."

His jaw tightened as anger rose within him. "Don't, Jake. Don't put Dani in the middle of this, because she doesn't belong there. This has to do with you and me or rather with your fear that what's developing between us will turn out badly. What have I ever done to make you think I want to hurt you, or abandon you, or whatever it is you are afraid of?" He tilted her chin up. "Answer me, Jake."

Tears glistened in her brown eyes when she finally looked up at him. "At least I am trying to deal with my past."

"And I'm not? I deal with it every damn day, Jake. Not a day goes by that I don't think about Paula and miss her and wonder what she would be like now if she'd survived. That doesn't go away, Jake. It doesn't hurt as much to think about her, but the loss is still there, not just of the child but of all the possibilities cut off because she isn't here. All the hopes and dreams and promises squelched because she isn't alive to fulfill them or rebel against them, or whatever she might have done."

"Oh really? Then why did it take you so long to tell me you'd been married and even longer for you to tell me you shared a child? I'll tell you why. You didn't want me nosing around in your past, stirring up feelings that are too close to the surface for you to deal with. Maybe it's easier living vicariously through someone else's child than to deal with your own loss. That's not fair to any of us, least of all Dani."

His eyes burned and his stomach cramped. He couldn't think of a single word to refute what she'd said. "That's a low blow, Jake."

"But I see it struck its mark."

His own eyes stung with tears but he blinked them back. "I'll take you home tomorrow, if that's what you want. I'll leave it to you to explain that to Dani any way you want to, as long as you don't tell her it was my idea."

He walked away from her and went to his office. He didn't bother to open the sofa; he lay on top of the cushions staring at the ceiling. All his energy seemed to have seeped out of him, leaving him drained and miserable.

He recalled the expression on Jake's face when he walked away from her. Hopeless, tearstained. What had she really wanted from him? For him to reassure her? To beg her not to go? For him to tell her that her fears were groundless? That last one he could have done least of all. Especially since he wasn't convinced of that himself. Maybe she was right that he was still a captive of the past. While the pain diminished, the guilt still ate at him. The guilt that his carelessness had caused Paula's death. For a long time it had seemed that was all he had left in him, guilt and pain and regret for not taking care of the one person in his life who had really needed him.

And if she was right, that he had a death grip on the past, what would he have if he let it go?

Thirteen

The next morning, Jake woke to feel something small and warm pressed against her back. A little hand rested on her arm. Dani must have snuck into her bed sometime during the night. Jake turned and looked down at the little girl. She had her father's deep-set brown eyes, her mother's high cheekbones and almond-colored complexion. She and Dani shared not one drop of blood, but Jake loved her as if she were her own daughter. Jake stroked a lock of Dani's hair from her face. She knew that if she lost Dani, it would devastate her. She would never be the same again. Perhaps she'd been too hard on Eamon for not wanting to share what had to be the most painful experience a parent could suffer. Maybe she was disappointed in him for finally exposing a flaw underneath the impeccable exterior.

Dani stirred and opened her eyes. "Hi."

"Good morning to you, too." Jake tickled Dani's tummy. "How would you like to help me fix breakfast? I'll let you crack the eggs."

"Okay."

Five minutes later, Jake had bacon sizzling on a skillet and bread in the toaster, and Dani was stirring six eggs to a rubbery death with a plastic whisk. "I think that's enough stirring," Jake said, reaching for the bowl.

Dani's eyes lit up. "Can I pour them in?"

Jake smiled. "Not until you're big enough to see over the top of the stove."

Dani made a face, but relinquished the bowl.

When the eggs were cooked she offered Dani the first taste, as she always did. "How are they?" she asked and waited for Dani's pronouncement.

"Good."

"Of course they're good. We make a great team. McKenna and McKenna at large." Jake spread her arms in a silent *tada!*

"What about Fitzgerald? Isn't Uncle Eamon part of our team, too?"

Dani looked up at her with such a hopeful expression that it broke Jake's heart. She dropped her hands to her sides and straightened. She sat across from Dani, leaned forward, and took Dani's hands in hers. "Sweetheart, I know how much you like Uncle Eamon, but we have to go home today."

"Why? Uncle Eamon wants us to go?"

The despair in Dani's eyes and in her voice tugged at Jake. "No, Dani. We have to go home because we don't live here. We were staying here until I got better, and I'm fine now."

"So why can't we stay here if Uncle Eamon doesn't want us to go?"

"Because we have our own life, our own apartment. That's where we belong."

"I don't care. I don't want to go. Can't we stay here, Jake, please?"

She saw it in her eyes, she was breaking Dani's heart, too, but she couldn't turn back. The only thing to do was hold firm. "No, we can't."

Tears welled up in Dani's eyes. "I don't want to go." Dani shrugged off Jake's hold and bolted from the room. A moment later, Jake heard a bedroom door slam.

She sat back in her chair and covered her face with

her hands. What a mess! That's what she got for wishing for things that could never be. She would get over it, but what about Dani? Since she couldn't answer that question, she went to Eamon's room and began to gather her belongings. Once she had her things packed, she'd start on Dani's.

After she'd stuffed everything into the one suitcase she possessed, she sat on the bed, tired and achy. She'd had her back to the door, so it surprised her to look up and find Eamon watching her with his shoulder braced against the door frame. His eyes were hooded, unreadable, but the coldness in his voice chilled her.

"You're really determined to leave today?"

"Yes. I think it's best for all of us."

For a long moment, he said nothing. She held her breath, hoping that he would say something to change her mind or put her fears to rest. He straightened from the door frame. "I promised Dani I would help her practice today. I'd like to keep my word to her."

"All right. I still have to pack her things."

"We'll be in the kitchen when you are ready to go."

The minute Jake got their apartment door open, Dani ran to her room and slammed the door. Jake supposed she would have a lot of that to get used to. Dani was angry with her, maybe rightfully so, and she hadn't the heart to chastise her.

Eamon set their suitcases on the floor, then stepped back. For a moment their gazes locked. He lifted his hand to graze her cheek with his knuckles. Unable to help herself, she leaned into his caress. "I'm here if you need me, Jake."

"I know." She ran her tongue along the seam of her lips. "I'm coming back to work next week."

He dropped his hand to his side. "No."

Her eyes widened and she pressed her lips together.

Eamon sighed. "What kind of man do you think I am? I'm not firing you. I think you should take some more time before coming back to the office."

"Please, Eamon. I can't sit around here doing nothing."

"All right, but I won't have you on the subway where someone could jostle you and injure you. I'll pick you up and bring you home. Take it or leave it."

She shook her head. "I'll take a cab. I promise."

Eamon lifted his hands in the only helpless gesture she'd ever seen from him. "Have it your way, Jake. But I suggest you rest up. All hell is going to break loose in the office on Monday."

With that cryptic comment, he turned and headed for the stairs.

Jake closed the door and turned to the stack of mail waiting for her on the hall table, hoping to divert herself from the events of the past day and the fact that Dani had locked herself in her room.

She took the mail to the living room sofa and leafed through it. One card with an Italian postmark drew her attention. The card was addressed to her, but she'd never heard of Marie-Therese Ramalla Troubat. Probably some distant relative trying to hit her up for money.

She pulled the card from the envelope and a single photograph slid out. The man in the picture was her uncle Jake. He had his arms around a slender brunette. She'd guess her age at mid-fifties, very pretty with twinkling eyes. Uncle Jake wore a tuxedo, the woman an off-white evening gown. The caption handwritten on the back read *The Big Day, 15 Octobre 2001*.

The Big Day. The words circled around in Jake's head as she opened the card. Whoever Marie-Therese was, she wrote with a small neat script that suggested a Catholic-school upbringing. Jake shifted in her seat and read.

My dear Jacqueline,

    I am so sorry to have to be the one to inform you of the unfortunate passing of your uncle Jacques. He suffered a heart attack in his sleep. His death was quick and painless, or so the doctors tell me.

    Jacqueline, I spent the last two years as his wife. They were the happiest years I have known. I only pray that I made Jacques half as happy as he made me. But when we wed, I told him that he had to give up his old life, his old friends, his old ways. I am so sorry he included you in the people he gave up for me. He spoke of you and your brother and little Danielle often. To some degree, he felt the three of you were better off without his influence. We were both saddened to hear of Daniel's passing.

    Please know that I am here for you, Jacqueline, should you need anything.

                  Fondly,
                  Marie-Therese Ramalla Troubat

By the time she finished reading the letter, tears streamed down her face. Uncle Jake was dead. Her one remaining relative was gone from her life forever. Jake swiped at her eyes. She'd always assumed Uncle Jake would pop up in her life sooner or later, as he always did, when she least expected him. She hadn't expected this.

Almost as surprising as his death was the fact that his marriage was what had kept him out of her life. What kind of woman was this Marie-Therese that she could have induced him to give up his bachelor ways? She picked up the picture and studied it. In the woman's dark eyes, she saw the hint of merriment and of challenge and, most of all, of love. Those sentiments were mirrored on Uncle Jake's face as well. Had he simply succumbed to a love that couldn't be denied? In her romantic's heart, that's what she wanted to believe.

In the end it didn't matter. All that mattered to her was that her uncle finally seemed to have found happiness. She shut her eyes and whispered a quiet prayer for his soul.

When she opened her eyes, Dani stood in front of her, a worried expression on her face. "What's the matter, Jake?"

Jake swiped at her eyes. "Nothing, sweetheart." Dani didn't need to know that a man she probably couldn't remember had died. "Why don't you go get your toys and put them away? Then I'll make lunch. Or better yet, we'll go out, my treat."

Reluctantly, Dani went down the hallway to where she'd left her things, picked up the bag that contained her toys, and went back to her room. Jake gathered up the mail and took it to her room to finish reading later. On her way back to the living room the phone rang.

"Hello," she said into the receiver, hoping the misery she felt didn't show in her voice.

"Jake, are you all right? Dani called me to tell me you were crying."

Jake cleared her throat. She wasn't aware Dani knew Eamon's number. "I'm fine. I got a letter telling me my uncle Jake died."

"I'm on my way over." The line went dead before she had a chance to tell him not to bother. Within a half hour, Eamon was at her door. She had planned to reiterate that she was all right and that he could go home. But once she pulled open the door and saw him standing there, a look of sympathy in his eyes, her resolve melted. He pulled her into his arms and she went to him, needing his warmth, his tenderness, and mostly his strength, as hers seemed to have deserted her.

He backed them into the apartment, enough for him to kick the door shut. "I'm so sorry, Jake," he whispered against her hair. "I know how much he meant to you."

Jake inhaled, fighting a fresh batch of tears. "We're all alone now."

She hadn't meant to voice that last sentiment, though that's how she felt, as if her last remaining connection to the world had been severed.

Eamon pulled back from her to cup her face in his hands. "That's not true, Jake, and you know it. You have Liza, and that pain in the neck Jim." He paused for a moment to brush the tears from her cheeks. "And you have me, if you want me."

If she wanted him. That had never been the problem. She'd wanted him from the very beginning. What she had trouble sorting out was what was good for her and Dani.

She stepped back from him. "Thank you for coming, but I have to get Dani settled."

His jaw flexed as if he might say something. Instead he sighed, suddenly looking weary and defeated. "Remember what I said about resting up." He let himself out, leaving the door to close on its own steam.

After turning the locks on her door, Jake turned and leaned her back against it. "Dani, come here," Jake called.

Dani slowly appeared from behind the wall. The expression on her face showed both worry and a fear of reprisal for having eavesdropped. "Are you mad at me for calling Uncle Eamon?"

"No, Dani, I'm not. I don't want you making any more phone calls without asking me first, though."

"Okay. Why were you crying?"

Jake crooked her finger at Dani. When she drew close enough, Jake hugged Dani to her. "I should have told you this before, but I didn't want you to be sad, too. I found out my uncle Jake died."

"Was he old?"

"Pretty old. You are too young to remember him, but he loved you very much."

"Are you going to cry anymore?"

"Not today." Jake tried to inject a note of excitement in her voice. "Today I think we should go have some lunch, then maybe go to the park. How does that sound?"

"Okay."

Jake snorted. So neither of them could muster much enthusiasm for the day. They were down now, but they'd get better. She and Dani were survivors. They'd survive this, too.

Jake hadn't mustered any more enthusiasm by the time she reached the office on Monday. However, her coworkers welcomed her back with the zeal of a parent receiving a prodigal child. She managed to smile and appear interested as staff members stopped in her office to fill her in on what had been going on in her absence and coax her into recounting her own story.

She noticed the absence of two people in the parade through her office: Eamon, whom she didn't expect, and Sandra, whom she did. From the first, her relationship with Sandra had been strained, but she hadn't expected an employee who reported to her to snub her, either.

Jim arrived a little before ten, shooed the others out of her office, and closed the door. Leaning his backside against the credenza perpendicular to her desk, he folded his arms. "I missed you last night when I dropped by Eamon's to mooch Sunday dinner."

"Dani and I moved back home."

"So I noticed. Why?"

Jake rocked back in her chair. "Why don't you ask Eamon?"

"Tried that. Didn't work."

So she wasn't the only one whom Eamon liked to keep in the dark. But if Eamon chose not to tell Jim anything, she wouldn't go behind his back and do so either. "It's

in the vault." She pantomimed locking her lips and tossing away the key.

"Who'd have figured you for a Seinfeld devotee?" Jim
huffed. "Look, you know I care about you, Jake, and I'm
permanently stuck with the big guy. I thought you guys
had something going there."

So had she until she realized how broadly Eamon's
past colored his present. "What can I tell you?"

Jim shook his head. "What are the rest of us poor
shlubs supposed to do if the hopeless romantics of the
world can't get it together?"

She wouldn't argue the descriptor of hopeless romantic for herself, but for Eamon? "I thought for Eamon
caring was a decision, not an emotion."

"Yeah, but once the decision is made, he gets pretty
pathetic. He actually thought he could squeeze some
warmth out of that ice queen he married. A thermo-
nuclear blast couldn't have thawed her out. I probably
shouldn't tell you this, but I don't think he shaved
yesterday."

She couldn't imagine Eamon anything less than impeccably groomed. Jake closed her eyes and rubbed her
temples with her thumb and middle fingers. "Why are
you telling me this?"

He shrugged. "Just wondering if knowing he was miserable had any affect on you."

Yes. It made her feel like something unpleasant stuck
to the bottom of someone's shoe. "I'm not trying to hurt
him."

"I know. Otherwise I'd have to t'row ya a beatin'." He
motioned as if he were delivering an uppercut to her chin.

Laughing, Jake shook her head. "I'm glad he has you."

"Remember to remind him of that the next time you
see him. He's under the impression I'm a pain in the
ass." Jim stood. "Now, I have to make an appearance upstairs before the axes start to fall."

Puzzled, her brow furrowed. "What axes?"

Jim winked. "Now it's my turn to be mysterious." He laid a finger against his lips and left her office.

With a sigh, Jake tried, without success, to settle down to work.

Sandra finally made an appearance in her office just after lunch. She stopped in front of Jake's desk, her stance confrontational, her eyes bright as if she were drinking or on the verge of tears. "I hope you're happy now. I've been fired."

Jake had been examining photographs to select one to accompany a travel article. She switched off the portable light box she'd brought into her office for the task and set the loop on the table. "What are you talking about?"

"As if you didn't know. Your *boyfriend* fired me and half the rest of the staff."

Jake was too shocked by her accusation to be concerned by Sandra's assumptions about her relationship with Eamon. "Why?"

"How should I know?" Sandra's derisive gaze traveled over her. "I guess I don't have to ask why you didn't get a summons up to his office."

Jake straightened to her full height and narrowed her gaze on Sandra. "And why exactly is that?"

"I should have had your job to start with. But you waltz in here, flashing yourself like a two-dollar whore. If I'd known I had to do the boss to get ahead, I might have given it a try."

That statement didn't even make sense. If Eamon had wanted to promote her, he would have done so before hiring someone else. Jake put her hands on her hips and glared at Sandra. "Unfortunately for you, Eamon possesses a thing called good taste. You might have offered, but he wouldn't have bitten. Now get out of my office and quit wasting my time. Unlike some of us, I have work to do."

She intended to get back to it, until she noticed Eamon standing in the doorway behind Sandra. When she'd first met him, she would have sworn he could look right through her. She'd seen his eyes darken in passion and twinkle with laughter. But never had she seen the glacial expression she saw in them now. She shivered, even though it wasn't directed at her.

Sandra must have noticed the change in her, as she turned to look behind her. A small cry of surprise escaped her lips.

Without preamble, Eamon said, "You have ten minutes to get yourself and your possessions out of this building."

"Wh-what about my last paycheck?"

"I'll have it mailed to you. Now get out."

Sandra sputtered, but after a moment she stalked from the office without saying anything.

Jake watched her angry departure, until Eamon captured her attention by stepping into her office and shutting the door. If he was as miserable as Jim claimed, she saw no evidence of that. If anything, he seemed controlled, detached, maybe. She pressed her lips together, wondering why he'd come to see her in the first place. And why hadn't he told her he intended to decimate the staff this way?

Trying to appear detached herself, she sat in her chair and looked up at him. "What can I do for you, Eamon?"

"How are you feeling?"

"I'm fine. I just love being accused of sleeping with my boss to keep my job. Why didn't you tell me you were about to put half the people here out of work?"

"It was a business decision, not a personal one."

Which meant he felt no obligation to share it with her. "I'm sure the people you fired are taking it personally. How could you do this now in the middle of summer? How are these people supposed to find work?

Half of New York is on vacation and the other half is packing to go."

"Would you have preferred that I waited until September? Then we could all be out on the street. I told you my situation, Jake. I told you things had to change. What did you think I meant?"

"I don't know." She hadn't really thought about it. But it ate at her that she was staying while others who had been at the magazine for years were not. "By the way, why am I not fired?"

The glacial look in his eyes returned. "I'm going out of town for a couple of days. If you need to reach me, Jim knows where I'll be." Without another word, he turned and left.

Jake slouched back in her chair and sighed. "Nice work, McKenna," she said aloud. She'd just implied that she thought he kept her around in hopes of sleeping with her. She didn't believe that for one minute, but she admitted that the way she'd asked the question could easily have given him that impression. Not only that, she'd questioned his decisions and accused him of being callous in the way he'd treated the staff. She didn't really believe that either. Sandra's attack had surprised her, and his presence had unsettled her and her mouth had been engaged before her brain got up to speed.

She did the only thing a woman in her position could do. She locked her office and headed to the Lancome Insitut de Beaute in Bloomingdale's on Fifty-ninth Street for a facial. Life always looked better with your skin exfoliated and your pores cleaned. Right now, life needed to look a whole lot better.

Jake got back to the office a little after three o'clock. She went straight to Eamon's floor, determined to apologize to him. When she got out of the elevator, she noticed the floor was under construction. Plastic sheeting and yellow tape marked a pathway through the floor.

Knocking on Eamon's door produced no response. Jake opened the door to the outer office and found no one. Jim sat behind Eamon's desk in the inner office. "Come on in, McKenna," he called to her.

With a sigh she obliged him, sliding into one of the chairs facing the desk. "I was looking for Eamon."

"He left already."

Just her luck. "Did he say anything about me before he left?"

"Other than to watch out for you while he's gone? No."

"Oh." She looked down at her hands. Even though she'd practically accused him of heaven knew what, he was still looking out for her.

"For what it's worth, I heard just about every word the two of you said to each other before he left." Her head snapped up and Jim shrugged. "So sue me, I was eavesdropping."

Jake shook her head. "What's your point?"

"For what it's worth, every one of the people let go today knew about it for the past two weeks. Today just made it official. Most of them have already found other jobs—with Eamon's help—so he's not exactly throwing anyone to the wolves. And if you are feeling sorry for Sandra, don't. Eamon offered to help her, but she refused."

Jake sighed. She should have known better than to judge Eamon so harshly. "Maybe you ought to throw me that beatin' and knock some sense into my head."

"Nah. Eamon's drummed it into my head for as long as I can remember that good guys aren't supposed to hit girls. How about we go pick up Dani early and I buy you girls some dinner?"

"You're on."

But as the night wore on, one question nagged at her. Where had Eamon gone and what was he doing?

Fourteen

After an exhausting five-hour drive, Eamon let himself into his house in Massachusetts. He didn't bother to turn on the lights. In the darkened room the white covers that shrouded the furniture surrounded him like so many ghosts. He wouldn't be surprised if one of them floated upward to mock him like the specter of times past. He'd bought this house way back when he still had hopes that he and Claudia and the baby growing inside her would be able to carve out some semblance of a normal family life. All he had left of that dream was broken promises and ashes and the lingering dread that all of it had been his own fault.

He wandered through the downstairs rooms, all the while knowing that he procrastinated. He had no need to reacquaint himself with the home he'd lived in less than six months ago. Steeling himself, he climbed the stairs and opened the door to the second room of the landing, Paula's room. He flicked on the light and surveyed the room. It had remained unchanged since the day she had died.

Eamon inhaled, feeling a tightening in his chest. Even three years later, it was there—all the pain, all the regret, all the self-loathing he'd drowned himself in so long ago. He crossed the room and sat on the window seat amid a throng of stuffed animals. He pulled one onto his lap, and examined it—a mother koala bear with a tiny baby clinging to its neck. It reminded him more of Jake and Dani than it did of Claudia and Paula.

Jake. An image of her flashed in his mind—the sight of her on Friday night when she'd accused him of using Dani to replace his own daughter. He'd wanted to tell her she was wrong, but he couldn't. He knew that his feelings for Jake and Dani were genuine, but maybe he'd deluded himself into thinking he'd left his memories behind when he left Boston. Maybe he'd simply put physical distance between himself and the source of his pain, but emotionally they were as close as ever.

Saturday night, for the first time in weeks, he'd slept in his own bed, or rather he'd lain down in his own bed. He'd be surprised if he had actually slept more than twenty minutes. Although he'd changed the sheets, her scent, her presence, lingered, taunting him with what he'd lost. And he'd known he could never get her back unless he could prove to himself and her that his past was behind him.

But how could he do that when, in this room, every argument, every harsh word, every bitter moment crowded in on him, bowing his shoulders? It had been evident, almost from the first, that Claudia had no intention of being a mother to Paula. She'd barely been home two weeks before she returned to work from maternity leave. She'd claimed that she couldn't stand to take any more time off or she'd be derailed from the partnership track she put herself on. He'd been the one to wake for late-night feedings, to take Paula to the doctor, to provide for her in every way.

Claudia had given birth to her, and that's where her concept of parenthood ended. When he'd confronted her once on why she'd bothered to have a child she treated with utter indifference, she floored him by telling him that a college friend of hers had died from a botched abortion and she was terrified of suffering the same fate. In her mind, birth had seemed the safer option.

Paula was nothing more than a possession to her. When she finally decided to leave him, she'd packed Paula into the car with all her other possessions and driven away. But, as usual, they'd been arguing. At first, he hadn't tried to stop Claudia from leaving, but he'd threatened to fight her for custody. Over the years, she'd given him enough ammunition to prove her an unfit mother ten times over. For the first time since he'd known her, she'd cried. Tears running down her face, she'd gotten into the car. Then he had tried to stop her, realizing that she was in no condition to drive anywhere, let alone with Paula in the car with her. She'd peeled out, leaving him in the driveway, wondering if he shouldn't follow her. He'd decided against it, figuring he'd be better off letting her have some time to cool off.

Ten minutes later, he'd heard the sirens. In the quiet neighborhood where they lived, sirens of any kind were unusual. With a growing sense of alarm, he'd gotten into his car and driven in the direction of the sound. Claudia had only made it four blocks before she'd crashed into one of the giant oaks that lined the road to the highway. Claudia had been killed instantly; Paula had hung on for three agonizing days in which he didn't sleep, didn't eat, didn't move from her bedside.

He remembered standing at the grave, dry-eyed, flanked on either side by his brother Jim and his uncle Eamon. Using a stage whisper, someone had commented to his companion about his stoicism. His uncle had clasped his shoulder and said in a voice that reached his ears only, "Everyone grieves in their own way."

But had he grieved? He'd thrown himself into his work in a way he hadn't since he was young and hungry and eager to make a name for himself. He'd closed off his heart the same way he'd closed the door to Paula's room and never entered it again. But had he ever really let the full force of his grief wash over him? He didn't think so, not until now.

He swiped at the dampness on his cheeks as he glanced around the room. It was past time that he put Paula to rest. He exhaled heavily and stood. He'd brought three boxes with him—one for things to be donated to Goodwill, another he would keep, and the third was for things to throw away.

By nightfall, he'd filled all three and left them by the front door. Although he'd brought food with him, he lacked any desire to eat it. That night, he slept on the couch in the living room. Since knowing Jake, he'd gotten used to sleeping in odd places. Besides, unlike his bedroom at home, this one didn't hold her scent or her memory. The lonely sofa suited him better now.

In the morning, he'd head home, to Jake. He could finally give her the answer she wanted. He only hoped it would be enough.

After work on Tuesday, Jake picked Dani up from the nursery and headed home. Dani's mood hadn't improved any, making Jake glad Liza had promised to stop by for dinner. Dani deigned to leave her room long enough to eat. She even managed to be civil, though Jake suspected Dani's change in attitude was for Liza's sake, not her own. After dinner, Dani went back to her room, leaving Jake and Liza to straighten the kitchen and brew coffee alone.

Liza washed and Jake dried the few dishes their meal had required. Jake paused as she drew a dish towel around the last of the royal-blue ceramic plates that served as their everyday dishes. "I swear, she's driving me crazy, Liza. I don't know what to do with her. The last few days she's hardly spoken to me and when she does she's downright surly."

Liza turned off the tap and dried her hands. "You gave her a taste of what real family life is like. For the first time she had a semblance of mother and father—even a dog thrown in to complete the picture. She resents you for snatching it back, especially since she doesn't understand why you did. Frankly, neither do I."

Jake slid the plate into its spot in the overhead cabinet and shut the door. "We couldn't stay there forever."

"I'm not talking about you moving back home. As my mother would say, what man will buy the cow if he can milk her for free?"

Jake got two mugs from the stand on the counter and filled them. She handed one to Liza. "Frankly I've always considered that comparison a bit obscene."

With a sigh, Liza pressed on. "What I meant is, I'm not averse to putting a little pressure on a guy to get him to come around, you know, give him a chance to miss you instead of being underfoot all the time. But from what you've told me, that man really cares about you. I might even bandy about the L word if I were feeling adventurous. So why did you shut him out? Why are you giving me indigestion instead of him?"

Without thinking, Jake answered, "Because I don't know where he is."

Liza leaned back against the counter. "Ah, now I see the problem. *He* turned the tables on *you*. All along, all you ever had to do was say boo and he came running. Now he's unavailable to you and you can't handle it."

"That's not true," Jake protested, although now that she thought of it, she acknowledged Liza might be partially right. "We didn't just come home. Eamon and I had a fight. I accused him of using Dani to replace the daughter he'd lost."

Liza shook her head. "Excuse me? What daughter?"

"You may need a seat for this." The women took their coffee and settled on the living room sofa. "Eamon was married. He lost his wife and daughter in a car accident."

"Oh, God, Jake, that must have been horrible for him. No parent wants to bury his own child."

"I know. His daughter would have been Dani's age now. I was afraid maybe the reason he and Dani got along so well is he saw his own daughter in Dani. He said as much himself. Doesn't the fact that it took him so long to tell me about his family suggest maybe he's got unresolved issues where his wife and daughter are concerned?"

Liza tilted her head to one side and then the other. "Maybe, but did it ever occur to you that he never had cause to sort through those feelings before he met you? You know how men are. Why examine an emotion today if you can put it off until tomorrow? Did it ever occur to you that maybe he told you because he was finally ready to let the past go?"

"I don't know, Liza, I don't know. In some ways I'm afraid to find out. What if I'm right and I've risked Dani's heart and mine for nothing?"

"Oh, please, Jake. Don't forget we were raised together from the cradle. I have never known you to be afraid of failure. You thrive on it. What scares you is success, because anything you gain can be taken away from you."

Liza paused, drawing in a deep breath. "We've both had our share of disappointments where men are concerned, where life is concerned, but I'll tell you something. If I found a man with one-eighth Eamon's character who showed me one-tenth the devotion he's shown you, I'd latch on to him so fast both our heads would spin."

Liza stood. "With that I'm going to bid you good night. I've got an early morning tomorrow and I'm fresh out of Rolaids. Just do yourself a favor and think about what I said."

After Liza left, Jake put Dani to bed, took a shower, and pulled on her terry cloth robe. A peculiar restlessness claimed her. She wandered around the apartment, unable to keep still. Her gaze fell on the day's mail sitting on the table in the hallway. She hadn't bothered to open any of it. She took the mail back to the sofa and leafed through it. At the bottom was an envelope bearing the return address of a Park Avenue law firm. When she opened it two letters slid out. The first came from a Donald Lawson, Esq., officially notifying her of her uncle's death and requesting that she come into the office at her earliest convenience to sign the forms that would release her portion of Uncle Jake's estate to her, assets that totaled one hundred and seventy-five thousand dollars. Jake stared at the stark-black figure on the white page. Where had Uncle Jake gotten that kind of money? Shaking her head, she reached for the second letter. One single word graced the envelope written in her uncle's bold script: *Jake.* She slid her index finger under the flap to open it. With trembling fingers she read the letter inside.

My dearest Jake,

If you are reading this letter, I am in the hereafter, wherever and whatever that is. Please don't mourn for me. I had a good life, filled with wonderful friends and great adventures. And know that I have always loved you, though I have not been around to show it. I obeyed my wanderlust rather than my common sense more often than I should have. I am thankful that at last one lovely lady captured my heart and helped me find what I had been looking for all of my life.

That's right, Jacqueline. The old bachelor fell in love. I know I have always avoided attachments, but once Marie-Therese got her hooks in me, she wouldn't let go. After a while I no longer felt the need to go anywhere.

*She has made this old man the happiest he has ever been.
I only hope I have made her half as happy as she has
made me.*

*And so, I hope you have not taken too much to heart
the ramblings of an unwise man and that you have
found happiness with a man who loves you. If you have
not, I urge you to give love a chance, Jake. With the right
man you won't be sorry.*

*Take care of yourself and Dani. I've left you a little
something to help you take care of her financially at least.*

Je t'aime, mon couer,
Oncle Jacques

Jake sat back and pressed the letter to her chest. So she
had her answer. Uncle Jake had traded *la vie* bohemian for
the love of a good woman. He'd found peace. She
couldn't have wished for anything more for someone she
loved. And what about herself? Had she found the right
man in Eamon? She only knew she was miserable without
him, as miserable as Jim claimed Eamon was without her.
That had to count for something.

Jake drew in a long breath and let it out in one quick
gust. She was going to chance it. Maybe life finally owed
her a little something for all it had taken away. Maybe this
one time she could want something and not have her
dreams turn to a handful of ashes right before her eyes.

Her decision made, an odd feeling of relief flooded
through her. Now if only Eamon would cooperate and
get his buns back to New York. She considered calling
Jim to ask him where Eamon had gone off to, then
thought better of it. Perhaps, wherever Eamon was, he
was working out his own issues regarding her.

Jake snorted. Wouldn't it be ironic if just as she realized she wanted to be with him, he'd realized she was too
kooked for him to deal with? It would be just her luck,
but it wouldn't be funny. Not funny at all.

* * *

After leaving Boston, Eamon drove straight to Jake's house, partly because he needed to see her and partly because he wondered what she'd say when he told her what he'd done. He'd thought the five-hour drive would have been long enough to calm him, but he arrived at her door feeling agitated and out of sorts. As he drove, his mind invented one scenario after another, all of which ended with her sending him away. So when she pulled the door open and he saw her standing before him in that skimpy robe, he couldn't think of a single comprehensible thing to say.

As if in slow motion, she stepped closer to him and wrapped her arms around his neck. She pressed her soft body against him and he was helpless to do anything but respond. His arms closed around her, drawing her nearer. He buried his face in her fragrant hair and inhaled, willing his suddenly rapid heartbeat to settle down.

He backed them into the apartment, enough so that he could close the door, then set her away from him. With a finger under her chin, he tilted her face up to him. He hadn't imagined the remnants of tears he'd seen on her cheeks. "What's the matter, sweetheart?"

"Where were you? Jim wouldn't tell me anything."

He ignored her question, more concerned that his absence had been the source of her tears. He swiped at the moisture with the pad of his thumb. "Tell me I didn't make you cry."

Without waiting for an answer, he lowered his mouth to hers. His tongue plunged into her mouth, hungry, seeking. Her hands wound around his back, her fingers digging into his flesh, urging him closer, obliterating what little control he had. He pressed her backward, against the wall, as his mouth devoured hers.

When he broke the kiss, he buried his face against her throat as he dragged air into his starved lungs. Her hands wandered over his back, soothing him, and her breath fanned his throat for an instant before her lips touched down just below his ear. "It's all right, Eamon," she whispered.

He squeezed his eyes shut and hugged her to him more tightly. *I love you, Jake.* Not for the first time, those words popped into his head. But fearing what her reaction would be to hearing them, he didn't speak them aloud. Instead he repeated them to himself, over and over like a litany against whatever perverse emotion gripped him. *I love you, Jake.*

She cradled his head in her palms, urging his head upward where she could look at him. When he obliged her, she scanned his face with narrowed, concerned eyes. "Tell me what happened."

He wanted to tell her, but he also didn't want to let her go. He picked her up and carried her to the living room sofa. He settled in one corner of it with her on his lap. He felt the trepidation in her and sought to alleviate it. He touched his fingertips to her cheek, then ran his hand over her hair. "I went back to Boston."

"Why?"

"I wanted to prove to myself that you were wrong about me, that I had put Paula's death in the proper perspective."

"Did you?"

"No. You were right about that. I think I've got a better handle on it now, though. I packed up Paula's things. I visited her grave. I haven't been there since the day we buried her. I think I was trying to convince myself that if I didn't acknowledge her death in any significant way, then it wasn't real. I can't say I'm totally okay with it, but I'm finally willing to let her go.

"And I'll admit to something else. Maybe I got along

so well with Dani because she reminded me of Paula, but Dani is her own person. If you forget that, she's more than happy to remind you."

Jake sighed. "She hasn't spoken two civil words to me since we moved back in here."

"I'm sorry. Do you want me to speak with her about that?"

"No, we'll work it out." Her tongue darted out to lick her lips. "Is there anything else you want to tell me?"

He realized he'd been stroking his hand up and down her thigh and stilled his hand. "I'm sorry I didn't tell you about what was going on at the office. Why do you think I wanted you to stay home? I knew, big softy that you are, you would feel guilty for keeping your job when so many others who had been around longer than you had were losing theirs."

"I didn't know anything about it until Sandra burst into my office accusing me of sleeping with you to keep my job."

"If that bothered her, it must have been a case of sour grapes—you apparently succeeding where she failed."

Jake's mouth fell open. "She came on to you?"

Eamon shrugged. "According to Jim she did. Honestly, I didn't notice."

Jake giggled. "That must have been a real boost to her ego."

Eamon shrugged again. He couldn't care less. "Just so you can't claim I am surprising you with anything, I want you to know one more person is leaving."

"Who?"

"Jim."

"You're firing your own brother?"

"Not exactly. Jim is itching to get out of here and I've already found someone to replace him." He paused a moment until she looked at him. "You."

"Me? You are kidding, right?"

He shook his head. "In case you haven't noticed, Jim hasn't been doing much around here but running up my phone bill and mooning over some woman who dumped him. You have made and executed every decision as far as the artwork for the magazine goes. I don't see why you shouldn't have the title and the pay to go along with the responsibility."

"Are you sure?"

"If you are wondering if my decision has anything to do with my feelings for you, it doesn't. You should know me better than that by now."

She gazed down at her lap, her teeth tugging on her lower lip. "What are your feelings for me?"

Her gaze met his. He shook his head. "No fair, Jake. You're the one who walked out on me, remember? Isn't there something you want to say to me?"

A tremulous smile turned up her lips. "I've come to the conclusion that my mother has a fool for a daughter."

He chuckled, stroking her hair back from her face. "Why would you say that?"

"For reasons too numerous to mention, but mostly for acting like an idiot these last few days. But I made you a promise, and I'd like to keep it."

"What promise was that?"

"To give you a chance to prove you weren't Stan. So far, I haven't been holding to my end of the deal."

He scanned her face, saw the trepidation evident there, but also the hopefulness and resolve. "What changed your mind?"

"I got a letter from Uncle Jake he sent me through his lawyer. That's why I was crying when you came in—not because of what he said, but because I miss him. I figure if my commitment-phobic uncle could take a chance on this love thing, maybe I should stop being such a chicken."

He closed his eyes for a moment as relief flooded through him. "Thank you, Uncle Jake."

She laughed and smacked his shoulder. "You rat."

A smile curved his own lips as he caught her hand and brought her palm to his lips. "Thank you," he whispered against her skin.

"For what?"

For the first time, when she'd had the option of shutting him out or letting him in, she'd chosen the latter. And while he was ahead in the game, he ought to get going while the getting was good. "I'd better go."

"Why is that, Eamon?"

Surely she'd noticed he hadn't been unaffected by her tenure sitting on his lap. In fact, the teasing smile on her lips assured him that she had. He surveyed her through half-closed lids. Her hair was tousled from having his fingers in it and her lips were slightly swollen from his kisses. Her eyes were languid and heavy-lidded. Her robe had parted to reveal a line of flesh that ended just above her navel. His groin tightened and his breathing hitched just looking at her.

With his hands on her waist, he set her off his lap, knowing if he put his hands on her in a more intimate way, he'd be lost. He stood and took her hand. "Walk me out."

She followed him, but when they reached the door, she slid her arms around his neck and pressed her body to his. A siren's smile turned up her lips. "Are you sure you have to go so soon?"

He unwound her arms from around his neck and took both her hands in his. "You know I want you, Jake. I've wanted you since the first day you walked into the office wearing that hideous blue dress. You've been driving me crazy ever since." He touched his fingertips to her cheek. "But you're the one with something to risk if I proved that to you now. Believe me, when the time is right, I'll be more than happy to show you." He kissed her mouth, then let himself out of the apartment while he still had the willpower to do so.

After Eamon left, Jake locked the door and leaned her back against it. She wrapped her arms around herself. For a moment she relived her conversation with Eamon, focusing on the intensity in his eyes when he'd told her he wanted her. If he wanted to take things between them slowly, she wouldn't object. In their own way, each of them needed reassurance. She hadn't understood that about him before. Just because he presented a cool, competent exterior didn't mean he didn't suffer from the same insecurities she did. He'd been scarred by his own losses and failures just as she had. He'd shown her that tonight with the fierceness of his kiss and the uneasiness in his eyes when he waited for her answer when he'd asked her how she felt about him. If she could help it, she wouldn't give him reason to doubt her again.

Smiling, she looked heavenward. "It's a start, Uncle Jake. It's a start."

Fifteen

The next morning, Jake woke to the sound of Dani's voice in her ear. "Can we invite Uncle Eamon to dinner tonight?"

Jake stifled a smile. Dani assumed she was asleep and was up to her usual tricks. In a sleepy voice, Jake said, "Sure, sweetheart," her usual answer to Dani's early morning interrogation sessions.

"Really?"

Jake turned over so that she lay on her other side facing Dani. Jake tickled her tummy. "Yes, really. I'll call him a little later and ask him to come over, okay?"

"Okay."

"What do you say we play hooky today? I'll stay home from work and you stay home from camp and we'll do something fun today. Just us."

"Cool!"

"Why don't you go get dressed and then we'll have some breakfast and we can figure out what we're going to do?"

"Okay." Dani scooted from the bed and out the door.

Jake turned to glance at her bedside clock. The digital display read six-twenty. Eamon would be awake by now. She dialed his home number and waited.

"Hello."

His voice sounded rough, sleepy. "Don't tell me I woke you."

"Jake? Is everything all right? How's Dani?"

It hadn't occurred to her that such an early morning call would alarm him. "Everything's fine." She sat up and rested her back against the headboard. "I wanted to let you know I won't be coming in today. Dani and I are playing hooky."

"I'm glad to hear it. Jim said that when you left the office last night you looked like, and I quote, 'death on a hot stick.' Maybe you came back to work too soon."

"Is that your way of saying, 'I told you so'?"

"No, I just don't want you to overexert yourself. Why don't you have Jim sneak you home some more work for a few more days?"

Jake laughed. "You knew about that?"

"Let's just say that neither you nor Jim should go into espionage. What are you and Dani going to do today?"

"We haven't decided yet? Why?"

"Maybe I'll join you."

"You?"

"What have I ever done to make you think I'm so stiff I wouldn't enjoy skipping work one day?"

She lifted one shoulder. "I don't know. But Dani would love it if you joined us. And so would I."

"Good. I'll be over in an hour."

Jake hung up the phone, showered, and dressed in a form-fitting sundress and a pair of low sandals. She finally had her waist back and didn't mind showing it off. Dani had dressed in a blue and white short set. The two of them met up in the kitchen for a light breakfast of cereal for Dani and an English muffin for Jake. The doorbell rang just as Jake was finishing up the breakfast dishes.

She glanced over her shoulder at Dani, who sat at the kitchen table. "You want to answer that?"

Dani slid from her chair to go to the front door. Jake followed, drying the last dish as she watched Dani open the door to Eamon. "Hi, Dani," he said.

"Uncle Eamon." Dani threw herself at him.

Eamon picked Dani up and hugged her, but Jake felt something electric rush through her realizing Eamon's gaze rested on her, assessing her in the short dress. Holding Dani in one arm he pulled Jake closer with the other. He kissed her cheek, then whispered in her ear, "If you were looking for a way to test my willpower, you succeeded."

She pushed away from him. "I did no such thing," she said, but her self-satisfied smile belied her words.

"If you say so." He set Dani on her feet. "What's on the agenda for today?"

Jake set the last dish in the cupboard and closed the door. "We still haven't decided."

"Can we go to Rye Playland, please?" Dani begged with her hands pressed together. "Please?"

Dani had been begging her all summer, but without a car they'd had no means of getting there. She glanced at Eamon. "What do you say to a day full of screaming kids, cotton candy, and riding the Tilt-A-Whirl till we throw up?"

He lifted one shoulder. "It's up to you, but I'll skip the throwing-up part, if you ladies don't mind."

Dani giggled. "Me, too."

"You go get a sweater, young lady," Jake said. "Just in case."

"All right." Dani clomped from the room.

Jake groaned. "What is the aversion kids have to sweaters? You'd think I'd asked her to eat broccoli or something."

"I wouldn't know." He closed the space between them. "But as long as she's gone I plan to take advantage of it." With his hands at her waist, he drew her closer and lowered his mouth to hers.

Jake leaned into him and wrapped her arms around his neck.

"Ugh, kissing again."

Jake looked over her shoulder at a disgruntled Dani. "It's one of the perks of being a grown-up, so get used to it." She pressed her mouth to Eamon's for a brief kiss to emphasize her point.

Eamon stepped back from her. "Are we ready?"

Jake grabbed her purse from the kitchen table and slung it over her arm. She nodded for Dani to join them. "Let's go."

On a weekday, the amusement park was crowded with camp groups that swarmed over the kiddie rides like noisy, matching-T-shirt-clad locusts. By midafternoon, Dani had exhausted the fare in the kids' section. He and Jake had taken turns riding with her on the ones that allowed adults. Now the three of them sat on one of the painted wood benches that lined the plaza, contemplating what to do next.

Eamon glanced over at Jake. If it weren't for her, he'd be in his office, poring over some boring figures, wishing he were with her. He'd been teasing when he offered to join them, but the incredulous tone in her voice when she'd questioned him had changed his mind. And, for someone who'd never skipped a day of work in his life, he had to admit, he'd enjoyed their day so far and hadn't thought of his obligations once until now.

He tugged on a lock of Jake's hair. "How about we get something to eat, then we can take a walk by the water?"

She smiled back at him. "You're on."

After a lunch of Nathan's hot dogs, Dani insisted on getting cotton candy, while Jake insisted on a plate of zeppolli, a fried sweet dough. They took their treats down by the water and sat in the grass. A few paddle boaters dotted the gently lapping water ahead of them. Dani sucked down her cotton candy in no time and zipped off to play with some children tossing a ball by the water, leaving the adults to fend for themselves.

Eamon stretched out, leaning back on his elbows, enjoying the peaceful scene before them. Jake sat beside him, her legs tucked underneath her, munching on the zeppolli.

"Want to try some?" Jake asked, extending a bit of the confection toward him.

"There's enough confectioners' sugar on that thing to induce a diabetic coma."

"Maybe, but it's delicious. Live a little."

He grasped her wrist and brought her fingers to his mouth. He nibbled the dough from her fingers. "Not bad." He licked the excess sugar from her fingers. "That's better."

She laughed and snatched her hand away. "We should go. In about twenty minutes all those day camps will start heading for their buses and we'll never get out of here."

"If that's what you want."

She surveyed him, a teasing smile on her lips. "You're awfully agreeable today."

"What does that mean?"

She tilted her head to one side. "You're not exactly Mr. Laid-Back. It's interesting to see you relaxed."

"You've never seen me relaxed before?"

"Not like this. You know, the grass stains will probably never come out of those pants."

"Exactly how uptight do you think I am?"

"I never said uptight, but face it, you're the only man I know that can wear a jacket in the middle of summer and not perspire."

Laughing, he rolled onto his side, facing her. He did feel relaxed. Ever since he got back from Boston, he'd felt as if a weight had been lifted off of him. And that he owed to her, since he would never have confronted his past if she hadn't challenged him to do so.

He cupped his hand over her bare knee. "Thank you."

"For what?"

Since he didn't have a simple answer for that, he pulled her down to him with a hand at her nape and kissed her. Eamon groaned as her tongue slid past her lips to mate with his. He should have known better than to start something in a public place. As always, the meeting of her lips and his turned into a combustible thing.

"They do that all the time." Jake pulled away from him and he sat up. Both of them stifled laughter at Dani's deadpan explanation of the adults' odd behavior to her two companions.

Jake reached for Dani and pulled her close. "Where have you been?"

"Playing."

"Ready to go?"

Since Dani looked ready to protest, he leaned over and whispered in Jake's ear, "How about we visit the arcade first? You haven't been to an amusement park if you haven't spent ten bucks trying to win a two-dollar toy."

"Okay," she said. "I play a mean skeeball."

Eamon helped Jake to her feet and the three of them walked back the way they had come.

Three hours later, Jake stood inside the doorway to her apartment, bidding Eamon good night. She knew he wouldn't come in and she didn't ask him. Although it remained unspoken between them, the enforced celibacy made being alone together difficult. Eamon cupped her face in his palm, and she leaned leaned into his touch.

He stroked his thumb over her cheek. "Do you think you can get a sitter for Friday night?"

"Why?"

He grinned. "I have this boring dinner to go to."

"And naturally, you thought of inviting me?"

"I thought having you with me might make the evening worth the price of the ticket."

Jake lowered her head, not doing a good job of hiding the blush that stole across her cheeks at his compliment. She tilted her head and slanted a glance up at him. "Very suave, counselor. In that case, I'd love to join you."

He leaned down and kissed her nose. "I was hoping you'd say that. It's formal. I hope that's not a problem."

She thought of the one formal dress she owned, a strapless, almost backless number that would surely make Eamon's eyes gape. "I think I can make do."

"I'll pick you up at seven."

"I'll be here." Bracing her hands against his chest, she leaned up for his kiss. His mouth settled on hers, gentle, teasing, but she wanted more. She slid her arms around his neck and pressed her body to his.

Immediately, he pulled away from her. "Let's not start something we can't finish."

She leaned her forehead against his chest, breathing heavily. "All right."

With a finger under her chin, he tilted her face up to his. "Two weeks, Jake. That's all." He kissed her forehead. "I'll see you Friday night." He slipped out the door, leaving her overheated and frustrated.

Jake closed the door and leaned her heated brow against the cool surface. No way in the world could she last two more weeks without imploding. Besides, what was the worst that could happen? She had no idea, but, in the spirit of her reborn adventurism, she decided to take her chances.

A slow smile spread across her face. Friday night, Eamon Fitzgerald was going to be in for a little surprise.

"Jake, would you please hold still?"

Jake closed her eyes and concentrated on standing in

one place long enough for Liza to get her zipped into her gown. She'd been restless all day, waiting for evening to come. Now that dusk had fallen, her nerves had become taut jangly things. She wondered what he'd do when she attempted to seduce him tonight. Knowing him, he'd set her aside, telling her all the logical reasons why they should wait. It galled her that he had so much willpower when she didn't have any.

"There." Liza stepped away from her. "Turn around and let me look at you."

Jake executed a slow turn and a half to end facing Liza. "What do you think?"

"Definitely killer. On a scale of one to ten, I'd give you a fifty-five."

Laughing, Jake turned toward the full-length mirror behind her door to see if Liza's rating held up. She smoothed her hands over her hips and down the narrow skirt. "Are you sure all this red isn't too much?" The hair she couldn't help. Even so, she'd pinned it up leaving wispy tendrils to frame her face. The red dress, well, she couldn't change that either. Maybe she should change her fire-engine-red lipstick for a more subdued color.

"Stop obsessing. You look great."

"Yeah, stop obsessing," Dani said from her seat on Jake's bed. "If I put on all that girly gook for a boy and he didn't like it, I'd slug him."

Jake and Liza shared a humor-filled glance. Liza tilted her head in Dani's direction. "The voice of experience speaks."

All three of them froze a second later when the doorbell rang. Jake's heartbeat accelerated and her mouth went dry. She glanced at her bedtime clock in time to see the numbers change from six fifty-nine to seven.

"Dum da dum dum," Dani said in a deep voice.

"I'll get it," Liza volunteered. "If you go to the door,

you'll probably jump on the man before he has a chance to say hello."

Not wanting to argue, Jake waved Liza toward the bedroom door. After Liza left, Jake grabbed her purse and followed. She stopped when she reached the wall on the other side of the hallway—the perfect place to eavesdrop. She heard Liza turn the latch, the door being pulled open, then Eamon's surprised baritone voice. "Hi."

She heard laughter in Liza's voice when she answered. "Hi yourself, Eamon. Are those flowers? I didn't think men brought women flowers anymore."

"I'm a throwback, ma'am."

"Come on in. Believe it or not, Jake is almost ready."

Jake was still digesting the fact that he'd brought her flowers when she realized she'd better hightail it back to her room if she didn't want Eamon to know she'd heard every word he and Liza said. She settled for the bathroom instead. After flipping on the light, she went to the medicine cabinet mirror to check her makeup. She took a deep breath, counted to ten, then left the room.

When she stepped out into the hallway, Eamon stood in the dining room facing her, one hand in his trouser pocket, the other holding a bouquet of pale pink roses. Her gaze wandered over him, drinking in the sight of his tall frame clad in an expertly tailored tuxedo. Of its own accord, her tongue traced a slow path along her bottom lip. Liza was nowhere to be seen, so Jake assumed she'd already joined Dani in the bedroom. Finally, her mouth formed one small word in greeting. "Hi."

As she walked toward him, his eyes darkened, with what emotion she wasn't sure. She stopped a few inches away from him. "It's the red, isn't it? It's too much."

"Turn around."

His warm baritone voice washed over her, heating her nerve endings. She gave him the same turn she'd given Liza, this time with a little attitude. "Well?"

"If anything, I'd say it was too little."

She tilted her head to one side and considered him. Was that a note of possessiveness she heard in his voice? "Do you want me to change?" she asked, just to test.

"Not on your life."

Smiling wickedly, she gestured toward the bouquet in his hand. "Are those for me?"

He extended the bouquet toward her. "How'd you guess?"

Their hands brushed as she took the flowers from him. She brought them to her nose and inhaled their powdery scent. "If you'd brought them for Dani, she'd probably be whacking them against the wall to find out how much abuse they could stand before the heads popped off." She cradled the bouquet in one arm. "Thank you, Eamon. They're beautiful. I'd better go put these in some water before we go."

She felt his eyes on her as she walked around the table to go into the kitchen. She found a vase right away and filled it with cold water. As she arranged the flowers and greenery, she heard Dani say, "Uncle Eamon," and his answering, "Hey, short stuff."

Jake pushed through the kitchen door carrying the vase. Both Liza and Dani stood in the dining room along with Eamon. "I leave the room for one second . . ."

"Dani wanted to say good night," Liza said by way of explanation.

"Come here, sweetheart," Jake instructed. Dani skipped to Jake's waiting embrace. "You behave yourself for Auntie Liza."

"Don't I always?"

"You don't really want me to answer that question, so say good night, Dani."

"Good night, Dani."

Jake ruffled her hair. "Just what I need, a three-foot Gracie Allen. I meant say good night to Uncle Eamon."

"Good night, Uncle Eamon."

"Good night, short stuff."

Jake glanced at Liza, who nodded in Eamon's direction. Jake picked up her purse. "I guess we'd better go."

Once he seated Jake on the passenger side of his car, he circled around the hood and slid behind the wheel. "Comfortable?"

She finished buckling her seat belt and sat back. "Very."

He started the engine. He'd considered hiring a car for the evening, but now he was glad he hadn't. He needed something to concentrate on besides the scent of Jake's perfume, and something to do with his hands. As much as he wanted her, he didn't want their first time together to be in the back of a rented car. He had other plans that didn't include plush leather upholstery. And after seeing her in that clingy red sheath, he no longer trusted himself to behave.

"So where are we going? I never bothered to ask and you never bothered to tell."

"Actually, I'm not sure. Or more precisely, I don't know what we are going to. Margot roped me into buying tickets to this thing." Since it was the first thing she'd ever asked of him, he didn't dare refuse. "I've never heard of the sponsoring organization, though, the Poets' Day Society." The name conjured up a roomful of staid intellectuals discussing Chaucer, which from what he knew of Margot, didn't seem all that far-fetched a prospect. Then again, he admitted he didn't know much about Margot, either. He snuck a glance at Jake. "All I'm sure of is that they'll feed us."

"Good enough. I'm starved."

So was he, but it had nothing to do with food. His hands tightened on the steering wheel. They'd stay long enough to eat, listen to a couple of speeches or whatever, and then he'd get her out of there and to his apartment where they could be alone.

The event was held in the second-floor ballroom of the downtown Marriott hotel. They were assigned to a table near the front of the room. As they approached, a dark-skinned woman of medium height wearing a black halter-style gown stood to greet them. "Eamon, Jake, I'm so glad you made it."

Eamon blinked. "Margot?" Laughter rumbled up in his chest. So much for his paragon of decorum. The slit on the left side of her gown could almost be considered indecent.

"I would like to present my fiancé, Albert."

Albert stood and extended his hand. "Pleased to meet you."

"Likewise." However, Eamon hadn't seen a navy blue tuxedo like Albert's since his senior prom. But he didn't want to deck the man until he made a grand show of kissing Jake's hand, no doubt as a means of peeking down her dress.

"Shall we sit, then?" Margot suggested.

Before claiming his seat between the two women, Eamon seated Jake next to a kid who looked barely old enough to shave. Margot introduced the younger man and his date as her nineteen-year-old niece, Margot, and her boyfriend, Max. "She's my sister's oldest, named after me, you know," the elder Margot confided.

Eamon chuckled to himself. He never would have guessed. The two women looked enough alike to be mother and daughter instead of aunt and niece.

He turned to Jake, who looked back at him with a bemused smile on her face. "Would you like a drink?"

"I think I need one."

He could believe that. "What would you like?"

"I'd love a glass of wine."

"Coming up." He excused himself and threaded his

way through the crowd to the bar. He joined the end of the line and surveyed the room. Far from being some stuffy gathering, the men and women around him seemed to be working-class people who'd put on their finery for one night. Besides that, the band was loud. At the moment, they were making a valiant attempt at turning the Bay City Rollers' "Saturday Night" into "Friday Night," but not quite making it.

He made it to the head of the line and ordered Jake's wine and a scotch for himself. He glanced back at their table to find that Jake had moved over into his seat. She and Margot appeared to be deep in conversation.

When he got back to the table he slid into Jake's seat and handed her the wineglass. "What are you two talking about?"

She took a delicate sip. "I found out what Poets' Day is."

"Oh, really? Let's have it."

"You've heard of T.G.I.F., right? Thank God It's Friday. It's sort of the British equivalent, except it stands for, Piss Off Early, Tomorrow's Saturday."

"Margot told you that?" He couldn't imagine that Margot knew the word *piss* existed, let alone hearing her say it.

"Actually Albert did."

That figured. Eamon glanced over at the man. Grudgingly, he admitted that despite his choice in attire, he had that sort of older-man rugged look that women found attractive, and Margot seemed to be entranced with him, so maybe he wasn't so bad. He turned his attention back to Jake. "What else did Margot tell you?"

"The Poets' Day Society is actually a group of friends that meets every Friday at O'Toole's over on Lexington for happy hour. This is actually a fund-raiser for one of the members whose daughter needs heart surgery but the family is uninsured."

Eamon sat back, not knowing what to say to that. Sometimes it surprised him, all the sorrow in the world, and yet all the altruism to counterbalance it. He stroked his hand down Jake's back. "Are you having a good time?"

She smiled, but before she could answer, the waiters started removing the salad dishes that neither of them had touched. Dinner was a choice of filet mignon, baked salmon, or chicken fiesta, whatever that was. Eamon selected the steak while Jake opted for the salmon.

"How is it?" Jake asked as he sampled the first bite of meat.

"It could use a few peppercorns."

She laughed and smacked him on the arm. "The salmon is excellent. Want to try it?"

He said nothing, but allowed her to feed him a sample of her food. He chewed, but tasted nothing, too caught up in her smile and her nearness to care about food. The band was on a break, but sooner or later they'd come back and play something he could actually dance to. He wanted to hold her. He wanted to get the hell out of there, but since Margot had told him through Jake that she had something to discuss with him, their escape probably wouldn't happen any time soon.

Finally, the band wandered back in and struck up a surprisingly good version of Eric Clapton's "Wonderful." He took Jake's hand. "Dance with me."

She glanced at the empty dance floor. "No one else is dancing."

"Then we'll be the first."

Shaking her head, she allowed him to help her to her feet. He laced his fingers with hers and led her to the floor. Once there, he pulled her into his arms. Knowing others probably were watching them, the lone couple on the floor, Eamon behaved himself, maintaining a discreet distance between them, when he really wanted to pull her closer and bury his nose beside her soft, fragrant neck.

His hand on her back flexed. "This isn't so bad, is it?"

"Not at all." A gamine grin lit her face.

"Why are you smiling like that?"

She shook her head. "Nothing."

"Tell me."

"I was just thinking that I nearly died when I realized the woman wearing that outrageous dress was Margot. That's not to say that she doesn't look fabulous, but I don't think I've ever seen her wearing anything that showed so much as her elbows before."

"I don't think I have either, and I've known her for ten years."

She laughed. "Albert certainly seems smitten."

"Does he?" Eamon wondered if the rest of the table were thinking the same thing about him where Jake was concerned. If so, he didn't care. Despite the possibility of onlookers, he pulled her closer and pressed his lips to her temple.

As he predicted, one couple after another joined them on the dance floor, until they were surrounded. Jake slipped her hand from his and slid her arm around his neck.

He wondered why Jake suddenly stepped away from him, until he saw Margot standing beside her. "I hope you don't mind me borrowing your beau for a few minutes," Margot was saying to her.

"Not at all." Jake winked at him. "See you at the table." For a moment, Eamon watched her make her way toward the tables.

A delicate cough from Margot drew his attention. Margot stepped toward him. "Shall we?"

Why the hell not? He pulled Margot into a loose embrace. "What brings you out on the dance floor?"

"I figured I'd better come out here before the two of you embarrassed yourselves in public. You two do make a dashing couple."

"Thank you, but I don't think that's what you wanted to talk to me about, is it?"

"What do you think of Margot junior?"

He hesitated to answer for a minute, wondering where Margot senior was headed. "She seems like a nice kid."

"She's a bright girl. She'll be graduating from Columbia with a journalism degree at the end of next year."

"And you want me to give her a job, is that it?"

"Yes, my job."

"Your job? And what will you be doing?"

"I'll be going back to Boston to be with Albert." She pressed her lips together. "You're going to hate me for telling you this, but the only reason I agreed to come to New York with you was to shake a little sense into Albert. He was a tad slow in realizing that he can't live without me. You know what they say about absence making the heart grow fonder."

"I see he's come around to your way of thinking. I'm happy for you, Margot. Though I am going to miss you."

"You're a dear." She leaned up and kissed his cheek. "I'm going to miss you, too."

The song ended. Eamon brought Margot back to the table and seated her next to Albert. To Jake, he said, "You want to get going?"

She put her hand in his. Now the night would really begin.

Sixteen

Just as they made it to the car, the overcast night gave way to the thundershowers the weatherman had predicted. Eamon slid into the driver's seat and fastened his seat belt. "So, where to?"

"I'm feeling a little tired. Maybe you should take me home."

She didn't seem tired. In fact, all night she'd seemed full of nervous energy, now even more so. Still, disappointment flooded through him knowing that his plans for the evening had come to nothing, considering that Liza and Dani were in her apartment. "Whatever you want," he said, hoping his dissatisfaction didn't show in his voice.

When they got to her apartment, he took her keys from her and unlocked the door. He held the door open for her to precede him. The apartment was quiet and the only apparent light came from the light panel over the stove. He gazed at Jake, who smiled at him from the other side of the threshold. She looked so lovely, the urge to pull her into his arms assailed him. He tamped it down, knowing that to do so would only add another level of frustration. He swallowed. "I guess I'd better go."

"Why would you want to do that?"

"I wouldn't want to wake Dani or Liza."

"You wouldn't. They're not here. Liza took Dani to her place."

Eamon's eyebrows lifted. They were alone then. A glimmer of hope stirred in him. Why hadn't she told him that before? "I thought you were tired."

She ran her fingers along his lapel, up and down, as if she was stalling before answering him. When she looked up at him, a siren's smile tilted up her lips. "I am tired. Tired of waiting. I want you and I know you want me."

Want? He'd passed want with her a long time ago and headed straight up to need. Right now, every particle of him blazed as if he were standing in an inferno, and she wasn't even touching him in any way that mattered. He started to tell her that, but before he got a word out, she leaned up to press her mouth to his.

He closed his eyes as he stepped closer to her, backing her into the apartment so that he could let the door close. Then he kissed her the way he wanted to. He pulled her closer with his hands on her hips. His tongue plunged into her sweet mouth and withdrew, in imitation of the more intimate act yet to come.

Yet, she kissed him back and clung to him with a desperation that seemed alien to the woman he knew. He pulled away from her and set her away from him against the hallway wall. "What's the matter, sweetheart?"

She lowered her head and gripped her fingers together. "I didn't want you to flex your willpower again and say no to me."

With a finger under her chin, he tilted her face up to his. "If you think it has been easy for me to keep my hands off you, think again. That wasn't willpower, that was fear. I was afraid I'd hurt you."

"What changed your mind?"

"I called your doctor."

Jake stared at him openmouthed. "Eamon! You didn't. What did she say?"

He chuckled low in his throat. "Be gentle." He leaned forward and softly kissed her cheek. "Does that qualify?"

"Yes."

He smiled, hearing that one breathless word. "How about this?" He touched his lips to the spot just below her left ear.

"Definitely."

"And this?" He trailed kisses down the side of her throat until he reached the juncture where her neck and shoulder met. She didn't say anything this time, but rewarded him with one of those erotic noises low in her throat, and her hands rose to grip his shoulders. He lifted his head and kissed her mouth, a sweet caress that nonetheless left him gasping for air. He pulled back and stared down at her.

"I should probably warn you that my room is a mess. Dani had her toys everywhere. I didn't have a chance to clean u—"

That's as far as he let her get before laying a silencing finger against her lips. She was rambling, and he wanted to know why. He brushed a stray hair from her face. "What is it now, sweetheart?"

She huffed and her shoulders drooped. "It's been such a long time, for all I know they could have reinvented sex and you need a computer chip or something else I don't have."

He laughed. "If they have, I wouldn't know about it. I haven't been with a woman in five years, Jake. If that's not a record, it's got to be damn close."

She laughed and threw her arms around his neck. "You poor baby. You're worse off than I am."

Didn't he know it! Her hips pressed against his, making no secret of how bad off he was. He ached to be inside her, but more than that, he wanted this first time between them to be magical. He wanted to prove to her that she, just the way she was, was sufficient for any man. He wanted to show her how much he loved her in actions since he feared to do so with words. He wanted to kiss her, and he did, but this time the urgency was in him. His fingers went to her hair, pulling out the pins that held the heavy mass in place. Her hair cascaded around them like a soft, crimson curtain. His lungs burned from the effort to drag in air. By the time he pulled away from her, they were both panting.

But they couldn't stand here in the hallway forever. He took her hand and kissed her palm. "Maybe we'd better see how messy your room is."

She smiled and laced her fingers with his. She led him through the dark apartment, through the dining room, where miraculously neither of them managed to bump into the furniture. A soft light seeped from her bedroom doorway. Once she got to the threshold of the room, Jake stopped and said, "Oh, my."

He came up behind her and surveyed the room. Not only was the space immaculate, but the bed had been turned down to reveal champagne-colored satin sheets. Several candles had been stationed around the room. The largest of which bore a yellow Post-It note that said *Light Me*. A tape player sat on her dresser, bearing an identical note that read *Play Me*.

"Liza?" he asked.

Jake glanced over her shoulder at him. "Obviously, she has little faith in my powers of seduction."

Eamon shook his head. Liza had a lot to learn. He slipped past Jake and went to her nightstand beside her bed where a crystal ice bucket rested. He plucked the note saying *Drink Me* from the bucket and dropped it to her nightstand. "I don't suppose we should let that go to waste."

"I guess not."

He lifted the bottle from the ice bucket and began to tear away the foil wrapping.

She strolled toward the dresser. "I don't suppose we should let these go to waste either." She found a lighter and lit most of the candles. After disposing of the lighter in the nightstand drawer, she turned off the single lamp that had lit the room, leaving only the glow of the candles. Finally, she pressed the play button on the cassette player. Almost instantly, Frank Sinatra's voice filled the room singing "The Way You Look Tonight."

She turned to face him, and smiled. His eyes wandered over her as he contemplated the appropriateness of the song's lyrics. He had never seen her look as lovely as she did now. Awash in candlelight, her skin glowed, her hair glistened, and the beading along the sweetheart neckline of her gown shimmered. But most of all, her smile got to him, one full of anticipation and promise.

She walked toward him just as the cork slid from the bottle. He filled one glass halfway and handed it to her, then filled his own. He set the bottle in the ice bucket and turned to her. "What should we drink to?"

"How about Ol' Blue Eyes, wherever he is right now?"

He clinked his glass with hers. He'd have toasted to Toulouse LeTrec if she'd wanted him to. He watched her as he drank, noting with interest how her body naturally moved to the music. When she set her glass down on the nightstand, there was a broad grin on her face.

"What's so funny?" He set his glass on the dresser beside hers.

"I was wondering if Liza left a Post-It note on the bed, too, and if so, what it could possibly have said."

He tried to smile, but all the humor in him had fled. With his index finger, he traced the outline of her bodice along her skin. "I think we can figure that one out for ourselves."

His hand slid down to cup her breast and she moaned. He rubbed his thumb against her erect nipple, but it wasn't enough. He wanted to feel her bare flesh against his. He wanted to see her, all of her. His fingers went to the zipper at the back of her dress and rasped it down. The crimson garment slithered to the floor, leaving her bare except for a pair of lacy red panties, a pair of thigh-high stockings, and her sandals.

He swallowed, drinking in her beauty with his eyes. Lord, she was perfect, with full, round breasts, a slender waist, and those long, long legs. He lifted her and laid her down on the bed and came down beside her. His mouth found hers as his hand roved over one breast and then the other. Her fingers gripped his shoulders, urging him on. He lifted his head to look down at her. The rapturous expression on her face got to him, too. He lowered his head again, this time to take her nipple into his mouth. She arched against him, and called his name.

"What's the matter, baby?" he whispered against her skin.

Her chest heaved and her fingers tugged at his lapels. "S-something is wr-wrong with this picture. I'm almost naked and you still have y-your jacket on."

"I can fix that." He rose from the bed and shrugged out of his jacket. He tossed it and his tie onto a chair, then toed off his shoes. Otherwise, he left his clothes as they were. He knew if he were as bare as she, he'd leap on her with all the delicacy of a two-ton truck. She deserved better than that from him. He knelt on the floor in front of her and slid off her sandals.

She leaned up on her elbows and watched him with a heavy-lidded gaze. "What are you doing?"

He leaned forward and braced his forearms on either side of her. "Fixing things." He rolled one stocking down her leg and kissed his way back up until he reached her inner thigh. Her hips bucked toward him, but he didn't give her what she wanted, not yet.

Instead he kissed the scar that ran along her pubic bone. He owed her that one from the time Dani burst in on them. Her hips rocked against him, and she moaned his name, but he didn't acquiesce. "Not yet, baby. Not yet."

He took his time rolling down the other stocking. When he'd pulled it from her body, he kissed the delicate arch of her foot, the curve of her calf, the back of her knee, the inside of her thigh.

She squirmed against him. "Stop torturing me."

He grinned hearing the urgency in her voice. But he was torturing himself as well. He slid her panties over her hips, down her legs, and from her body. For a moment, he simply stared at her. Fully nude, she was more beautiful than he'd ever imagined. Then his fingers tangled in the thatch of curly red hair that shielded her femininity. He parted her and brought his mouth down to her.

She gasped and wrapped her legs around his shoulders, holding him to her. He lapped at her soft, moist flesh, perfumed with the scent of her arousal. His tongue delved inside, sampling her sweet juices, shallowly at first, then deeper and more demanding.

"Eamon!"

He knew she was near the edge by both the urgency in her voice and the tiny shivers in her legs as they tightened around him. She was ready for him, more than ready, but, perhaps selfishly, he wanted to bring her to climax first. If he were inside her now, he wouldn't last two seconds.

He replaced his tongue with his fingers and drew her clitoris into his mouth to suckle her. She shouted his name and convulsed around him, her hips bucking, her legs trembling against him. He slid his hand beneath her hips to hold her steady as he continued to lave her with his tongue. His fingers, still inside her, flexed and she convulsed again, more violently than the first time. "Eamon," she whimpered, and he had to admit it didn't do his ego any harm hearing his name on her lips that way.

When her tremors subsided, he lay down beside her and pulled her against him. She buried her face against his neck. Her chest heaved and her heart beat rapidly against his own. He stroked his hands over her hair, down her back, in an effort to soothe her. "Are you okay?"

She nodded, but burrowed closer.

He brushed her hair back from her face and tried to get her to look at him. "What's the matter, sweetheart? Tell me what I did."

She exhaled and her breath fanned his cheek. "You didn't do anything. I . . ."

She trailed off, and it hit him. She'd told him about her former fiancé, the cold fish who expected her to be just as frigid, but he hadn't really paid attention. Did she expect him to judge her as harshly, and more importantly, had she been holding back from him all this time for fear of his reaction?

He gritted his teeth as self-directed anger flooded through him. He'd wanted to pleasure her, but in so doing he'd also made her embarrassed of her own uninhibited response. In protecting his own vulnerability he'd compromised hers.

"Jake, look at me."

Slowly she turned her head toward him and opened her eyes.

He saw the apprehension in her gaze and longed to ease it. "Let me get this straight. You are upset because you let me know how much I pleased you? Do you hear how ridiculous that sounds?"

Her nose was back in his neck again. He stroked her hair. "Just so you know, I wouldn't mind if half the people on Pluto just heard you scream your head off."

She lifted her head. A hint of a smile turned up her lips. "There aren't any people on Pluto."

"You know what I mean." He ran his hand down her body to cup her derriere in his palm, then he gave her flank a gentle tap. "I just want to make you feel good, and I'm sorry if I didn't."

She offered him a lopsided grin. "Oh, you did. Boy, did you." Her fingers went to the buttons of his shirt. "Any chance you plan to lose this?"

"Could be." He kissed the tip of her nose, then set her away from him so that he could rise. He stripped out of the remainder of his clothing in about three seconds and tossed it onto the chair. While he did so, she arranged herself between the satin sheets. She leaned her head against her upturned hand watching him. "Is that better?" he said.

"Much." Jake let her gaze travel over him, from his muscled chest and abdomen to his groin, heavy with his erection. Lord, he was a beautiful man. In the candle-light, his eyes had darkened to a deep, exotic blue. Even though he'd just given her *the* most explosive orgasm of her life, she wanted more. She wanted to have him inside her, to hold him while he came inside her. Just the thought of it made her insides quiver and her body's juices flow. She pulled back the sheet to reveal herself as both an enticement and an invitation.

He paused long enough to sheath himself; then he came to her, covering her with his big, warm body. She shivered and wrapped her arms around him. He leaned up on his elbows and gazed down at her. "Hi."

"Hi," she echoed, not knowing what else to do. Simply having him there cradled between her thighs started a quickening in her belly. Unable to keep still, she moved against him. He groaned and buried his face against her ear. "I need you, Jake. Now."

"Yes." She shivered as he entered her, slowly, mad-deningly, until he filled the length and breadth of her. For a moment he didn't move, but he trembled beneath her fingertips. "Oh, God, Jake," he whispered against her ear. Then just as slowly, he withdrew from her, only to sink against her again.

She wrapped her legs around him and her fingertips dug into his back. Perspiration broke out along her skin as her hips undulated in concert with his thrusts. Her neck arched and she called his name, wanting the sweet torture to end, wanting it to go on forever.

"Yes, baby."

She opened her eyes and looked up at him. The intensity in his gaze sent a shiver through her. She cupped his face in her palms and brought his mouth down to hers for a wild, erotic kiss. He thrust into her again as his tongue thrust into her mouth, pushing her over the edge into wave after wave of pure ecstasy. She clung to him, as his own release overtook him, making his back arch and his body tremble. He collapsed against her, his breathing hard and fast, his heartbeat as erratic as her own. For a long moment they lay together, recovering.

He was the first to move. He lifted himself on his elbows and looked down at her. "How are you feeling?"

Too weary even to open her eyes, she smiled. "Check back in a few minutes when I can breathe again."

He laughed and rolled onto his back, pulling her to his side. He rubbed his hand up and down her back. "My sentiments exactly." He exhaled heavily. "Thirsty?"

She nodded.

He leaned over her to reach the champagne. That brought one of his nipples into her line of view. She leaned forward to trace her tongue around its edge. She grinned, when his entire body jerked in response.

"Behave yourself, woman, if you don't want me to spill this."

"If you do, it will be the most easily removed liquid that's been spilled in here. Try getting red Hi-C out of a beige carpet." She accepted the glass he handed her and held it for him to fill it. When he did, she drank deeply. "Where's yours?"

He refreshed her glass, nearly draining the bottle. "Right here." He lifted the bottle to his lips and drank a swig.

Her mouth dropped open. Eamon Fitzgerald drinking from a champagne bottle? No one would believe her if she told them, not that she would. "Where's a camera when you need one?"

He looked back at her, the picture of innocence. "What do you mean?"

She drew in a breath, inhaling the scent of their love-making that still hung in the air. Sometimes she thought he did things like that just to shock her. "You don't even drink beer without a glass."

"Not true." He wiggled his eyebrows comically. "Maybe you're rubbing off on me." He leaned down to cover her mouth with his.

She sank back against the pillows, savoring his kiss, until something wet and cold drizzled on her belly.

Laughing, he pulled away from her. "You objected to my former drinking vessel." He leaned down to lick the champagne from her navel and all the other directions the bubbly liquid had traveled.

Her back arched and a throaty sound of pleasure escaped her lips.

"Did you like that, baby?"

Before she could answer, a fresh wash of champagne trickled between her breasts. And then Eamon's mouth was on her again, sweeping the liquid from her body with his lips and tongue. Unable to keep still, she squirmed and felt herself slide sideways on the slippery sheets. "Eamon."

He took her glass from her and a second later she heard the clink of it being set on the nightstand. His hand cupped her breast and his tongue, icy cold from the champagne, circled her nipple. She squeezed her eyes shut, letting the sensations wash over her. Her head spun, and she realized that was because she was hanging half off the bed. "Eamon," she warned.

His response was to roll onto his back and pull her on top of him. That only made the problem worse, as it edged them closer to the foot of the bed. She sat up, straddling his waist. But when his fingers delved between her thighs, she lost all ability to concentrate on anything but what he did to her. And when he lifted her and set her down on his erection, she lost it. She bucked against him as her entire body shivered. His arms closed around her, pulling her down to him, as they slid from the bed to join the covers on the floor.

For a moment, they clung together laughing. As their laughter subsided, his hands roamed over her back. "Are you all right?"

"I'm not sure this is what the doctor meant by being gentle." She leaned up to see his face. But he was still deep inside her, and the motion of rising sent a shiver of pleasure coursing through her body. She braced her hands on his chest and lifted herself above him. She lowered herself slowly. Eamon's chest rumbled with a groan of pleasure and she smiled. "Everything seems to be in working order, though."

His hands gripped her hips, guiding her, helping her set a slow, deliberate pace that drove them both mad. Jake moaned as one hand rose to explore her body, first her breasts, then lower. His hand splayed over her belly before his thumb delved between her thighs to stroke her soft, slick flesh. She stiffened as her orgasm claimed her, arching her back, sending a shock wave of pleasure along her nerve endings. She collapsed against him, clutching his shoulders as his body contracted beneath hers. She closed her eyes and inhaled, trying to breathe normally. After a moment, Eamon settled the covers around them.

With some effort, she lifted her head to look down at him. "Shouldn't we get back in bed?"

"It's safer down here." He kissed the tip of her nose. "Go to sleep, Jake."

Despite the wisdom of his words, she lay awake, even long after his soft snore began to drone in her ears. Despite his slumberous state, his arms still held her. She snuggled against him, this man she loved, though she feared to acknowledge it too deeply, to dwell on it too much in her mind. And not because she worried that he didn't return the depth and breadth of her feelings, even though she did. More importantly, she didn't want to jinx herself or tempt whatever Fates might attend such mortal matters.

But now, while he slept, she couldn't resist one little flight into the face of providence. She leaned up to whisper in his ear, *"Je t'aime,* Eamon."

His arms tightened around her, but he slumbered on. Smiling, Jake laid her cheek against his chest. It would be all right. It had to be.

Seventeen

Jim was waiting for him when Eamon let himself into his apartment the next morning. Jim sat on the sofa, his feet propped on the coffee table. Eamon shrugged out of his jacket and tossed it onto the sofa beside Jim. "I didn't think you were going to be here until this afternoon."

"I decided to come by early to find out how Margot's snore-a-thon went last night. It never occurred to me that you would come slinking back home this morning in the same clothes you had on last night."

"Don't start," Eamon warned. He was in no mood to discuss Jake or anything else with his brother right now. He wasn't in the mood for Jim's cavalier sense of humor or Jim's penchant for obnoxious questions. But a mutual obligation to their uncle made Jim's presence necessary and also precluded Eamon from seeing Jake for the rest of the weekend.

"I haven't begun to start." Jim grinned and folded his hands over his chest. "So, you and Jake finally did the deed. It doesn't look like she put too much of a hurtin' on you."

That's where Jim was wrong. Jake's uninhibited love-making had moved him to a greater passion than he'd felt with any other woman, and her vulnerability had touched him.

Then there were the three words she'd whispered to him while he'd drowsed with her in his arms. *Je t'aime,*

Eamon. I love you, Eamon. Or he thought she'd whispered them to him. By the time his brain had roused itself enough for the English translation of what she'd said to take shape, Jake had fallen asleep. He couldn't bring himself to question her about it in the morning. What could he have said, anyway? By the way, did you tell me you loved me while I was sleeping last night or did I dream that because it was what I wanted to hear?

Besides, if she'd whispered those words to him when she thought he couldn't hear, he assumed that she hadn't really intended to share her feelings with him in the first place. He sighed, noting the curious look on Jim's face. To throw his brother off the scent, he said, "Give me a moment to change; then we can go."

"Whatever you say, big brother."

That's what Jim said, but Eamon suspected Jim wasn't through with him yet. Not by a long shot.

Jake had just finished washing the breakfast dishes when Liza and Dani burst into the apartment. Dani seemed full of energy; Liza looked as if someone had dragged her over a twenty-mile course—uphill.

Jake dried her hands on a dish towel and bent to hug Dani. "Did you have a good time, sweetheart?"

"Auntie Liza let me watch cartoons all night."

"Tattletale," Liza shot back.

"Why don't you go put your things away? I want to talk to Auntie Liza."

"Okay." With a wave to Liza, Dani skipped from the room.

Liza slumped into one of the kitchen chairs. "The next time I say I want kids, please remind me of this moment."

Jake giggled. "That bad?"

"I made the mistake of promising her she could watch this *Johnny Quest*-athon they had on one of the cartoon networks. Who knew it had so many episodes. I think I passed out on the sofa on the one with the camera that looks like a big red daddy longlegs. And to think I used to have a crush on Race Bannon."

While Liza spoke, Jake went to the coffeemaker and poured Liza a cup of the still-warm liquid. Jake set it in front of Liza and slid into the opposite seat. "That's what you get for being such a softy. Even I can get Dani to go to bed by ten o'clock."

Liza sipped from her cup. "Enough about me. How did it go last night? Did my handy reference guide help?"

Jake's cheeks colored. She'd known Liza would get around to asking her about the previous night. They'd always shared confidences before. Yet she didn't feel comfortable discussing her evening with Eamon. "How did you get all that done with Dani underfoot?"

"How do you think I got stuck watching nonstop *Quest?* I told her if she sat quietly on the sofa I'd let her watch whatever she wanted. I got off easy, considering it could have been WWF." Liza sighed. "I'm not asking for the gory details, you know. A thumbnail sketch will do."

An irrepressible grin spread across Jake's face and the urge assailed her to tell Liza that she finally knew what scream-your-head-off, sweat-rolling-down-your-back sex was like. Not only last night, but this morning, Eamon had brought her to such shattering climaxes that she'd probably woken half her neighbors.

Instead, she got up and poured herself a cup of coffee. She turned to face Liza, who watched her avidly. "All I'll say is that Eamon left here a half hour ago. So, yes, your reference guide came in handy. Just next time go with plain cotton sheets. We fell out of bed."

Liza covered her cheeks with her palms. "You didn't!"

"We did, though neither of us was complaining at the time."

"When are you going to tell him that you love him?"

"I did. In French. When he was asleep. I'm working my way up to English and conscious."

Shaking her head Liza stood. "I am so happy for you, sweetie. But I gotta go."

Jake sighed and set her coffee cup on the counter. Of the two of them, Liza was the one who had always sought out love or at least a bit of romance; Jake was the one who eschewed it. Somehow it didn't seem fair that Jake stood on the brink of having what Liza had always wanted.

Jake embraced her friend. It had occurred to Jake to introduce Liza to Jim, whom Eamon described as mooning over some woman. Maybe those two could do some good for each other. But Jake had ruined that possibility herself. She'd made the mistake of relating some of Jim's exploits to Liza. Now, rather than wanting to date him, Liza wanted to string him up for the sake of all womankind.

As they separated, Jake said, "Thanks. For everything."

Liza winked at her. "All in a day's work, but next time you two are on your own."

Jake grinned. "I think we can manage from here on in."

"Never doubted it for a second." Liza let herself out the door, closing it softly behind her.

For Eamon, the following week dragged on slowly. He moved downstairs into the corner office opposite Jim's, so he saw Jake every day. Although he picked Jake up every morning and brought her home every night, they had little time alone together. By mutual assent, they restrained from making love with Dani in the apartment. Ever since Jake's illness, Dani had woken at odd hours needing reassurance from Jake. They didn't want to chance her waking and walking in on them. By Friday night, the strain of being so near to her and not being with her was making him a little crazy.

Friday nights some of the staff met at a bar around the corner to share a drink and enjoy the free buffet. This week's get-together also served as a farewell party for those members leaving the staff. Eamon had never shown up to one of the Friday night gatherings before, though he had been invited. He figured his employees probably went there to blow off steam about work, and as he was the boss, they probably blew off about him, too. But knowing Jake would be there this time, he went.

By five-thirty, when he walked in the door, the gathering was in full steam. Destiny's Child wailed from the stereo speakers, and several couples were crowded into the little dance space created by pushing some of the small square tables against the wall. He spotted Jake almost immediately. She sat on one of the tall stools that lined the bar. The three kings, as she'd gotten him to think of them, as well as a few other male staffers surrounded her. A wild possessiveness seized him, a feeling as alien as it was unexpected. The men surrounding Jake must have sensed it too, as they disappeared as soon as he made his presence known.

Jake swiveled around to face him. "You should add 'ability to clear a room' to your list of talents."

She smiled up at him. He wanted nothing more than to drag her out of there to some place where they could be alone instead of surrounded by people. Instead, he lifted the drink from her fingers and set it on the bar. "Come dance with me."

She tilted her head to one side. *"You* want to dance to *this?"*

"Why not?"

She shrugged. "Doesn't seem like your style."

He couldn't argue with her, so he didn't bother. He held out his hand to her. "Come on." His voice sounded harsh to his own ears, but she put her hand in his and slid from the stool.

On the dance floor, he pulled her closer with his hands at her waist. When her arms looped around his neck, he pulled her closer still. Her perfume tickled his nose and her warmth heated his body. He tugged on a strand of her hair. "Now does it seem more like my style?"

She laughed. "A little."

He grinned. "That's because in my head I'm hearing 'The Way You Look Tonight' and remembering you coming apart in my arms."

She clamped her hand over his mouth and stared up at him wide-eyed. "I thought you were the one who wanted to maintain some decorum in the office."

"There's not a person here who doesn't know that something is going on between us."

"So, that's what this dance is about? Staking a public claim?"

"Maybe. Maybe I just wanted to hold you." He pulled her closer, closing the discreet distance he'd maintained between their bodies.

With a sigh of pleasure, she sank against him. For a time, they clung together, oblivious of the others. One of the more animated dancers jostled them, and he led Jake back to the bar to where she left her purse. His hand traveled upward to squeeze her nape. "Let's get out of here."

Jake nodded. "It's almost six o'clock. I'd better go pick up Dani."

"No need to. I talked Jim into giving you the night off. He's taking Dani to my place."

"Oh, really? I wondered why he wasn't here."

"You don't mind, do you?"

"Not at all. Let's go."

After saying their good-byes to the others, Eamon drove them to Jake's apartment. Once inside, Eamon pulled her into his arms. "What's the matter, sweetheart? You haven't said two words to me since we left the bar."

"There's nothing wrong with me, but you have definitely got to work on this control issue of yours."

"What control issue would that be?"

She shook her head as if she couldn't believe what he'd said. "You plan everything, without ever consulting me first." She pulled away from him, to go into the kitchen. She dropped her purse on the table.

"What are you talking about?"

"Who decided Dani and I should stay at your house after I got out of the hospital? You."

"You didn't have anywhere else to go."

"Not true, and you know it. You could have hired someone to stay with me here, but you never mentioned that and I was too out of it to think of it for myself."

He braced his shoulder against the wall, watching her. She didn't seem angry with him, so he wondered where she was going with this. "Are you accusing me of manipulating you into staying with me?"

"You never asked me if I wanted to go to your house on Montauk. You simply packed up the car and we left."

"And you didn't have a good time?"

"Of course I did, but that's beside the point. Even when we make love . . ." She trailed off, shaking her head.

"When we make love, what?"

"Wouldn't you say that every relationship involves a certain amount of give and take?"

"Yes," he said hesitantly, wondering what she was leading up to.

"It seems to me your definition of give and take is that you give and I take. There's a certain amount of control in that, wouldn't you say?"

"Maybe." He crossed his arms. "What are you suggesting?"

"I want you to let *me* make love to *you*."

Desire sizzled through him as quick and as hot as a lightning bolt. "Were you expecting me to object to that?"

"No. But honestly, I don't think you can do it." She walked toward him, slowly, her hips swaying, a seductive grin on her face. She stopped right in front of him and grasped his hands in hers. "Do you really think you can lie still and let me have my way with you?"

He gulped. "Not a problem."

"We'll see." She leaned up and pressed her mouth to his. He groaned as her tongue slid into his mouth and he moved to put his arms around her.

She broke the kiss and at the same time pushed his arms back against the wall. "See, two seconds into it and you can't even control yourself."

"I'm not even allowed to touch you?"

"Not unless I tell you to."

"Are there any other rules I should know?"

"I'll let you know as we go along." She tugged on his tie and pulled him down to her for a brief kiss. "We are now going to the bedroom."

"Lead on, MacDuff."

"Don't get cute on me."

"I wouldn't dream of it."

Once they stood by her bed, which had thankfully been made up with cotton sheets this time, she slid her arms around his neck and brought his mouth down on hers. Her fingers slid under his lapels, pushing his jacket from his shoulders. Next they went for his tie, loosening the knot and pulling it from his body. When she'd gotten the first two buttons of his shirt undone, she reached around him and freed his shirt from his waistband. "I have to hand it to you. I didn't think you'd last this long."

Neither did he. His hands fisted at his sides, fighting the urge to touch her. "Weren't you the one who thought I'd use my willpower and refuse to make love to her last week?"

Her hands wandered over his chest, then returned to

his buttons. "That was different. You thought you might hurt me. Under those circumstances, who wouldn't find it easy to refuse? But that barrier has been removed."

She spread his shirt and her fingers roamed over his bare chest. He gritted his teeth as her thumbs strummed over his nipples. Her lips made a trail of soft, moist kisses along his collarbone. But when she lowered her mouth to lap her tongue over his nipple, he groaned her name.

"Yes, Eamon?"

Her warm breath fanned over his moist, heated skin. Her hand slid lower to cup his erection and he jerked. She squeezed him and his eyes drifted shut and his breathing hitched. Then her hands were at his waistband unfastening his belt. He sucked in his breath as she pushed aside his clothes to free him. His eyes squeezed shut as her soft fingers caressed him. "Jake."

"Sit down."

The bed was directly behind him. He sat and undid his shirt cuffs as she removed the remainder of his clothing. He tossed the shirt onto the pile with the rest. His eyes burned and his body hummed as he watched her strip out of her blouse and skirt. She sat down on the bed to roll off her panty hose. He couldn't resist skimming his hand over her bare stomach.

She smacked his hand away. "No touching, counselor. I'll have to cite you with contempt."

He leaned back against the pillows and pulled her on top of him. "Cite away." His fingers went to the front clasp of her bra and unfastened it. Her breasts spilled out into his hands. He rolled her nipples between his thumbs and index fingers. He was rewarded with one of those throaty sounds he loved, but she pushed his hands away.

She slipped out of her bra and tossed it to the floor. "Behave yourself," she warned. She leaned down and took his nipple into her mouth. He sucked his breath in through his teeth from the sheer pleasure of having her mouth on him. But she wasn't finished with him yet. She trailed a path of soft, moist kisses across his chest to suckle his other nipple. Her mouth and her hands roved lower, over his abdomen and lower. She knelt between his legs with her hands resting on his hips. "Think you can stand a little more?"

He looked at her with half-closed eyes. A lopsided grin lit her face. She was enjoying having him at her mercy. In truth, he didn't have any complaints either. "Maybe."

He knew what she intended to do, but when she took him into her mouth, he nearly came off the bed. His fingers gripped the bedcovers and his eyes squeezed shut as her mouth moved over him. His heartbeat trebled and a sheen of perspiration broke out on his skin. His hips rocked upward and he called her name. He didn't know how much of this sweet torture he could take without losing it completely. And he wanted to be inside her, to please her, to hold her while she came in his arms.

She took pity on him, coming to straddle his waist. She leaned forward to retrieve a condom from the dresser. He took it from her and rolled it onto his shaft himself. He didn't trust his own reaction if she put her hands on him again. While he did so, she removed her panties and positioned herself over him. He groaned, a low, guttural sound, as her body enveloped him.

And then she started to move over him, not the slow, deliberate pace he would have set, but a wild ride that stole his breath and robbed him of any control whatsoever. His hands gripped her hips, not to control her, but as a means of hanging on as she drove them both to the brink of ecstasy. He was touching her, but she was beyond objecting, beyond anything except seeking the rapture just beyond her reach.

She leaned over him, bracing her hands on his shoulders. He sat up and took her nipple into his mouth. Her fingers dug into his shoulders as she contracted around him, calling his name. He pulled her down, crushing her to him as he thrust into her over and over again, prolonging her orgasm. But he couldn't hold back any longer. He squeezed his eyes shut as his own orgasm rushed over him like an all-consuming wave that left no part of him untouched. He pressed her to him as his back arched and his body spasmed, rocked by the power of his release.

For a long time, they lay together, each trying to recover. As their bodies cooled, he pulled the edge of the blanket over to cover them. He stroked his hands over Jake's back. Her breathing had normalized a little, but her heart beat rapidly against his palm. "Are you okay?"

She lifted her head and looked down at him. "I'm fine. A little disappointed to find that the man I'm in love with has so little self-control, but otherwise I'm fine."

Every nerve ending in his body froze. He cupped her smiling face in his palms. "What did you say?"

"I said I love you, Eamon."

She buried her face against his neck. He hugged her to him. "I love you, too, Jake."

"I know."

He tilted her so that she lay beside him where he could see her face. "How do you know?"

"Liza told me. She said no man went to so much trouble for any woman he didn't love."

He chuckled. Maybe he'd have to revise his opinion of what Liza knew and didn't know.

She touched her fingertips to his cheek. "But it can't be lopsided like it has been. Every time I need something I don't want you to come charging in providing it—a job or a place to stay or whatever. I'm a grown adult. I can take care of myself."

"Baby, I know that." He stroked her back, examining his own motives. "You know, all my life, I've been the responsible one. When my parents died, I went from being a little kid to being almost totally responsible for myself and Jim. We lived with my uncle, but he was busy trying to keep a roof over our heads and run the magazine that had been my parents' dream. The day-to-day stuff of getting to school and putting food on the table and keeping Jim out of trouble, that fell on me.

"And as a lawyer, people literally put their lives in my hands. The decisions I made, the advice I gave could mean the difference between a life in prison or a life on the streets. It was an obligation I took seriously. I can't turn it off as easily as you would like."

"I'm not asking you to turn it off, just moderate it a little. Believe me, I appreciate everything you have done for me, but either we are in this together or each of us will end up alone."

"I know, Jake." He trailed his index finger along her cheekbone. "Maybe you could do something for me?"

"What's that?"

"Order us some dinner. I'm starved."

She shook her head. "You are such a man."

"Don't you forget it."

She laughed. "I've got menus for pizza and Chinese, or I could cook something for you."

"That won't be necessary. Pizza will be fine, with pepperoni. Spicy foods are supposed to be an aphrodisiac."

She shook her head again. "What am I going to do with you?"

He winked at her. "Hurry back and you'll find out."

Jake pulled on her robe and padded out to the kitchen barefoot. She found the menu and ordered the pizza, which would supposedly be there in twenty minutes. After she clicked off the cordless phone, she lingered at the kitchen table. She'd gone and done it.

She'd told Eamon she loved him. While she relished
hearing he loved her from his own lips, a shudder of
foreboding shivered through her.

Jake sighed—she was being ridiculous. God or the Fates
or the universe had better things to do than monitor her
happiness only to snatch it away. She stood, straightening
her spine. Eamon was waiting for her. There was no telling
what that man might accomplish in twenty minutes.

Eighteen

Eamon woke with a start just after daybreak. He'd dreamed that he and Jake were being consumed by an inferno. He rubbed the sleep from his eyes. The warmth that had wakened him came from a shaft of bright morning sunlight, the cocoon of covers, and the heat of Jake's sleeping body.

He rose from their bed and padded to the half bath in the corner of the room. He relieved himself, washed his hands and face, and squirted a glob of toothpaste into his mouth. He rinsed his mouth and turned off the tap. As he did so, his gaze caught on his reflection in the mirror above the sink. God, he looked like hell. Rubbing his palm over his chin, he lamented the lack of a razor. He tended to look more like Grizzly Adams than Don Johnson if he didn't shave in the morning.

He flicked off the bathroom light, but paused in the open doorway, watching Jake sleep. She'd sprawled out in the space he'd abandoned. Her sweet derriere pointed upward, taunting him. She shifted again to lay on her side facing him. "Good morning."

"Did I wake you?"

"Not at all. I'm usually up this early on Saturday. I try to get some work done before Dani wakes up."

"What sort of work?"

"Cleaning up, mostly. Or I use the time to sketch or sew."

"You sew? What do you know, you're a Jake-of-all-trades."

She groaned. "How else do you think I manage to dress myself? I'm a poor working girl."

"Lord knows you can't spend much on fabric."

She laughed. "Let me know if you plan to stand there all day. I'll get my sketch pad."

"How about you join me in the shower instead?"

"You've got a deal."

Under the warm spray of the water, they took turns lathering and rinsing each other's bodies. Once they stepped from the shower, he toweled her dry, then wrapped another around his waist.

Jake slipped into one of the robes she kept on the back of the door. "The other robe is for you. It's one of my brother's but I'm sure it will fit. Take your time. I'm going to make breakfast."

His body shivered, taking that for the threat it was. She really was a hazard in the kitchen. For her next birthday he was giving her cooking lessons from the CIA. He shrugged into the robe, surprised to find a razor in one pocket and a toothbrush in the other. He shook his head. This transparent woman he'd fallen in love with was suddenly full of surprises.

They ate snuggled in a corner of the living room sofa. Eamon took a last sip from his coffee cup and placed it on the coffee table. "I should get going if you don't want me to be here when Dani gets home."

She grasped his biceps. "Don't go. If you are going to be a part of our lives, Dani needs to get used to seeing us together. Maybe you can make yourself useful later and put a lock on the bedroom door."

"Maybe." But he contemplated her use of the word *if*. If he was going to be part of her life. As far as he knew, he wasn't going anywhere. The way she pressed herself against him suggested she didn't want him anywhere but with her. So why did that one word bother him so much?

"Speaking of Dani, her birthday is next week. She wants to have her birthday party here, just a few friends from school, and of course you and Jim and Liza. I'd do it at McDonald's or the Pumpkin Patch, except it doesn't really pay unless you have ten kids or more. And if you do have more than ten kids you pray for a lobotomy."

Eamon chuckled. "I might have a special guest for the celebration."

"Unless it's The Rock you may be disappointed by the reception you get."

"I'm not worried."

She giggled. "I was talking about me, not the kids. Have you seen that man?"

"Oh, really?" He tickled her and she squirmed and straddled his lap. With her arms around his neck, her mouth claimed his. She brushed aside the fabric of their robes and her body enveloped him, and for a while all he could think of was the rapture to come.

It was late afternoon when Jim finally showed up with Dani. When Jake opened the door, Dani flew into her arms. "Guess where Uncle Jim took me."

Jake sniffed. "From the smell of it, I'd say the local pigsty."

"We went up to the Bronx Zoo," Jim explained. "In the children's section you can feed the animals. Dani was very popular with the geese they've got running around loose."

Jake looked Dani over. "You are filthy, young lady. You are getting into the bathtub right now."

"Aww, Jake," Dani protested.

Eamon chuckled as the two of them passed him on the way to the bathroom. His humor died when he saw the suddenly grim set of Jim's face. "What's the matter with you? The ewes didn't swoon when you passed by?"

Jim slid into the seat at the dining room table Jake had vacated and shot him a castigating look. "I wanted to say this with the two of them out of the room. Yesterday when I went to pick up Dani at camp, I think someone was watching her."

Eamon sat up, giving Jim his full attention. "What do you mean?"

"You know how they have that little yard in the back where the kids play until the parents pick them up?"

Eamon nodded.

"When I got there yesterday, I noticed a woman, short, maybe five-two, black hair, standing by the fence looking in. I'd swear she was looking at Dani, though she had sunglasses on. When I walked toward her, she got into the backseat of a gray Mercedes and drove away. I didn't get the license plate number."

Eamon leaned back in his chair. Both the make of the car and the fact that the woman had a driver suggested a person of some means. The only woman Eamon could think of who might have an interest in Dani was her mother. Jake once told him that Dani's mother had come from a poor family and hadn't taken a dime from her brother when she left him. But six years was a long time in which anyone's fortunes could change.

Then again, Jim could be totally wrong and the woman he'd seen had simply enjoyed watching children play, but he didn't think so. He focused on his brother. "Thanks for telling me. Do me a favor and don't say anything to Jake about this."

Jim stood. "If that's how you want it, but I think you should say something to her. What if this woman is some sort of psycho?"

"I'll take care of it."

Jim shrugged. "It's your call, but I think you should tell her."

Eamon locked the door after Jim left. It would be easy enough to find out if Dani's mother was the woman Jim had seen. Easy too to make sure no one, not even Dani's mother, got to her. If he found out that this woman posed any threat to Dani, then he'd tell Jake. There was no point in worrying her if it turned out to be nothing.

Remembering Jake's words from the previous night, he knew she wouldn't appreciate what he was doing. He didn't care. His first priority was keeping Jake and Dani safe. If he offended her sensibilities by doing so behind her back, then so be it.

He only hoped Jake saw it that way when she found out.

The morning of Dani's birthday party, Jake woke content with her life and excited about the day ahead. Eamon had spent several passion-filled nights with her that week, last night included. Her body tingled anew just thinking of all the wild and wicked things they had done to each other in this very bed where they slept.

Oddly, the nights Eamon spent with her were the only ones Dani slept straight through. Maybe having both of them there gave Dani an added sense of security. Jake didn't know and didn't care. All was right in her little corner of Greenwich Village; that was enough for her.

Like most mornings he stayed with her, Eamon had wrapped himself around her in spoon fashion. His snore sounded in her ear, but the way his hands explored her body suggested he must be at least partly awake.

His lips touched down on her temple. "Morning."

"Morning yourself." Her breathing hitched as his hand delved between her thighs. "What do you think you are doing?"

"While you were asleep I was copping a cheap feel. Now that you're awake, I'm making love to you."

She laughed and reached back to caress his stubbly chin. "As long as we make that distinction." Her humor died and her eyes squeezed shut as he thrust into her. Out of necessity, she bit her lip instead of crying out like she wanted to. They'd made love in a variety of positions, in the shower, on the living room sofa, even once against the wall in the hallway. Their lovemaking had been wild and erotic and slow and gentle. But somehow this time seemed different from all the rest. His hands on her body and his movements within her were tender, almost worshipful. Before she knew it, she tumbled over the precipice wrapped in his arms. Afterward, unaccountably, she felt like weeping. She turned in his arms and buried her face against his chest.

His arms closed around her, warming her, soothing her—until he leaned down to kiss her cheek. "I need to talk with you about something."

Judging by the solemn timbre of his voice, it wasn't a pleasant something. She shook her head and burrowed closer to him. *Not now,* her mind screamed. She'd known from the beginning that this couldn't last. She'd known something or someone would come along to destroy the only true happiness she'd known in years. While she knew she could handle almost anything he might tell her, she couldn't bear to hear it now. Not when only moments ago she'd thought everything in her world was finally okay.

But her innate curiosity wouldn't let her remain in ignorance. She mustered her courage and whispered against his ear, "Does this have to do with us?"

His arms closed tighter around her and lips touched down on her shoulder. "Indirectly. It has to do with—"

She covered his mouth with her fingertips. "Will it affect the outcome of today?"

He shook his head. "Probably not."

"Is anyone sick, dead, or dying?"

"Not so far as I know."

"Then can we talk about it later? In a little over five hours, six seven-year-olds are going to be running all over, wrecking the place."

"If that's what you want. But I really do need to talk to you tonight."

"I promise." She snuggled against him, until a loud knock sounded at the door.

Dani's voice, muffled and indignant, reached them. "The birthday girl is awake out here, you know."

Jake rolled her eyes. "The fun begins."

As expected, Liza was the first to arrive. Jake opened the door to her a little after ten o'clock. Jake did a double take when she saw her friend. Liza had cut her shoulder-length black hair into a spiky pixie style.

"When did you get that done?"

"Two days ago." Liza fingered the hair at her nape as she entered the apartment. "You hate it."

Jake shut the door. "Not at all. It's different."

"I wanted a change, but I'm still not used to not having hair." Liza set her bag down in the kitchen as the two women entered it. "Where's Dani?"

"She and Eamon are still perfecting the magic act they intend to dazzle Dani's guest with. Or Dani plans to dazzle them. I think Eamon's just hanging on for the ride."

Liza laughed. "That poor man."

"Oh, make no mistake, he's enjoying every minute of it. But Dani can be a bit much to handle."

"Don't I know it! Now, what can I help you with?"

By noon, they had decorated the apartment with every manner of Spiderman paraphernalia, including a giant web Jake had crocheted from gray yarn and hung in the archway leading to the dining room. Jake had set out chips and dip to snack on. Later pizza would arrive for the kids along with an assortment of Italian dishes for the adults. After all the preparations were complete, the two women enjoyed a moment of solitude at the dining room table.

Jake checked her watch. Eleven forty-three. "T minus seventeen minutes and counting."

"Now you're scaring me," Liza said.

"Not to worry. I've got a couple of bottles of merlot chilling for after the little people leave."

"I knew there was a reason I liked you."

Jake laughed, but the doorbell sounded. Somebody's mother must be anxious to get rid of her little darling for the afternoon. Jake winked at Liza. "Show time."

Nineteen

Three hours later, after pizza, pasta, and cake and ice cream had been consumed and most of the apartment had been demolished, Jake stood at the doorway helping Dani bid her last guests good-bye. After she closed the door, Jake turned to Dani. "Did you have a good time, Dani?"

"It was the best, Jake." Dani threw her arms around her. "Thanks, Jake."

Jake gave her a squeeze. "You're welcome, sweetheart."

Dani turned and ran to Eamon, who sat at the kitchen table with Liza. "And thanks for being my assistant, Uncle Eamon."

He lifted her onto his lap. "You're welcome, short stuff. You did a terrific job."

Jake leaned against the archway wall. Dani had done a great job. Dressed in a black cape Jake had sewn for her and a tiny top hat Eamon had found for her, Dani had performed the marvelous feats of turning a silk scarf into a handkerchief, "removing" a knot from a rope, and putting a pencil through a paper cup full of water. But the most well received trick was her grand finale where she used a chick pan to produce a trayful of Hershey's Kisses. The kids had gobbled them up and gone on a sugar rampage after that.

The doorbell rang again. Jake's gaze slid to Liza. "Could someone have forgotten something?"

Liza shrugged. "Not that I know of."

"Jim!" Jake said when she opened the door to find him on the other side holding a large shopping bag. "I was beginning to hate you for blowing off Dani's birthday."

"Not a chance." He embraced her with his free arm. He leaned in to whisper in her ear, "I can do without the kids, though."

"Uncle Jim." Dani ran up to embrace him. "What did you get me?"

"Dani," Jake scolded. "It's not polite to ask people things like that."

Dani looked back at her, seeming to digest that. "Did you get me something, Uncle Jim?"

Jake shook her head in surrender. "I give up."

"Of course I brought you something." Jim presented the package. "Happy birthday, munchkin."

Dani accepted the heavy bag from him. "Can I open it now, Jake?"

"Sure."

"Maybe I better carry it," Jake volunteered.

Dani scooted ahead of them into the kitchen.

Jim draped an arm around Jake's shoulders as the two of them followed. "Where's the big guy?" Jim asked.

"Right here." Eamon stood to greet his brother. "It's about time you showed up,"

Jim stopped midstride and his hand fell away from Jake's shoulders. But his attention didn't seem to be on his brother. Jake followed the line of his gaze to Liza, who was still clutching her glass. Liza stared back at Jim with a stunned, openmouthed expression on her face. Of the two of them, Liza recovered first. She took a step away from him. "You."

Jim's brow furrowed as he shook his head. "What the hell have you done to your hair?"

And then the contents of Liza's glass found its way into Jim's face. A horrified expression came over Liza's face and her mouth worked but no sound came out. Suddenly, she whirled and fled from the kitchen.

Jim grabbed a Spiderman napkin from the table and ran it along his face. "Excuse me." He stalked out of the kitchen the way Liza had gone.

For a moment the three remaining in the kitchen said nothing. Then Dani broke the silence. "Somebody's got issues."

"Dani!" both Jake and Eamon said in unison.

Jake looked at Eamon. Dani had simply voiced the thought on all their minds.

Eamon shrugged. "I have a feeling we've just discovered the mystery woman Jim's been mooning about for the past two months."

Jake sighed. And the mystery man Liza lamented leaving during her trip to Florida. Although Jake had known at some point that both of them had been in the same state at the same time, it had never occurred to her that they had met there when she couldn't even get them together in New York where they both lived. The irony of it brought a smile to her lips. "What do you suppose they're doing?"

"If she's got any sense, she's knocked him into next week by now."

As Jake recalled, Liza had already tried that. "Just what I need, bloodshed to go along with that grape juice stain in the carpet." Then to divert everyone's attention she said, "Dani, why don't you open Uncle Jim's present?"

Jake needn't have worried about where Dani's interest lay. She had already worked free part of one flap of the wrapping paper. Eamon lifted the rectangular gift from the bag and set it on the table so that Dani could attack the wrapping paper in earnest. Once Dani got most of the paper off, she shouted, "Yes."

"Oh, no," Jake said, staring down at the partially revealed X-Box carton. Dani had been begging for one since the video game system had come out, but a six-hundred-dollar toy hadn't been in the family budget. Nor was Jake certain she wanted Dani exposed to a game like this so early. She'd rather Dani spent most of her time reading or doing projects with Jake as she did now. The video game would change that. "I'm going to kill him."

"Stand in line." Liza pushed through the swinging doors to enter the kitchen.

"Come on, Dani. Let's see if between you, me, and Jim, we can't figure out how to hook this thing up," Eamon suggested.

Once the two of them cleared out, Jake motioned for Liza to sit, then poured each of them a glass of wine. She extended one to Liza. "You're only allowed to have this if you promise not to throw it at anybody."

Liza took a sip and placed the glass on the table. "I can't believe I did that. It was such a shock seeing him and when he made that comment about my hair, I freaked."

"To put it mildly." Jake slid into the seat next to Liza. "Now forgive me if I'm wrong, but the last time we discussed this mystery man of yours, you were feeling guilty for having run out on him the way you did. You finally see him again and you throw your wine in his face? I don't get it. What changed things for you?"

"You did. You told me all about Eamon's younger brother, Love-'Em-and-Leave-'Em Jim. Pardon-Me-If-I-Can't-Commit Jim, I-Have-the-Mentality-of-a-High-School-Senior Jim. Forgive me for being Not-Going-There-Again Liza."

Jake sighed. "Me and my big mouth. I only told you those things about Jim to cheer you up, as in at least you're not pining away over this guy. Sure, Jim is all the things I told you about him, but that's not all he is."

"Well, that's all he is to me."

While Liza sipped her wine, Jake sat back, studying

her friend. For all her bluster, Liza didn't seem angry, just upset. Color suffused her cheeks, and her eyes seemed overly bright, but not with the sheen of tears. Liza's fingers trembled slightly as she set her glass on the table, making Jake wonder exactly what had gone on in her bedroom to make Liza so agitated.

"By the way, what happened to that lovely shade of red lipstick you were wearing up until a few moments ago?"

Liza's hand flew up to cover her lips. "He kissed me. Mostly to shut me up, I guess. And fool that I am, I let him. Good Lord, Jake, does that man know how to use a pair of lips!"

"It must be a family secret."

Liza shot her a castigating look. "Don't try to humor me out of this, Jake. Here I was beating myself up for deserting a decent guy, when that's what he *does*, Jake. He probably would have sent me a thank-you note for disappearing and saving him the trouble of throwing me out."

Jake shook her head. "I know for a fact that's not true."

Liza stood. "Whatever. I'm going to fix my face, say good night to Dani, and go home. I can't deal with this right now." Liza snatched up her purse from the table and headed out of the kitchen in the direction of the bathroom.

Jake rested her elbows on the table and put her face in her hands. It had been an exhausting day and it was only five o'clock in the afternoon. While everyone else was occupied, she might as well start cleaning up. But just as she rose from her chair, the doorbell sounded.

She opened the door to a stylishly dressed older woman, probably in her late fifties, with graying black hair and a dimple in each cheek. "Can I help you?"

"Is this the McKenna residence?"

"Come in, Barbara. You're in the right place."

Jake hadn't heard Eamon approach, but suddenly he

was beside her welcoming a stranger into her home. Eamon had mentioned a mystery guest, but who was this woman? The woman turned and motioned to someone behind her as if directing them to come along. A few moments later, an older man appeared in the doorway, tall, with salt-and-pepper hair, a handsome face, and familiar ice-blue eyes.

"Jake," Eamon said, "I'd like you to meet my uncle Eamon. Uncle Eamon, this is Jacqueline McKenna, who makes us call her Jake."

"It's a pleasure to meet you." Jake extended her hand, then froze noting the vacant look in Eamon's uncle's eyes. "Welcome."

"And this lovely lady is Barbara Blake, Uncle Eamon's companion."

"Flatterer," Barbara accused before extending a hand toward Jake. "I'm pleased to meet you, although I have to confess Papa and I were a bit surprised at first when we heard Eamon was seeing someone named Jake."

Jake laughed. "I can imagine you would be. Please come in."

Barbara started to cross the threshold, but Uncle Eamon had a death grip on her arm and he wasn't budging. A look of stubborn apprehension came over his face. "Barbara, where are we? Who are these people?"

For a moment no one spoke. Jake focused on Eamon. His jaw was tight, his body rigid. Clearly he hadn't expected that reaction from his uncle.

Barbara broke the silence. "That's your nephew, Eamon, and his girlfriend, Jake. We are in her home."

"Nephew?" The elder Eamon gazed at the younger, a concentrated look as if he was trying to remember something, but he allowed Barbara to lead him into the apartment. Jake watched them for a moment, noting that Jim had come out of Dani's room and waited at the end of the hallway. She'd let Jim take care of his uncle for a moment. Her concern now was for Eamon. When he started to follow the older couple, she grasped his arm and turned to face him.

"I thought your uncle was in Europe."

"He was, until two weeks ago."

"And I suppose Barbara, the woman who calls him Papa and looks at him as if he's Michaelangelo's *David,* is the gold digger you told me about. Why didn't you tell me about your uncle's condition? Is it Alzheimer's?"

Eamon nodded. "I've never seen him like that before. He's always known who I was at least. Barbara says he's deteriorated in the last couple of months, and I see now that she's right."

Jake slipped into his arms and hugged him. "I'm so sorry, Eamon."

His arms closed around her and he buried his face against her neck. "I wanted to introduce him to Dani. She told me she never knew any of her grandparents. I thought she might enjoy meeting him. I'm not sure that's such a good idea now."

"Dani will handle it just fine. How are you doing?"

"It's hard, Jake, watching someone you think of as strong and vital wither away. I remember when we came to live with him when we were kids. At a time when he should have been a young, carefree man, perhaps looking to start a family of his own, he put his life on hold to take care of us. We were devastated, Jim and I. To cheer us up, he told us stories of the places he wanted to go and the things he wanted to see. With two small children to take care of, all it ever amounted to was dreams."

He sighed and leaned back against he wall. "In many ways, he lived a George Baileyesque sort of life—sacrificing his own desires for the needs and responsibilities of others. Once Jim and I were on our own, he still felt obligated to make the magazine, which had been my father's vision, viable."

"That's why you sent him to Europe?"

Eamon lifted one shoulder. "Jim and I did. We thought we could give him back a little of what our presence in his life cost him. The only problem is, now I'm not sure he'll even remember it."

She didn't know what to say to him, so she simply held him, resting her cheek against his chest. She realized, too, that she'd misjudged him. Up until that moment, she'd assumed when Eamon took control of the magazine his primary concern had been that his uncle had been squandering the family fortunes, either through incompetence as he'd first led her to believe, or because of illness as she now knew. He was a more complex man than she gave him credit for being.

Jake lifted her head and gazed into his eyes. She finally knew the adjective she wanted: inscrutable—like she could study him for a million years and never really know what made him tick. At the moment she didn't need to understand him. "I love you, Eamon," she whispered.

He tugged on a strand of her hair and his smile grew cocky. "I know."

She tilted her head to one side. "Who do you think you are—Han Solo?"

"Right now, I'm whoever you want me to be."

"How about the man who helps me entertain his relatives and roust mine out of their hidey-holes?"

He shook his head. "Why don't you see what the crowd in the living room is up to? I'll take care of Dani and Liza."

"It's a deal."

Fifteen minutes later, after she had served everyone their food or drink of choice, Jake took a seat on the sofa next to Liza. She had no idea what Eamon had said to Liza to get her to stay, but she was grateful he'd succeeded. She hadn't wanted Liza to leave in such an agitated state. Even now, Jake sensed a brittleness in

Liza, and the studious way she avoided looking at Jim, who watched her from across the room.

Jake leaned closer to Liza. "Where are Eamon and Dani?"

"Probably still defending the earth from virtual attack by alien invaders. They got the video game hooked up and Dani launched into it like a pro."

"It figures. Next she'll expect me to go broke buying fifty-dollar video games."

Just then Eamon appeared in the hallway holding Dani's hand. He brought her over to where his uncle sat. "Dani, this is my uncle Eamon. Uncle Eamon, this is Dani, Jake's niece."

Jake held her breath, wondering what would come of this encounter. Dani stepped forward, appearing to study the old man's face. "Are you very old?" she said finally.

Uncle Eamon chuckled. "I suppose so."

"Do you have fake teeth?"

"Dani," Jake scolded. She'd let the first question slide, but the second was too much.

Uncle Eamon waved a hand at her. "Let the child be." He sat forward a little, and Jake noted a new clarity in his blue eyes. "Why do you want to know?"

"I saw a man on TV take his out and all he had left were gums."

"That must have been something."

"Oh, it was. So, do your teeth come out?"

Jake didn't hear the answer to Dani's question, as her attention was diverted by Eamon coming to sit on the arm of the sofa beside her. He took her hand and held it on his lap. "I'll give Dani this, she's persistent."

Jake laughed. "I think your uncle likes her."

"He always was a sucker for kids. That's why it's such a shame he never had any of his own."

"What do you mean I didn't have children of my own? Every gray hair on my head I owe to you and that brother of yours." Uncle Eamon nodded in Jim's direction. "If that doesn't make you a parent, I don't know what does."

Eamon leaned closer to her and said in a stage whisper, "Did I also mention he always had the ears of a bat?"

"I needed them to keep up with the two of you, always plotting some mischief."

For the next hour, Uncle Eamon recounted humorous stories of raising Eamon and Jim, most of which either one or the other refused to own up to. Feeling Eamon's tension ease helped Jake relax, too. Even Liza had loosened up a bit thanks to the good company and another glass of merlot. This room held all the people Jake loved and those she could grow to love, her own little makeshift family, bonded not by blood but by affection. She glanced around the room at the smiling faces, heard the laughter, and grew content.

Eamon squeezed her hand and nodded toward his uncle. Dani had fallen asleep in his lap and Uncle Eamon appeared to be running out of steam as well. Although she hated to end the evening, she didn't want to tire him further. And with any luck, there would be other evenings like this.

Eamon lifted Dani into his arms, and together Jake and Eamon saw the guests to the door. Jim left on his own while Barbara and Uncle Eamon promised to drop Liza at her apartment. Jake closed and locked the door, then turned to face Eamon. "Despite a rocky beginning, that went well." And for Eamon's sake, she was glad his uncle had regained lucidity rather quickly.

Eamon winked at her. "I'm going to put the Denture Queen in her bed. Then I'll help you clean up."

"Sounds like a plan." Jake started to straighten the kitchen table when a knock sounded on the front door.

Jake made a face. "Who put the sign for Grand Central Station on my door?" She pulled open the door to find the person she least expected to see again in this world. Jake surveyed the woman who stood on her doorstep. Her straight black hair had been cut in a style shorter than Jake remembered it. Her designer outfit and Coach handbag bespoke a wealth she hadn't known as Dan's wife. Her face bore a confident expression that would have been alien to her six years ago. Jake's first, childish impulse was to slam the door in her face. Instead she straightened her spine and fastened one of Eamon's stares on the woman. "It's been a long time, Sylvia."

Twenty

"Yes, it's been a long time, Jake. Too long."

Jake shook her head. To her mind it hadn't been long enough. "What do you want, Sylvia?"

"I was hoping to see Dani on her birthday. Is she still awake?"

"No." But even if she were, Jake would never allow Dani to have contact with this woman without preparing her first.

She looked away and for the first time her confidence seemed shaken. "Could you please give this to Dani for me, then?"

Jake focused on the FAO Schwarz shopping bag in Sylvia's hand. A large package wrapped in Power Puff Girl wrapping paper filled the bag. "What is it?"

"A birthday present for Dani. A collector's-edition Barbie."

"Dani doesn't play with dolls."

Sylvia swallowed. "She's a beautiful little girl, Jake. You've done a wonderful job with her."

"Somebody had to." And then a thought occurred to her. "You've seen Dani."

"Just from the other side of the school yard fence. I never spoke to her or even approached her." Sylvia sighed. "Look, Jake, I know this isn't the best of ways to come back into your lives. I probably should have called first or found some other way to let you know I was back in New York. It took me all day to muster up the nerve to show up here now . . ."

Did Sylvia honestly expect her to feel sorry for her? "Then you spent your day worrying for nothing. There's nothing here for you, Sylvia, not anymore. I will pass on your gift to Dani, if she wants it. We have nothing more to discuss."

Sylvia set the package down on the inside of the door against the wall. "That's not true, Jake." Sylvia pulled a business card from her purse. She extended it toward Jake. "If you don't want this ending up in court, I suggest you have your attorney contact mine."

Jake stared at the card a minute before taking it. Sylvia turned and walked away in the direction of the elevator. Jake shut the door and leaned against it, crushing the card in her fist. In all her imaginings of gloom and doom, she hadn't expected this. She'd always assumed that if the Fates wanted to punish her, they'd take away her lover, not her child. To find Eamon and lose Dani, that was too high a price to pay.

She sank down to the floor, her back braced against the door. Tears pooled in her eyes and she let them spill down her cheeks unchecked. She drew her legs up and rested her cheek against her knees. Did she really have Eamon, either? Even now, she wondered how much of her attractiveness to him was based on the fact that she came with a ready-made family to replace the one he'd lost. If she lost Dani, would she lose him, too?

The only thing she knew with certainty was that if she lost either of them it would devastate her. To lose them both would kill her. The only question she needed answered was how much life intended to take away from her.

"Jake?"

Eamon returned to the kitchen expecting to find Jake there. But the kitchen was empty and virtually unchanged since he'd last seen it. "Jake?"

He got no answer, but he heard her sniffle. He found her seated by the front door, her knees drawn up, her head down. Although she faced away from him, it was obvious she was crying.

Alarm rippled through him, as he strode toward her. He sat beside her and pulled her into his arms. "Jake, sweetheart, what happened? Who was that at the door?"

"Dani's mother. She brought her a birthday present. And this." Jake held out a crumpled business card. "She suggests I have my lawyer call her lawyer if I don't want a custody battle in the courts."

Eamon uncrumpled it and read the name of a lawyer who worked for a prominent Park Avenue firm. *Damn!* Ever since he'd discovered that the woman Jim had seen was definitely Dani's mother, Eamon had known that she wasn't simply curious about her daughter. She wanted something, and the only motive ruled out was money. Her new husband came from one of the wealthiest black families in Atlanta.

"Eamon, I can't lose Dani, I can't. She's all I have left of my family."

"Listen to me, Jake, I'm no expert in family law, but I doubt any judge in his right mind would award custody to a woman who abandoned her child for six years."

"You lawyers," Jake accused. "You think just because a thing is legal that makes it right. I'm not talking about being afraid that the courts will award Sylvia custody, at least not mostly that. What if Dani wants to be with her mother? Think about it, Eamon. As much as you love your uncle, if it came down to a choice of being with your mother or being with him, which would you choose?"

"Obviously my mother. But then I have memories of my mother. She always smelled like flowers and she loved pistachio ice cream and she read every word Isaac Asimov ever wrote. I remember one time when I was eleven,

I threatened to run away because I thought my father had punished me unfairly. She said I could go, but I could only take with me things that I'd bought with my own money, because otherwise that was stealing—and that included the clothes I was wearing."

"What did you do?"

"I stalked up to my room and slammed the door. I wasn't crazy enough to leave the house naked at four o'clock in the afternoon. But later that night when she brought dinner to my room she told me she was glad I'd changed my mind, because if I'd left it would have broken her heart."

"Don't you see, Jake? Dani doesn't have any memories of Sylvia. In years to come when Dani recalls the woman who was her mother, she'll be thinking about you."

He ran his knuckles down her cheek, in a soothing caress. "I'm so sorry it's come to this. When I found out Dani's mother was in New York, I figured she'd want to see Dani, but I never expected her to show up here today."

Jake pulled away from him enough to see his face. "You knew? For how long?"

"Last week, Jim spotted a woman watching the children in the camp's play yard. It turned out to be Dani's mother."

"And you didn't bother to tell me this?"

"I tried to this morning. If I'd had any idea she'd show up here today, I would have tried harder to get you to listen to me."

"Okay. I'll give you that, but what about the other six days you've known? I told you I wouldn't stand for you taking over my life again like this." She rose to her feet and backed away from him. "I think you should go now."

He stood, too, and took a step toward her. "I can't do that, Jake. You're being unfair to me. I don't know any other man who in my position would have done anything differently. And not because I wanted to control you, but because I wanted to protect you and Dani. At first, I didn't know if there was anything to worry about."

"That was for me to decide, don't you think? Now I want you to leave."

He knew that when she found out she'd be angry with him, but he hadn't expected her to take it this far. Although her insistence on shutting him out on a personal level stung, he feared leaving her unprotected on a professional level more. He took a step toward her and she retreated. She had nowhere much to go, as her back hit the door. He cradled her face in his palms, forcing her to look up at him. "Let me help you, Jake. You need me. You know you do. This law firm Sylvia hired is no fly-by-night outfit. If they can, they'll come after you like a Mack truck. Let me help you."

"I'm not a fool, Eamon. I'm not going to refuse your help, because I don't have anywhere else to turn. Call her attorney. Set up the meeting if you like. Do whatever you think is necessary. But I want you to leave—now."

Her eyes glistened and her lower lip trembled. She seemed on the verge of tears again. Perhaps he'd pushed her as far as she would go tonight. "All right. I'll go. Call me if you need me."

She opened the door and he stepped into the hallway. She looked so forlorn that he hated to leave her. She must have read his thoughts on his face. She whispered one word, "Go." Then she closed the door.

Eamon stood there for a moment, his hands braced on either side of the narrow door frame, fighting the urge to bang his forehead against the wood surface. His being on the outside of the door rather than inside with Jake was his own fault. No matter how he'd rationalized his actions at the time, he'd known he should have told her sooner. Part of him wondered now if he'd chosen this morning to tell her knowing that with Dani's birthday party later that day, she wouldn't want to hear any news that wasn't pleasant.

Sighing, Eamon straightened. At least she'd allowed him to act as he saw fit on her behalf legally. He'd already put in a call to a friend of his, a colleague who specialized in family law, and was waiting for the call back. This Sylvia was in for the fight of her life if she sought to pursue custody of Dani. As far as he was concerned, both Jake and Dani were his now. He wasn't going to let anyone take either of them away from him. Not even Jake.

Two days later, Jake awoke feeling groggy. She hadn't slept much the last two nights, and keeping a happy face on for Dani had been a strain on her, too. Dani had accepted Sylvia's gift with a minimum of curiosity about its sender and a total lack of enthusiasm for the present itself. If it came to it, Jake would tell her Sylvia's true purpose in showing up, but she was hoping, perhaps blindly, that it wouldn't.

And now that Monday morning had arrived, she'd have to face Eamon as well. She hadn't heard from him since he walked out of her apartment the night of Dani's party, but she doubted that would stop him from showing up this morning to drive Dani to camp and her to work. She'd missed him terribly, despite her anger, and even that had abated over time. Distance from him had given her a little perspective, and she realized that to some degree she'd overreacted.

Yes, Eamon should have told her about Sylvia, but asking him to leave hadn't given her anything but two lonely nights spent in an empty bed. If the situation were reversed, she couldn't say that she wouldn't go to the same lengths to protect him. Though they might come at life from different angles on the surface, underneath she and Eamon were the same in many ways.

Eamon rang the doorbell just as Jake finished clearing

the breakfast dishes from the table. Dani ran to open the
door before Jake could get there.

"Hi, Uncle Eamon," Dani said cheerfully, pulling open
the door.

"Hi, short stuff." Eamon scooped her up. "Ready to go?"

"Almost. I've got to put on my sneakers."

"Well, get to it." He set Dani on her feet. She scooted
off, calling, "The two of you be nice till I get back."

Jake dried her hands and tossed the dish towel onto
the counter. That was Dani, perceptive as ever. Although Dani questioned her about Eamon's absence
the day before, she'd figured Dani suspected something wasn't right between them. Jake huffed out her
breath in several short puffs and turned to face Eamon.
He surveyed her through heavy-lidded eyes, and the
set of his jaw was grim. It disturbed her to know she'd
put that expression on his face. For a moment, neither
of them said anything; then both of them started to
speak at once.

"You go first," Jake said.

"I spoke with a friend of mine who specializes in family law. From what I told him, he seems to think Sylvia
might have a case for getting custody of Dani. If it's all
right with you, I'd feel more comfortable having him
represent you, even at this meeting with Sylvia's lawyer.
As I said, this isn't my area of expertise. And Hal is willing to do it for free. He owes me a favor."

For a moment, Jake stared at him, shaking her head.
She'd told him he could do whatever he felt was necessary, yet he was asking her to make the decision. A man
truly interested in controlling her or the situation would
have done as he pleased and told her about it later.

Biting her lip, Jake walked to him and slipped her
arms around his neck. "I'm so sorry, Eamon. I never
should have asked you to leave the other night. I don't
know what got into me."

His arms closed around her, squeezing her tight, warming her. His breath feathered across her skin as he lowered his head to kiss her temple. "I do. You're scared, Jake. You have a right to be. And I didn't help by keeping what I knew from you. You're right about that."

"You know, the thing that bothered me most was knowing I was blithely dropping Dani off at a place where Sylvia could have gotten at her. What if Sylvia had tried to take her?"

"Impossible. At least after I knew about Sylvia. I had someone watching the play yard since Jim saw her."

She smacked him on the arm. "You think of everything, don't you?"

"I try."

She pulled back from him so that she could see his face. "Do you really think hiring your friend will make a difference?"

"Yes. Hal's the best. And if nothing else, it will keep you from having grounds to sue me for malpractice."

She smiled, which she supposed was the reaction he'd been going for. "Okay. Then we'll do it." She exhaled, letting her shoulders droop. "I can't believe this is happening. Part of me thinks I'm trapped in one of Dani's nightmares and eventually I'll wake up."

"It'll be okay, Jake. I promise."

Jake shook her head, knowing he couldn't guarantee any such thing. But she loved him for trying to get her to think he could. When his mouth claimed hers, she closed her eyes and reveled in the tenderness of his kiss. When she pulled away, in the periphery of her vision she noticed Dani standing in the center of the kitchen. She turned to look at her, wondering how long she'd been standing there and how much of their conversation she had heard.

Hand on hips, shaking her head, Dani said, "I can't leave you people alone for five minutes."

Despite her words, Jake could tell by the grin on Dani's face that she was happy that all was right with the two most important adults in her life. Suddenly Jake wanted to laugh. Maybe Eamon was right. Maybe everything would be all right, because she simply couldn't imagine her life without Dani in it. "Come here, you," Jake said. Dani ran to her and Jake hugged her to her side. "We'd better get out of here," Jake said, "before all of us are late, not just me."

"Sounds like a plan." Eamon stepped away from her to open the apartment door. "Let's go."

Twenty-one

During the day, Eamon made arrangements for Hal to stop by Jake's that night. He showed up at nine-thirty, bearing a chocolate cheesecake. As the three of them devoured the dessert, Hal had Jake produce every legal document she possessed and grilled her with questions, most of which Eamon never would have considered important.

After a while, he sensed Jake needed a break. He stood and took a position behind Jake's chair. He squeezed her shoulders. "Why don't you check on Dani?"

Jake glanced back at him. She considered him for a moment before rising, probably figuring correctly that he wanted her out of the room for a few minutes. "I'll be right back."

After she left, he returned to his seat and turned to Hal. "What do you think?"

"For one thing, you're a damn lucky man. Any chance there's more like her at home?"

"None whatsoever, but I meant what do you think about the case?"

"Not good. You've got a young girl, barely twenty, signing away her parental rights a couple of weeks postpartum. On top of that you've got an older, perhaps domineering, husband in the picture." Hal shrugged. "These things always turn on the mental state of the parent at the time rights were terminated. I'd say she's got a good case for claiming duress."

"And the fact that she had no contact with the child for six years bears no weight?"

"It does. But you add to that the fact that Jake shares no blood relationship with the child. She's unmarried, never held the same job for more than a year, and if your average judge saw her in the outfit she has on now, he'd probably have a massive coronary induced by a raging hard-on. Forgive my bluntness, but she's not exactly what most of us think of when we remember dear old Mom."

"So, I'll buy her a suit only Grandma Moses could love. Are you saying it's hopeless?"

"Not at all." Both men looked up as Jake slid into her seat. "I got remarkably little information from her attorney when I called him. My gut says out-and-out custody may not be what she's after. Maybe a visitation agreement, for the time being. Since she hasn't seen the child in such a long time, her attorney may feel it might eventually go better with a judge if she reestablishes contact first."

Hal stood. "Besides, you never really know how these things will go until you get before the judge. Everyone is supposed to be concerned with what's in the best interest of the child. But sometimes the only real interest is how much fairness you can buy with either money or influence."

And unfortunately, Eamon mused, Sylvia and her new husband had both. Eamon draped an arm around Jake's shoulder as the two of them walked Hal to the door.

Once on the other side of the threshold, Hal turned to them. "Don't worry, folks. I'm going to do some digging and see what I can find."

Eamon extended his hand for Hal to shake. "Thanks again."

"Not a problem." To Jake, he added, "If you ever get tired of this guy, you just give me a call."

Jake looked up at him and grinned. "So far, he's still interesting, but I'll keep that in mind."

With a wave, Hal started toward the elevators. Eamon shut the door, then followed Jake into the kitchen. He wrapped his arms around her from behind. "Leave the dishes. I'll wake up early and take care of them. Come to bed."

She didn't argue with him. Once they were under the covers, she snuggled up against him, running her hand over his chest. In spite of, or maybe because of, the events of the last few days, he needed to be with her. By the fervor of her kisses, she obviously needed him, too. Their coupling, more physical release than lovemaking, was brief, rough, and highly erotic.

Afterward, he held her against him, stroking her soft, lax body. As for Hal's recitation of Jake's deficiencies in trying to maintain custody of Dani, Eamon couldn't do anything about the others, but there was one aspect of her profile he could rectify. He leaned down to whisper in her ear, "Marry me, Jake."

Immediately her head snapped up. "What did you ask me?"

"I asked you to marry me."

Her eyes narrowed, studying him. "Why? Because Hal said I'd have a better chance of keeping Dani if I had the prospect of being married?"

He wanted to be honest with her, so he told her the truth. "Partly." But mostly he'd asked because he was in love with her. Dani's custody situation only gave him an excuse to ask sooner than later.

She shook her head. "No. No, I won't marry you." She shifted onto her side facing away from him.

He shifted so that he lay behind her spoon fashion. "Why not?" For a long time she said nothing. He didn't realize he'd been holding his breath until he released it when she spoke.

"Please, Eamon. I have enough to deal with without this."

He rolled onto his back and expelled a heavy breath. He hadn't expected her to leap for joy at his proposal. Given her past experiences and her inherent free-spiritedness, he hadn't expected that getting her to agree to marriage would be a walk in the park. But neither had he expected her to stomp on his proposal with both feet. He wondered if the current situation was her only reason for refusing him. Especially since she rolled over and pressed herself against his side.

Eamon closed his eyes and circled his arms around her. For now, he'd have to settle for what he could get.

The meeting with Sylvia's lawyer was scheduled for Thursday at ten o'clock. By the time the day and the appointed hour rolled around, Jake's nerves were jangled and her temples ached from the tension of the last few days. What was the point of this meeting anyway? If Sylvia wanted Dani back, why hadn't she simply filed the necessary papers and been done with it? Why did she have to torture Jake with the possibility that maybe Sylvia wanted something else?

She glanced up at Eamon, who sat beside her in the taxi, then at Hal, who sat by the other door of their taxi. They each seemed to wear the same resolute expression—two lawyers with their game faces on. Lord, she wished she were capable of wearing her emotions anywhere except on her sleeve.

The taxi drew to a halt on the corner of Forty-seventh Street and Park Avenue. Now it was time to get out and face whatever gauntlet Sylvia chose to throw down before her. Jake knew that nothing would be settled at this meeting, either good or bad, but it could be a beginning, a declaration of war that could end with her losing custody of Dani. The thought alone sent a shiver of dread down her spine.

With Eamon's help, she stepped out of the cab into the bright morning sunshine and glanced up at the tall glass and steel building before her. Somehow the view and the churning of her stomach reminded her of the day not too long ago when she had stepped out of a cab in front of the building where she now worked. She'd been terrified then, more afraid of being offered a job than coming home without one. But that had worked out fine. She felt Eamon take her hand. This time at least, she wasn't alone.

If Jake had harbored any doubts about the wealth of the law firm Sylvia had hired, they would have evaporated as they stepped off the elevator on the thirty-fourth floor—polished dark wood paneling, plush carpet, and a faux or maybe not-so-faux marble receptionist's desk that boasted the latest in telephonic and computer technology. A young woman led them to a glass-enclosed conference room. "Mr. Allen will be with you shortly," the young woman said and left them.

Hal rested his briefcase on the surface of the cherrywood table that dominated the room. "And so it begins. I hate this posturing crap."

"Relax, Hal," Eamon said. "Jake probably threw their schedule off by actually getting somewhere on time."

"You rat," she shot back. "I haven't been late to anywhere in months."

Eamon nodded toward the secretary they had passed on their way to the conference room. "Besides, Little Miss Nosy out there is probably reporting everything we're doing, so I suggest we all looked composed."

Easier said than done, Jake mused. The churning of her stomach and the pounding in her head made anything close to being composed impossible. She wanted to pace or scream or maybe both, but more than anything she wanted this to be over. Worst of all, she suspected both men knew it.

"Why don't you sit?" Eamon suggested.

Jake shook her head. She knew her nerves would never allow her to sit quietly in one place. "I think I'll freshen up instead."

"Don't be too long," Eamon said.

Jake left the room and asked directions to the ladies' room from the secretary outside the conference room. Once inside the lavish ladies' room just off the conference room, Jake surveyed herself in the large rectangular mirror over the bank of pastel-pink sinks. She ran her hands under warm water and pressed her fingertips to her pale cheeks.

She could get through this. She had to for Dani's sake, though in many ways the situation seemed unreal to her. Despite the confident aura Sylvia had displayed the other night, Jake still thought of Sylvia as the insecure girl her brother had married seven years ago. While the two of them had never been close, Jake had always believed there was a bit of affection between them. Way back then, Jake would never have imagined the two of them would find themselves wrangling over the child of the man they both had loved. Even though her animosity toward Sylvia had blossomed and grown in the intervening years, Jake had never been able to bring herself to truly hate her, probably because deep down Jake saw enough of herself in the other woman to sympathize.

Jake sighed. None of that mattered now, anyway. Obviously, Sylvia wasn't that girl anymore. Seeing another woman enter the ladies' room, Jake reached for a paper towel to dry her hands. She'd already been gone long enough. As she started toward the door, she heard the lock of the bathroom door turning and realized the woman at the door was Sylvia. Sylvia straightened and faced her. "I need to talk to you. Alone."

Jake stopped midstride. "What do you want now, Sylvia? Isn't it enough that you threatened to take Dani away from me in my own home? Isn't it enough you dragged me into your lawyer's office? Whatever you have to say, you can say it in front of my attorney, who by the way is waiting for me."

Sylvia held up her hands as if to forestall Jake's leaving. "You have to believe me, Jake, this isn't the way I wanted things to go. I only arranged for you to come here because I wanted you to take me seriously. I knew you wouldn't unless you realized I had a case for getting Dani back."

"So, what do you want, Sylvia?"

Sylvia turned plaintive brown eyes to her. "I want you to understand. I'm not a bad person. I've made some wrong choices in my life, and I regret them. I'm trying to atone for them." An olive-green chair sat to the right of the door. Sylvia sank into the chair and put her face in her hands. "I want you to understand."

For the first time, Jake actually felt sorry for her. She had missed all of her daughter's life. If the loss had affected her so deeply, why hadn't she come back? Why wait until now to try to make amends?

Sylvia lifted her head and Jake saw the sheen of tears in her eyes. "I know you loved your brother, Jake. So did I. I was sorry to hear about his passing. But he was a very hard man to live with. I was such a baby when I met him, barely eighteen. I worked at this hole-in-the-wall diner where he and his friends used to come for lunch. I was such a mousy thing, I was surprised he even noticed me. At first, we were just friends. He was the one who encouraged me to go back to school and get a decent job. I'm not ashamed to admit that he was like a god to me then, older, handsome, caring. I was so in love with him it was disgusting."

Sylvia swiped at her eyes. "After I left the diner, we didn't see each other for a long time. Then one night, at a party given by a friend, he was there. We left together, and, well, let's just say we took our friendship to a new level that night. He asked me to marry him three months later and I was ecstatic to say yes."

"Then what happened?"

Sylvia lifted her shoulders. "As happy as I was, I was just as terrified. I had been on my own since I was sixteen. I'd never depended on anyone but myself before. When I met Dan, he sort of took over my life and helped me find direction. But once I did, I resented his continued attempts to control me. Isn't it always that way, the thing you love at the beginning is the thing you hate at the end?"

Jake thought of Stan, who had attracted her because he treated her as if she were special. Eventually she'd chafed at him treating her as if she were so special he didn't allow her to be human. "I guess."

"Did you ever wonder why Dan wanted to marry me? I did for a long time. Really, I had nothing to offer him, but a warm body. After all, what would a twenty-seven-year-old man want with a girl too young to vote? It occurred to me that he wanted someone in his life he could control, someone who needed him and would never leave him. He'd lost his mother, his father, and you, well, you flitted around as you pleased. He wanted someone who would stay."

Jake stared out the window, unable to refute any of the claims Sylvia made. Dan had always been a bossy big brother, always trying to tell her what to do, whom to pick as friends, how to live. She'd simply blown him off and done as she pleased. She could imagine that a girl in Sylvia's position, eager to please the man she loved yet somehow assert herself, would have found Dan's attitude daunting.

"Then why did you leave him?"

"When I found out I was pregnant with Dani, I was terrified. I knew I had no business being anybody's mother. I could barely take care of myself. Being pregnant made me vulnerable in a way I never had been before. I had always supported myself. The idea of giving up my job to stay home with Dani and to rely on someone else financially, even for a short while, was the scariest prospect to me.

"If you've never been poor, if you've never had to wonder where your next meal was coming from, you don't understand. And Dan didn't help. He insisted that I stop working at the beginning of my third trimester. He thought he was being protective, when in reality, all he gave me was the opportunity to sit around and think of all the horrible things that might happen. Having money gives a woman power, if nothing else to help decide how it's spent. What if Dan cheated on me or frittered away our money or walked out on us? I'd be left with nothing considering I had less than a thousand dollars in the bank. How would I survive? It sounds so frivolous now.

"When Dani was born, I panicked. I knew I couldn't be this perfect wife and mother clone Dan wanted me to be. I gave Dan the divorce he wanted and signed away my rights to be Dani's mother, figuring she'd be better off without me. I knew Dan would be a good father to her. And——" Sylvia smiled. "I knew she would have you. You would check Dan's heavy-handedness and he would provide the two of you with the structure you needed. I wasn't wrong."

Anger rose in Jake hearing the note of satisfaction in Sylvia's voice. She'd been right, but at what cost to everyone? "Don't sound so pleased with yourself, Sylvia. You're not the one who fed her or changed her or worried when she was sick, or tired yourself out just trying to keep up with her. All you did was give birth to her."

"And I've had to live with the consequences of my decisions ever since. There hasn't been a day when I haven't thought of Dani, haven't wondered how she was doing, how much she'd grown, if she was happy. There hasn't been a day when I haven't wished I had been stronger all those years ago, strong enough to see that I could handle whatever life dished out without running away."

The hairs on the back of Jake's neck rose as Sylvia's words washed over her. Now she knew what she and Sylvia shared in common. Like Sylvia, Jake had lived most of her life as if waiting for the proverbial other shoe to drop, fearing she wouldn't be able to withstand whatever life threw at her. But now that she thought about it, she, unlike Sylvia, had always risen to the challenge, she'd always survived. So why was she still so afraid?

She couldn't live like that anymore.

"Why did you decide to come back?"

"I'm pregnant, Jake. And happy. I couldn't imagine bringing a new child into my life while I had never made amends with my first one. What was I supposed to tell this child about his or her sister? I'm not seeking custody of Dani. I couldn't do that to her or you. But I would like to be part of her life. I would like my two children to know each other. Brice and I would like to help provide for her financially, if you will let us."

For a moment, Jake didn't know what to say. Relief flooded through her, realizing that Sylvia wasn't trying to take Dani away from her, but rather asking permission to be part of Dani's life. But if she said no, would Sylvia simply walk away? And then there was Dani. If Sylvia had truly changed, didn't Dani deserve the chance to know her mother, if that's what she wanted?

Jake sighed. "This is a lot to digest in fifteen minutes."

"I'm not asking you to make a decision today. I'm just

grateful that you listened to me. I'm not sure I deserved even that much from you."

Jake nodded. In her mind, the decision rested with Dani. She couldn't force Dani into a relationship with Sylvia any more than she could deny her one if that's what she wanted. "I'll be in touch."

"Thank you."

Jake unlocked the door and opened it, not entirely surprised to find Eamon waiting on the other side. When he saw her, a slow grin spread across his face. "Good Lord, you ladies take a long time in the bathroom."

She closed the gap between them in the secluded hallway and slid her arms around his neck. She rested her cheek against his chest as his arms closed around her. "How long have you been standing out here?"

"Only a few minutes. I got to meet Sylvia's husband. He seems like a nice guy. The others sent me out here to make sure you two weren't scratching each other's eyes out while no one was paying attention."

Jake smacked him on the arm knowing no one had worried about any such thing. "I could have taken her."

His hand drifted upward to stroke the side of her face. "What did you tell Sylvia?"

Obviously Eamon had been filled in on what Sylvia had intended to say to her. "I said I'd call her. I need to talk with Dani first."

"Then let's get out of here. Being around all these stuffed-shirt lawyer types is giving me the heebie-jeebies."

"You're a stuffed-shirt lawyer type."

"I used to be. Then I met this crazy lady with wild red hair and sexy clothes who turned my whole world upside down. Have I ever thanked you for that?"

"No, but you will." She took his hand and led him down the hall. "Just as soon as I get you home."

Epilogue

Jake stood in Eamon's apartment at the large living room window, overlooking Central Park. Uncle Eamon and Barbara had joined them to ring in the New Year, each wearing a glitter top hat and blowing noisemakers when midnight struck. Eamon had volunteered to escort the revelers down to their cars, which gave Jake a few minutes alone to stare out at the city and wonder what the future held for all of them.

She worried about Liza and Jim, each of whom had declined her invitation to tonight's gathering, each fearing seeing the other. But Dani seemed to have come into her own. Sylvia's husband came from a large southern family with lots of cousins near Dani's age. For the last three days, Dani had been running hog-wild and basking in the warmth of a family that welcomed her like the prodigal daughter she was. As happy as Jake was for Dani, she had to admit that when she'd called Dani right after midnight to wish her a happy New Year, hearing Dani say she missed her and couldn't wait to come home had done her mother's heart good.

And then there was Eamon. When he'd proposed to her, they'd been in the throes of worrying about losing Dani. She'd refused him, because she could not see herself spending the rest of her life wondering if he'd asked her to marry him to help her keep Dani rather than because he truly wanted to.

He hadn't mentioned marriage since then, and considering the way she'd stomped on his first proposal, she couldn't blame him. When he got back, she intended to screw her courage to the sticking place and ask him herself.

Minutes later, she heard him approach and then his arms slid around her waist, pulling her back against him.

He lowered his head so that his breath fanned against her ear. "What are you doing standing here?"

"Just thinking."

"About what?"

She ran her hands over his arms. "The new year and what it has in store for all of us."

"I've been thinking about that, too." He turned her in his arms so that she faced him. "Look, Jake, these past few months we've been living like nomads between one apartment and the other. I love you, Jake. I love Dani. I want us to be a family, officially. I want us to pick one apartment and live there."

"What exactly are you saying?"

He brushed his knuckles against her cheek. "Marry me, Jake. I'm housebroken, I clean up after myself, I make a decent living. I've got a cute dog."

"Calling that animal cute is like saying Godzilla is cuddly." She cupped his face in her palms and touched her mouth to his. "Of course I'll marry you, Eamon. I love you."

"You say that as if I should have known what your answer was going to be. The first time—"

She placed a silencing finger against his lips. "The first time you asked me, I thought you only did so out of obligation. I couldn't do the same thing to you that your first wife had done, no matter how much I wanted to say yes at the time." She laughed. "In fact, I was planning on asking you myself since you hadn't said anything."

"Are you crazy, woman? If you knew how many times

in the last few months I've wanted to ask you but didn't, you'd know just how pathetic the two of us are."

Laughing, Jake hugged her to him. "I have to warn you that Dani has already put in her bid for a baby brother. She even has a name picked out for him, though she refuses to tell me what it is."

"As long as she doesn't want to call him Eamoni, I'm fine with that." He lifted her into his arms and carried her to the bedroom. He lay down on the bed with her beside him. He stroked her hair away from her face, then kissed her eyelids, her cheeks, then finally her mouth. When he pulled back, he propped his head on his hand and looked down at her.

"So Dani wants a baby brother, does she? That puts a strain on things."

Her eyes narrowed. "What do you mean?"

"We don't want to slip up and give her a sister. We'll never hear the end of it. We've got to get it right the first time."

"And how do you plan to do that?"

"The same way you perfect a magic routine," he said as his mouth lowered toward hers. "Practice, practice, practice."

Dear Readers,

I really enjoyed writing *Could It Be Magic?*, which was actually the second book I started working on after *Spellbound*. Somehow I got distracted by Michael and Jenny's story, *Always,* but I was glad to get back to finishing the story. I hoped you enjoyed reading it.

My next book is *Not the One,* a continuation of the Thorne family saga, in which Nathan Ward's sister Nina finds love with Dr. Matthew Peterson. You met both of these characters in *Once and Again.* So many people wrote me to tell me they wanted Nina's story and that I had to pair her up with the pediatrician that took care of her niece Emily, that I decided to give it a go. *Not the One* will be out in fall 2003.

And for those of you who are wondering—yes, I plan to write Liza and Jim's story and tell you what went on at the house in Florida.

I would love to hear from you. You can contact me at DeeSavoy@aol.com or at P.O. Box 233, Bronx, NY 10469. Or stop by my website at www.deirdresavoy.com.

All the best,
Dee Savoy

ABOUT THE AUTHOR

Native New Yorker Deirdre Savoy spent her summers on the shores of Martha's Vineyard, soaking up the sun and scribbling in one of her many notebooks. It was there that she first started writing romance as a teenager. The island proved to be the perfect setting for her first novel, *Spellbound*, published by BET/Arabesque Books in 1999.

Spellbound received rave reviews and Savoy was named Best New Author of 1999 and the first Rising Star author of Romance in Color. She also won the first annual Emma award for Favorite New Author, presented at the 2001 Romance Slam Jam in Orlando, Florida. This year, Savoy has been nominated for three Emmas, including Author of the Year.

Savoy's second book, *Always,* was published by BET/Arabesque in October 2000. *Always* was a February 2001 Selection for the Black Expressions Book Club. *Once and Again,* the sequel to *Always,* was published in May 2001, and was also selected by the Black Expressions Book Club. *Midnight Magic,* the third book in the Thorne family saga, was a 2001 Holiday release.

Savoy's fifth book, *Holding Out For A Hero,* was published in September 2002. The cover of *Holding Out For A Hero* features fictional hero NYPD detective Adam Wexler and real-life hero firefighter Paul Haney, the winner of the 2001 Arabesque Man Contest. *Holding Out For A Hero* was also picked up by Black Expressions.

In her other life, Savoy is a kindergarten teacher for the New York City Board of Education. She started her career as a secretary in the school art department of Macmillan Publishing Company in New York, rising to Advertising/Promotion Supervisor of the International Division in three years. She has also worked as a free-lance copy writer, legal proofreader, and news editor for CLASS magazine.

Deirdre graduated from Bernard M. Baruch College of the City University of New York with a Bachelors Degree in Business Administration.